SINGLE DADDY say WHAT?

DENVER ROYALTY

Sheridan Anne
Single Daddy Say What? - Denver Royalty (Book 3)

First Published in 2023

Anne, Sheridan
Single Daddy Say What? - Denver Royalty (Book 3)

Cover Design: Sheridan Anne
Editing: Heather Fox
Formatting: Sheridan Anne

DISCLAIMER

Single Daddy Say What? was previously published as Sean - Denver Royalty (Book 3) 2018-2023

The content of Single Daddy Say What? remains the same with new edits and tightening up of each chapter. The story within has not changed. Simply received a facelift plus new interior formatting, title, and cover.

Chapter One

SEAN

The sound of my daughter's wheezy breath fills the room and it fucking kills me to hear as she struggles to find peace in her sleep. Her asthma has been playing up a lot lately. We've already been to the hospital three times this month, and I fear it's only getting worse.

It's a battle we fight all year round, but the second winter set in, it was like torture for my little girl—in and out of the hospital when she should have been running around with her cousins, exploring the snow, and living the fullest life any three-year-old should. Instead, she sits and watches the other kids from the window, longing in her beautiful blue eyes.

All she wants to do is run.

God, she must think I'm a monster telling her no all the time. I just don't know what to do. I wasn't built to do this on my own.

I lay on her bedroom floor, reaching up to hold her little hand as she tries to sleep. Shadows dance across the ceiling, and all I can do to hold it together is stare at the picture of my dead wife on her bedside table.

My beautiful Sara.

She was ripped away from me three years ago, and I've spent every minute wishing I could get her back. I would sell my soul to the fucking devil just to hold her one more time, to feel her in my arms and hear her telling me she loves me. Sara was my sunshine, and ever since she's been gone, I've been living in darkness. If it weren't for Georgie . . . I don't know where I'd be right now.

I miss her so damn much. I never planned for her to be nothing but a memory I struggle to hold onto. She was my rock, my world. When I lost my parents, she was the one to help me find my way, and now I'm barely keeping afloat. Without her, I'm an empty shell, and I crave to be the man I once was, but it's not possible.

My heart aches just thinking about her and that emptiness inside of me only grows. But after three long years, I'm used to it. There comes a time when a man has to get on with life. He has to find a way to carry on, find a wave to survive, and for me, it was my daughter.

Sara hemorrhaged after an emergency C-section, and despite their vigorous efforts, the doctors couldn't save her. I'll never forget that day. It's forever ingrained in my memory—what was supposed to be the most magical day of our lives, turned into pure devastation.

Every day without her is a challenge. I need her to tell me what to do. Am I doing the right thing with Georgia? Am I raising her the way she wanted? Have I given her the life that she would have wanted for her child?

Just give me a fucking sign, baby. God, I need you.

It kills me that our last hours together were during torturous labor, that she was fearful of what was to come and was in the greatest agony of her life. But knowing she had a chance to meet our daughter before she passed is bittersweet and something I'm sure Georgie will hold onto for the rest of her life. Hell, I know Sara held onto the image of her sweet baby girl in her arms as she took her final breath.

A vicious coughing fit tears through my sweet girl, and I rip my gaze away from the photograph of Sara. I fly to my knees, scrambling to the side of Georgie's bed and desperately trying to sit her up. She clings to me, gasping for air as her lungs scream for Ventolin.

Tears fill her eyes, and it fucking kills me.

"Shhh, my sweet girl," I soothe, reaching across to her bedside table and grabbing her inhaler and spacer. I place it to her lips and she instantly breathes in the life-saving Ventolin with slow deep breaths, something that's become more than routine over the past couple of weeks.

My chest aches watching as she takes her slow breaths, listening to the soothing sound of my voice as I coach her through it. There's nothing worse than watching your only child struggle to breathe—the most basic human instinct, and the fact that I can't magically fix this for her only makes me feel as though I'm failing her. I'm her daddy, her whole world, and I can't make her better or make the pain go away.

The moment she's completed her treatment, I pull back and rest the inhaler on her bedside table, right where I can find it when this inevitably happens again.

Georgie looks up at me with big tears welling in her eyes, and it fucking destroys me. She clambers out of her bed and straight into my arms, and I grab the blanket to wrap around us both, not wanting her to get cold. "Daddy," she cries, snuggling her face into my chest as I hold her tight, desperately wishing there was some way I could help her, but sometimes, this is all she needs.

"You're okay, baby girl," I soothe as I rock us back and forth, trying to help her get back to sleep. Honestly, I think my words act more as a comfort to myself, reminding me that she's still here in my arms, still breathing.

She can never be alone. If there was no one there to help her when she had an attack. Fuck, I can't even think about what could happen. I would never forgive myself. When she gets older, she'll be able to read the signs and know when to slow down and take her Ventolin, but now, being so young, her life is literally in the palm of my hands.

My little girl is the spitting image of her mother, and every time I look into those big blue eyes, my heart shatters all over again. She has the same strawberry blonde hair, the same soft curls, and after a long day at preschool, she even has the same feisty attitude.

Georgia saved my life, and I fear the day she grows up and moves out. I can't wait to see the young woman she will become. I just hope

I'm raising her right, that she aspires to be as amazing as her mother was. Though, I know my little girl. No matter what she wants to do or be, she will be extraordinary. I just hope that one day, she'll find an intense, all-consuming love like I had with her mother, and I hope to God that she never has to know the pain of losing that.

Georgia cries in my arms as I try my best to calm her. The asthma attacks scare the living shit out of her, and rightly so. She's too young to understand what's actually happening and the dangers of it, but she knows she doesn't like it, and fuck, I know she can sense how they destroy me.

She's the perfect little daddy's girl. She's just as attached to me as I am to her. She's my world, just as I am hers, and I wouldn't have it any other way . . . apart from Sara. I'd give anything to be able to give my little girl her mom, but instead, we live through her memory, through the stories I tell her, and the pictures I hold so dear.

I tell Georgia about her mommy every single day. I know she would never be able to remember her from their one precious moment together, but at least she can know her through me. There's so much I look forward to sharing with her—the day we got married, when we first fell in love in high school, and the day we discovered she was pregnant with Georgie.

When my sweet girl finally begins to calm and her tears run dry, I brush my hand over her head. "Are you okay, baby?" I ask as a yawn rips through her.

"No," she pouts, her bottom lip wobbling and unintentionally breaking my heart.

"I know," I tell her, keeping one hand on her back as I reach for her water bottle.

She greedily takes it from my hand, lifts it to her lips, and demolishes the entire thing before dropping it onto her carpet. Another yawn rips through her and, seeming settled now, I get up off the ground, lift her back into her bed, and tuck her in as I get in bedside her, hoping like fuck the worst has passed.

The soft melody of *Twinkle, Twinkle, Little Star* comes flowing from my mouth the same way I know Sara would have if she were here, and after twenty minutes of wheezing, my sweet Georgie finally falls back to sleep.

Confident this is it for the night, I get comfortable beside her, propping my head up under my arm as my daughter snuggles in close, knowing that tonight is going to be another sleepless night for me.

If another asthma attack comes on, I won't be taking my chances. I'll be rushing her straight down to the hospital for the fourth time this month. This is getting ridiculous. There must be something more I can do for her, but until then, this will be our lives.

She's asleep for at least half an hour when the sheets become all too warm, and I let out a heavy sigh, realizing she's just wet the bed. I should have known better than to let her drink so much water, especially when we're right in the middle of toilet training.

I can only imagine the perfect little smirk Sara would give me if she were here now.

For the fourth time tonight, I wake my daughter. I get her cleaned up and into new pajamas before stripping her bed and throwing the wet sheets in the washing machine. Ten minutes later, I'm in my own bed with Georgie curled into my chest.

I start on *Twinkle, Twinkle, Little Star* again and sigh in relief when she finally falls into a deep sleep with even, steady breaths, allowing me the chance to finally get some rest.

Chapter Two

GIGI

I am exhausted.

I fall down onto the nurses' couch as I wait for my best friend to finish her shift. Mine was supposed to be over three hours ago, and I'm only just finishing up now, but that's life working on the maternity ward. It's been a huge day, though it usually is. We've delivered eight babies, three of which turned into emergency C-sections, two were elected water births, leaving the other three as straightforward vaginal births. They were mostly easy, apart from the lady who was screaming from the second she walked in and wouldn't give in until the baby was all but yanked out of her.

Trying to work out if I should start heading home or wait for my roommate, I pull my phone out and send a quick text to Mel, who works as a nurse in the pediatric ward.

Gigi – I'm finished for the day. How are you doing?

She texts back almost immediately.

Mel – Just finishing up now. Be there in 10 minutes.

Thank God.

All I can think about is getting home and crashing. It's been a massive week filled with extra shifts, new babies, screaming mothers, and everything gross that goes along with being a midwife, but I wouldn't have it any other way. I'm firm in my belief that being a midwife is the best job on earth, and while it can be incredibly stressful, and sometimes downright devastating, it's also incredibly rewarding. It's also the best birth control any woman could ever need.

Scooching down on the nurses' couch, I put my feet up and am just about to fall asleep when Mel barges in, looking way too chirpy for the end of a twelve-hour shift. "You ready?" she sings, making her way across the room to her locker and quickly riffling through for her things.

Mel hooks her bag over her shoulder as I get up onto my sore feet and scoop my things off the floor beside me. "I was ready hours ago," I tell her with a yawn as we walk out the door together. We head out to the staff parking lot, stopping to say a few goodbyes along the way, and eventually collapse down into my beat-up car, thankful that we both have the whole weekend off.

"I heard you had an exciting day," Mel grins as I start up my car and back out of my spot, doing my best not to crash into anything along the way.

"You heard about that, did you?" I cringe, knowing damn well this was going to come back to haunt me.

She lets out a booming laugh as she searches through her Spotify playlist for something to listen to. "How could I not? It was the talk of the whole hospital all day," she says with a stupid smirk. "Is it true though? The newbie spilled the piss bag all over you?"

"Shut up," I groan, confirming what she already knows to be true. "I had to rush straight into a C-section after, so I didn't even get to shower first, just had to throw on new scrubs and wipe myself over with disinfectant wipes. It was awful."

"Yuckkkkk," she groans, scrunching up her face in disgust. "You're so gross."

"Tell me about it," I say as I pull up at the liquor store for our traditional Friday night drink, though something tells me I'm going to need a little more than just one tonight. "It was nearly an hour before I could get cleaned up."

"That's the beauty of nursing," Mel says with a sigh as we get out of the car.

We hurry through the parking lot, and as we enter the liquor store, Mel looks down at the baskets, probably wondering if we'll need one for this particular shopping trip. "How messy are we planning on getting tonight?" she questions, already reaching for a basket.

"Depends if you have any plans for tomorrow," I mutter, moving ahead and searching the aisle as if I don't already know what I'm getting.

Mel practically skips to catch up with me, stopping to grab a bottle of Bailey's along the way. "My only plan is nursing a hangover."

"Music to my ears," I say, leaning down and grabbing a bottle of Moscato before thinking better of it and grabbing a second. "You know what, I think we'll be needing both of these."

Mel laughs as I place them into the basket. "Good thinking," she murmurs as she heads around the other side of the store to fill up on chips and candy. After throwing in a few extra odds and ends, we make our way to the checkout. Once we've loaded our spoils into the car, we dash across the road to the pizza place and order takeout.

Twenty minutes later, we push through the door to our small apartment and come crashing down on the couch, pizza and Moscato in hand. Mel and I have been living together since we were newbies at the hospital, both fumbling around like idiots hoping we didn't cause more harm than good. We both started in the emergency room, but since then, we've professionally worked our way up and gone separate ways.

Mel absolutely adores children, hence why she works in the pediatric ward, and while I love kids too, I have a preference for newborns. They're my weakness with their tiny little toes and fingers. I'd love to have one of my own one day, but it's a real shame I can't find anyone willing to make that happen. Don't get me wrong, there are plenty of men out there willing to fuck me first, but the moment things start getting serious, they're out the door and onto the next girl.

Me and men simply just don't mix. Hell, sometimes I wonder if Mel and I should just bite the bullet and become the hottest lesbian couple known to humankind, but unfortunately, pussy just doesn't turn me on the way a big dick does.

Every guy I've dated has turned out to be a complete loser. First, there was Johnny, my high school sweetheart, who wasn't so much of a sweetheart after I caught him screwing our science teacher in the backseat of his shit-box car. Then there was the string of guys through college who were only interested in sex. Then came the star of my devastations, my ex, who tried to climb into bed with Mel seconds after being with me. Like, seriously? What the hell was going through his head? Did he honestly think he could get away with that shit?

So here we are, two very single ladies, scarfing down pizza on a Friday night, absolutely wasted. Sure, we could go out to a bar to try and find the loves of our lives, or we could sit here and get shit-faced with our feet up. Yeah, it's a no-brainer, really. I know which option I'm taking.

"Oh," Mel gasps, breaking me out of the disastrous thoughts of my failed love life. She jumps off the couch and dashes around our apartment searching for her handbag. I watch with wide eyes, having no idea what the hell is going on, and when she finds it by the front door, she dumps the contents of her bag out onto the coffee table.

"What the hell are you doing?" I ask as she finally finds a little slip of paper and holds it up in triumph, clutching it tightly between her fingers before crashing back down beside me on the couch.

Mel grabs the TV remote and starts looking for something on the screen as she pulls her legs up under her on the couch, trying to get comfortable. "It's lottery night," she practically sings, waving the little slip of paper toward me and making me realize it's a lottery ticket. "We're about to win ten million buckeroos."

"Oh, shit yeah," I grin as I sit a little straighter on the couch, my knees bouncing in excitement despite knowing the likelihood of actually winning. "Here we come McMansion in the hills."

"McMansion?" she scoffs. "You need to think bigger. I'm buying an island."

I roll my eyes and laugh before pausing and glancing her way, my face scrunched up in question. "Is ten million even enough to buy an island? I mean, maybe you could just buy a section of the island and rope it off so tourists don't come and shit on your beach."

"Huh, good point," Mel says as she finally finds what she's looking for and we see the numbers already on the screen. We check twice before all our hopes and dreams are well and truly shattered. Hell, we weren't even a little bit close.

Mel holds up her glass and clinks it against mine. "Here's to living in poverty," she says with a fake grin.

I can't help but laugh as I lift my glass to my lips and take a big drink. "We're not doing *that* bad," I tell her, needing to defend what little we have.

"I know," she sighs as she tears up the lottery ticket and throws it behind the couch, watching as the tiny pieces float to the floor like snowflakes. "Don't get me wrong, I love the life we have here, but there's just something thrilling about the idea of living on a private tropical island with a hunky piece of man meat worshipping my body all day long. Just picture it, lying naked on the beach, getting all hot and sweaty, then going to bathe under a natural waterfall. Obviously, we would fuck again right there under the cascading water."

"Shit," I sigh, seeing the ultimate dream so well. There's no denying it, I want it too. Only I'm not sure about the fucking on the beach. I couldn't imagine anything worse than having sand thrust up my coochy.

Getting up from the couch, I take the empty pizza boxes into the kitchen before grabbing the second bottle of Moscato and refilling our glasses. "I wouldn't mind my own tropical island," I tell her as I flop back onto the couch. "But I think I'm still down with the mansion, the family, and a hot husband who'll do all kinds of nasty things to me every morning before work."

"Ugh," she groans. "You'll still work? You'll be filthy rich. You won't need to work. You could hire people to work for you."

"And leave my maternity ward to the likes of whores like you? Hell no!"

Mel scoffs. "You can take your maternity ward and shove it up your ass. Pediatrics is where it's at."

I roll my eyes as my phone beeps on the coffee table with a new notification. When I reach forward to scoop it up, I find a new match on my Tinder account—something I'm beginning to regret having downloaded in the first place. "Oooooh," I say, opening the app to ogle tonight's selections. Turning toward Mel, I show her my screen. "You up for a little hunky piece of man meat?"

Leaning toward me, she peers at my screen, excitement flashing in her eyes. "Ooh, hell yeah," she grins, finishing off her drink before scooching right over beside me as we swipe through our options.

"Nope. Nope. Nope. Oh, hell no," she says, taking over the swiping, before getting a little too excited and pulling out her own phone to do the exact same thing. We're a few minutes into swiping when her whole face scrunches in disgust and she holds back a gag. "Check out the mullet on this one."

"What's wrong with it?" I ask, choking back a laugh. "You don't like a little business in the front and a little party in the back?"

"Oh, you know I love a little party in the back," she grins.

She gets busy swiping again, and I realize she's going to end up with a hot stranger in her bed tonight. But I don't blame her, as long as the guy doesn't ask for a threesome or steal our shit, then I'm down with it, and honestly, I don't expect anything different. This is just her and I love her for it. She's spontaneous, horny, and doesn't give a fuck what anyone thinks about her.

I wish I was a little more like her. I'd love to have that carefree attitude, to be able to put myself out there the way she does, but I can't help it. I need control in my life. So until I'm able to find that kind of excitement of my own, I'm happy living vicariously through her.

I get back to business when I stop on what must be the most attractive man I've ever seen. "Holy shit," I mutter, choking on my

Moscato as I take him in. He stands by a pool with a beer in hand, wearing nothing but a pair of shorts and showing off his sculpted body—one that was clearly handmade by the angels of heaven. "Why, hello Sean," I say as I take in the chest, the abs, and the deep V leading down to what must be the sweetest kind of sin.

"Huh?" Mel grunts, tearing her greedy gaze away from her screen and feasting it on mine. "Oh, sweet baby Jesus" she breathes, her eyes widening. "Swipe right, Gi."

"What? No," I shriek. She knows perfectly well that I never actually participate in this shit. I just like to look. I mean, who knows what kind of creeps a woman could run into on apps like this.

"Why not?" she demands. "Look at the guy. He's sexy as hell, he's wearing a watch that probably costs a bomb, he has a body that you're already drooling over, and I can tell just by looking at him that he's killer in bed. He looks like the kind of man to shake hands with your daddy, only to have you calling him daddy between the sheets."

I shake my head, somehow already blushing at the thought of having this man dominating me in the bedroom. "How could you possibly know that?"

She puts her finger up to her temple. "Trust me," she grins. "I have a sixth sense for finding the good ones."

"Really? So, where's your good guy?"

"Come on, girl. You know me better than that," she says. "I'm not interested in the good ones. I like the bad boys who will destroy my pussy before destroying my heart."

I should have known better before asking.

"You're such a horny skank," I laugh, rolling my eyes. "But no. This one is all yours. I'm a good girl. There's nothing I could do or say to that man that he hasn't heard a million times before from a million girls just like me. But you, you could rock his world."

"I hate the way you put yourself down like that," she tells me. "You are honestly so fucking beautiful, any man would be lucky to have you, especially this guy. Swipe right, Gi. Give yourself a shot. Who knows, he might be the one you get your stupid mansion and filthy married sex with. But I'm good. I already have my screw for the night," she tells me, a wicked grin stretching across her face. "He'll be here in half an hour."

"Shit, Mel," I laugh as she gets up to refill her glass again. "You work fast."

"Sure do," she grins excitedly as she comes up behind me and plucks the phone out of my hand, instantly swiping right on Sean while I scramble to get my phone back.

"Fuck, Mel," I shriek, finally curling my hands around the phone, but it's far too late now. The damage has been done. "What did you do that for?"

"Because your bitch-ass never would have done it yourself," she says. "I want you to get your filthy husband sex and it's never gonna happen if you don't put yourself out there. Besides, you and I both know that you're going to spend all night staring at his picture and committing it to your mental spank bank. At least this way, you might get the chance to see him for real."

Ahhh, fuck. Fuck. Fuck. Fuck.

I should have expected this.

Mel gives me a cheesy, triumphant grin before dashing up the hallway. "I'm going to shower before my date shows up," she yells over her shoulder.

"I don't think you can classify that as a date," I call back.

"Fine," she says before correcting herself. "I'm going to shower before my latest screw shows up."

"That's more like it," I laugh.

Being that girl who couldn't possibly let a perfect stranger she'll never see again walk into a messy home, I get up and start cleaning up after us and putting our apartment back together. As I'm finishing my quick clean, Mel comes out of the bathroom in the sexiest lingerie I've ever seen and struts her stuff, giving me the full effect. "What do you think?" she questions, turning around to show me the way her ass sits in her thong, especially proud of it after spending hours in the gym.

"Not bad," I tell her. "If you're lucky, I might even screw you too."

She rolls her eyes before heading into her room and coming out wearing her silk robe, and I shake my head, realizing she isn't even going to pretend to do the whole date thing. She's keeping it simple—make the walls shake, then kick him out without any promises to do it again.

Mel goes to drop onto the couch when there's a knock at the door, and she sends me a wicked grin before starting across the apartment to answer it. Pulling it wide, she takes one look at tonight's challenge, decides she likes what she sees, grabs him by his shirt, and pulls him into the apartment. His eyes go wide as he takes her in. Within seconds, her legs are wrapped around his waist, and he's walking them down the hallway toward Mel's bedroom as she points out which room is hers.

With Mel getting busy, I slip into the bathroom, making sure to lock the door behind me before running a bath. After going all out with candles and bubbles, I slip into the warm water and do my best to relax. Only Mel was right about one particular Tinder account that keeps flashing in my mind.

I've never been on a Tinder date before, and the idea is honestly freaking me out. What if the guy matches and actually wants to go out? What then? I definitely don't have the guts to follow through on that, especially not with a guy who looks like a walking sex machine.

Who am I kidding? If he even gets in touch with me, it's going to be for a quick screw and nothing more. He might take me out first, but we all know his end game is with me on my knees and his dick halfway down my throat. Though, it might just be worth it.

A guy that looks like that isn't interested in dating and settling down.

The question is if I'm willing to give him what he wants or if I'm too fucking scared to live a little.

Chapter Three

SEAN

Georgie and I have been spending the day with my family at my sister's new place. Cassie and Jaxon have been building this property for what seems like a lifetime, and it was finally finalized a few months ago, and I can't lie, it's fucking beautiful. Naturally, my brother, Carter, built and designed it for them. He made sure it was absolutely perfect for our little sister because honestly, nothing else would have been acceptable. And as expected, his crew has done an incredible job. She may be married and moving on in her life, but she'll always be our little sister, and my brothers and I will never stop caring for her.

To me, there's nothing better than spending the day with the whole family since it just keeps getting bigger.

Carter and his new wife Bri have their twin boys, Nate and Parker, who are already growing into little ice hockey lovers. They came along at the perfect time for Georgie. She really needed other kids to bond with, and the fact that they're twins and just as rough as she is was a bonus. And speaking of bonuses, I'm pretty sure Brianna is pregnant again, though neither of them has said anything.

Ten months ago, Cassie and Jax welcomed their little bulldozer, Hudson, into the world, who must be the funniest little guy I've ever met. Then, of course, Logan and his wife, Elle, had a beautiful little girl, Lilly, who's only six months old. And I swear, my Georgie fell in love with her the second she was born. After having three boy cousins, she loved that there was a new girl to play with. And by play, I mean, she pushes her around in a toy stroller and treats her as though she's one of her dollies.

Seeing my siblings take on parenthood is one of the best experiences life has to offer, but what's better is watching the five kids come together and have each other's backs. The bond they're creating will last them a lifetime. It's literally the most beautiful thing I've ever seen.

Hearing my little Georgie girl calling for me, I scoop up the snacks and hurry back out to the yard, then just as the older kids dive in, my phone chimes with a notification. I quickly get the younger kids sorted with their snacks before digging into my pocket and finding my phone. I dread checking it. My firm knows that weekends are for my family, and I'm going to be pissed if they even attempt to drag me away, but sometimes it comes with the territory of being the best criminal attorney in the country.

Glancing down at my phone, I find a notification on the screen and stare at it in confusion. "What the fuck is this?" I grunt to anyone who'll listen, not recognizing the app it's come from.

Cassie peers over my shoulder before snatching the phone out of my hand, a cheesy as fuck grin plastered across her face. "Ooh," she teases. "You have a match on Tinder."

"A match on what?" I question, trying to grab my phone back.

Cassie's head snaps up, and she looks at me as though an alien lifeform just stepped out of my body and asked her to suck its dick. "What do you mean *a match on what?*" she questions. "It's Tinder. Have you been living under a rock?"

"Cass," I groan, getting frustrated and taking my phone back. "What the fuck is Tinder? And why the hell is it on my phone?"

"It's a dating app, dude," Carter explains as the grin widens on Cassie's face, making me realize that she had everything to do with this. "It searches for matches in your area, and you have to swipe right on the girls you're interested in. If they like you, you'll match."

"Right," I grunt, still very confused as I fix a heavy stare on my little sister. "But that doesn't explain how the fuck it got on my phone."

"Guilty," Logan says with a cringe as he raises his hand, making my head whip around to him in shock. I should have fucking known. "I thought it was time for you to start getting back out there."

"What?" I question, anger starting to pulse through my veins. The idea of trying to move on from Sara makes me want to double over in agony. "That's none of your fucking business."

I mean, shit. Who the fuck does he think he is? I don't want to date. I'm not even a little bit ready for that. Hell, I'm not even remotely interested. With work and looking after Georgie, I don't have time for it, nor do I want to. I might not be content with how the past few years have gone without Sara, but it works for Georgie and me.

Besides, what would Sara think? I can't just find some random chick from a dating app and insert her into her daughter's life. I have a child and a dead wife to think about. The thought of it just feels wrong, like they're wanting me to replace Sara.

"Dude, chill out," Logan says, his hands up in surrender. "I didn't mean anything by it. I swiped right on a few chicks for you and if they decide to match, then you can go from there. If not, whatever. I just thought dating could help to . . . I don't know . . . liven you up again."

"What's that supposed to mean?" I snap, not liking where this is going.

"You're just . . . since Sara passed, you've not been yourself. I just ha—"

"What the fuck do you expect?" I roar, flying to my feet and cutting off whatever bullshit was about to fly out of his mouth. "My wife fucking died. Of course, I'm not myself. She's gone, and I'm left to raise a child on my own. I don't want to date. I don't want some other woman in my life. And I sure as fuck don't want Georgie thinking someone else is her mother. What I want is for my wife to come back to me so I can stop hurting all the damn time."

Logan presses his lips into a tight line, and I see the pity in his eyes. I get it. Ever since he found Elle, he's obsessed with wanting everyone else to be as happy as he is, but for me, that just can't happen again. You don't find love like that twice in one life. I had my shot, and now it's gone.

Unable to handle the pitying stares, I turn to Cass and throw my phone into her lap. "Please, get this shit off my phone," I beg her, my chest straining with the pain.

She gives me a sad smile and thankfully gets on with it before handing my phone back to me. Then not wanting my daughter to see me falling apart, I check she has everything she needs and grab my drink, heading across the yard to the pool that overlooks the beautiful Denver cityscape. I desperately need to calm down, but I'm not sure if I'm angry with Logan for trying to push me when I wasn't ready, or if I'm angry with Sara for leaving me in the first place.

She's the only woman I've ever been with, the only woman I've ever loved. We started dating in high school, and for the twelve wonderful years we spent together, I never once considered being with someone else. Why the hell should I now?

I stand by the pool for at least twenty minutes before I hear someone approaching, and I turn to find Logan. Before I can give him a piece of my mind, his hands go up in surrender again. "I just want to talk," he warns.

I scoff and glance back at the view before lifting my drink to my lips and finishing what's left in the bottle. "Not sure if you caught on, but I'm not in the mood."

"No shit," he grunts, moving in beside me and mimicking my stance against the pool fence. He stands in silence for the shortest moment, as if trying to figure out what to say, before finally saying whatever the hell it is he feels he has the right to say. "We just want you to find your happiness again," he murmurs.

"My happiness was with Sara," I grunt, refusing to meet his eye. "It's gone. She took it with her when she died."

"We know that, and I don't want you to take this the wrong way, but Sara's gone, and you've been this depressed, broken version of yourself ever since," he says, making me wonder who this we is he's referring to. "You have no joy in your life, and we fear that's hurting you more than you know."

"I have Georgie," I remind him.

"I don't mean Georgie, and you know it," he says. "She's amazing and has been your rock over the last three years, but that's the love of a parent to his child. You shouldn't rely on your daughter for your own happiness. It's your job to give her joy, not the other way around. That's an awfully big burden for a child to carry."

Guilt soars through my chest, knowing he's right, but I'm not even close to being able to admit that.

"What about your heart, Sean?" he questions. "Don't you deserve to find that love again?"

"Logan," I groan, turning to face him, feeling my world crumbling beneath me. "I don't *want* to find it again. The idea of replacing Sara . . . I can't do it."

"Why the hell not?" he argues. "You know how good it can be.

Sara would want you to be happy. You're holding onto a ghost, hoping that one day she might come back to you. She's never coming back, Sean."

Anger rips through my soul, an inferno burning beneath the surface. "Don't tell me what Sara would want," I snap.

"Sean, just think about it, alright," he tells me before clapping me on the back, trying to calm me down. "You can't live the rest of your life pining over someone who's gone. You need to move forward and at least try. Be an example to Georgie. Let her know that it's possible to find happiness after tragedy."

"Just replace Sara, huh?"

Logan looks horrified at the thought, his eyes widening as if fearing he's taken it too far, and honestly, he took it too far the second he decided to step into my business. "Never. Sara is the mother of your child and was your wife, the first woman you ever loved. We all fucking loved her. No other woman could ever replace that. I just don't want you to spend the rest of your life alone. You're only thirty and deserve to have joy in your life. I'm not telling you to replace Sara, but you should make space for someone new to share your life with. You're fucking lonely, Sean. You could have more kids like you always wanted. Sara would be okay with it, and you know, I bet Georgie would be too. She loves you more than anything, and I know she's only three, but she's smart. She knows you're hurting, and I bet, more than anything, she wants to see just how fucking bright you can shine."

Logan gives me a tight smile, and with that, he turns on his heel and heads back up to the house, leaving me with a million traitorous thoughts running through my head.

Could Logan be right? The thought kills me that he could be. Don't get me wrong, it's not like I've never thought about it before. I just hate it, like really fucking hate it. But what about Georgie? She needs a mother figure in her life, someone who she can grow with, someone who can teach her all the things I simply can't as a man. I know she has all her aunties, but what about someone who would love her as a parent would? Someone who's there for her after a shitty day at school. Someone to hold her hand when she has her first heartbreak. Someone to confide in and teach her what it means to be a woman, someone she can rely on, someone to love.

Fuck.

Logan's right.

I don't know about the whole dating a chick for my own happiness bullshit because that's a long shot, but there's no doubt in my mind that Georgie needs a mother figure in her life, something more than Cassie, Elle, or Bri could offer. But fuck, it kills me to think Georgie might forget her real mom, forget what really matters.

Over my dead body.

I push the thought aside. It's ridiculous. I don't want to date. I want to continue the way I am, not needing a woman in my life to take up space and lay where Sara used to lay, hanging clothes where Sara's used to hang, cooking in the kitchen that Sara so carefully designed and loved.

Fuck no. I can't do it.

Turning back, I head up to the house, throwing my empty bottle in the trash on the way, noticing everyone else has gone back inside. I pause at the back door and take a breath, knowing the second I walk through it, all eyes will be on me. I can't just crumble where I stand in front of my entire family, I need to pull myself together.

Making my way inside, I grab a new drink and silently take a seat among my family, right where I can watch the kids play. I keep my eyes trained on Georgie, the oldest, and watch as she dominates whatever game they're playing—perks of being the biggest.

No one mentions the topic of me dating, doesn't even breathe the word *Tinder*, and I'm finally able to relax, but there's no denying I'm a tortured soul.

An hour later, I scoop Georgie up in my arms and head out to my truck. I've been shit company, even worse as we sat down to eat, unable to stop thinking about Sara and the possibility of trying to make room for someone new.

I buckle Georgie into her seat, and she reaches up to place her little hand on my cheek. "Wuv you, Daddy," she says with a heavy sigh before squishing her face into the side of her car seat trying to get comfortable. And I can't help but wonder if Logan was right. Can Georgie really sense just how much I'm hurting?

I look down at my angel and finally see reason. I need to try for her. She deserves the world, and right now, she only has half of it. I'd do just about anything to make sure she has everything she ever wants, and I guess that includes someone who'll love her like a mother.

Damn you, Logan.

With a sigh, I close the door and walk around to the driver's side.

I get in and start up the engine, and I'm hardly halfway down the driveway before Georgie is fast asleep in her car seat. It's been a long, exhausting day for such a little thing, but with all the sleepless nights lately, she's been incredibly tired. Add that to her preschool days, and the poor kid is wrecked.

Her light snores fill the cab as I drive home in silence, and ten minutes later, I pull up in front of my place. I go about pulling Georgie out while trying not to wake her, and honestly, this shit is harder than taking the fucking bar exams.

Taking her straight up to her room, I lay her down in her bed before sitting beside her, wanting to be close so I can watch her breathing. Then before I even know what I'm doing, I pull my phone out and attempt to download that dating app when I realize Cassie never deleted it, just moved it across to the next page so I couldn't see it.

I should have known better.

Opening the app with shaky hands, I bring up the profile of the girl who matched with me. Her picture hits me first. She's cute. Petite with light brown hair and green eyes. There's something familiar about her, but I just can't place it. She looks lively like she knows how to have fun, but can I date her? Who fucking knows.

I should try . . . but maybe I should wait a little longer first. Maybe I'm taking this too fast.

Shit. I don't fucking know.

I'm not ready for this.

With Sara, it was so easy, I just knew right away. She had just transferred to our school, and I practically bombarded her until she'd agreed to go out with me, but this woman . . . She's not Sara.

Nobody is.

Chapter Four

GIGI

I rush around the busy emergency room, absolutely exhausted. I've been put on a double shift, and it's killing me. I spent the day up on the maternity ward, doing what I do best, only to be asked to cover the night shift in the ER. Due to my inability to say no, here I am, practically dead on my feet. The only good thing is that this means I can take tomorrow off.

My only saving grace is that the ER is crazy busy, which is making the time fly past. So far, I've had a woman with a broken leg who decided to try snowboarding in the middle of the night, a man with a fractured eye socket who was in a bar fight, and a little girl whose mother thought she had a snake bite. Turned out to be two little red pen marks that came right off with alcohol wipes. I mean, it's none of my business how the pen marks got there, but judging by the shit-eating grin on the little girl's face, I have my suspicions.

Shit got exciting ten minutes ago when a man came in with stab wounds. I desperately wanted to work on him, but I just missed out. Don't get me wrong, it's a total travesty, but at the same time, it would have been awesome. I, however, got stuck on clean-up duty after the stab victim left a trail of blood from one end of the ER to the other. Someone's got to do the dirty jobs, and tonight, it's me. As if getting the piss bag spilled all over me last week wasn't enough.

I'm five hours into the second shift and it's well past midnight. I'm exhausted, but thankfully things have finally started to slow down. Taking a short break, I move around the reception desk and flop down in the desk chair as I let out a heavy sigh, desperately wishing for a quick power nap to keep me going.

With the quick downtime, I can't help but check my phone, glancing at my Tinder app for the hundredth time for tonight, just in case I missed the notification, but let's be honest, there was no notification. I've been holding out hope for something that's never going to happen.

The guy clearly isn't interested, or maybe he hasn't checked his Tinder account. Who knows. Maybe he accidentally went and dropped his phone down a storm drain, and in this cold Denver weather, it's stuck in a block of ice and he's just waiting for it to thaw before he can finally respond. Yeah, that's definitely it. Let's go with that.

Trying to maintain some level of professionalism, I put my phone away and grab a stack of paperwork to get a head start on patient reports. I'm halfway through when Sue, my supervisor, sticks her head around the corner and gives me a tight smile. "Oh, here you are," she says.

Glancing up, I meet her stare. "Do you need something?" I question. "I'm free for the time being."

"Oh, it's nothing important," she says. "Just checking if you wanted to go and have your break while we're quiet?"

"Oh, sure," I say, putting the paperwork into a neat pile and getting to my feet. I make my way out from around the reception desk as Sue scurries away, and just as my stomach starts to grumble with the promise of food, a commotion sounds at the door. "Perhaps not," I grumble before hurrying to investigate what the hell is going on.

A man barges through the ER doors with a child limp in his arms. "HELP," he roars, the agony in his tone almost bringing me to my knees. "She can't breathe."

Fuck.

Instincts and training have me springing into action, and I race toward the man, immediately scooping her out of his arms and onto a gurney. "What's wrong with her?" I question as my skilled gaze starts assessing, trying to figure out what the fuck is going on.

I hear shallow breaths, and my first thought is choking. There's no sign of trauma, so I rule out a crushed windpipe and prepare to remove the blockage, my brain going a million miles an hour as I come up with other likely scenarios.

"Severe asthma," the man rushes out, putting my mind at ease and giving me the information to be able to treat his little girl. "She's already had a few doses of her Ventolin tonight."

Shit. This isn't good. "Page the doctor," I call, seeing Sue hurrying back down the hall toward us.

The girl's eyes flutter, and the tears staining her cheeks kill me. She must be terrified.

Because she looks so young, I tilt her chin up and check her airway for any foreign objects. After seeing nothing, I agree that it's definitely asthma and hope like fuck that we don't have to intubate her. "How old is she?" I question.

"Just turned three."

"Okay, tell me about her night. How many times have you administered Ventolin?"

The man starts rushing through the details of their night, and I listen closely as I place a pulse oximeter on her tiny finger and wait for her reading. "Any allergies?"

"No, none that I'm aware of."

Sue rushes in and closes the curtain behind her to give us a little privacy. "I'm going to need a corticosteroid injection," I tell her, seeing the reading on her oxygen levels dropping steadily.

Sue jumps straight into action and prepares the injection as I remain with the little girl, positioning her in a way to make it just a little easier to take a breath, but fuck, she must be so uncomfortable. Seeing the needle, the man balks, his eyes going wide with horror, looking between the needle and his little girl, knowing this is bound to scare her. "What's that for?" he questions.

"A steroid injection," I explain, getting antsy as I wait for the doctor to hurry up and save this little girl. "It will act the same way as the Ventolin. It'll help relax the muscles around her airway."

He nods, and when the doctor still hasn't arrived, I don't give it a second thought as I work on saving the little girl. The man takes her hand and squeezes, and I pull on a pair of gloves and quickly insert the needle, hating the way the little girl flinches in pain.

I lightly rub the injection site, willing the medicine to work its magic, realizing it's been such a rush, I haven't even had a chance to ask her name.

Within seconds, the little girl takes a breath. It's not a great breath, but it's enough to give her small body the oxygen it so desperately needs. "Thank fuck," I mutter under my breath, my heart pounding as her oxygen level improves a little.

The father rushes into her, crushing her into his big chest as tears of relief fill his eyes. He should probably give her the space she needs, but I'll allow a small hug. After all, what parent wouldn't be desperate to hold their child in this situation? I'm not a parent myself, but I can only imagine the unconditional love that comes along with the territory.

"Oh, thank God," he sighs with relief, but as her breathing deepens, he still holds onto her as if she's about to slip right through his fingertips.

The little girl cries in his arms as I pull off my gloves and find her a glass of water. I hand it over to the father, and he takes it eagerly before holding it up to the little girl's lips. Once she's done, the man places the plastic cup down on the end of the gurney before finally looking up at me.

My eyes widen as my heart starts pounding erratically, having no fucking idea what to say.

It's the Tinder guy.

Sean.

No fucking way.

Hoooooly shit. Why does the ground never come and swallow you whole when you need it?

Embarrassment begins flooding me as my greedy gaze attempts to sail up and down his body, knowing exactly what's hidden beneath his shirt, but damn it, my professionalism just has to come in and ruin a good thing.

"Thank you," he says with every ounce of emotion in his body radiating out of his dark, dreamy eyes.

I'm completely thrown off, and it's obvious by the way he's looking at me that he has absolutely no idea who I am. And if he does, he's way too caught up with his daughter to make the connection. And there I was sitting at the reception desk barely an hour ago, wondering why he hadn't connected with me through Tinder, and it was because he was in the middle of trying to save his baby. How fucking shallow does that make me?

Giving him a tight smile, I try to shake it off. "That's what I'm here for," I tell him before turning away and giving him some privacy with his baby girl. Just outside the curtains, I start filling out a chart, realizing I still haven't asked the little girl's name.

What the fuck is wrong with me? One look at the sexy Tinder dude and I've turned into a frazzled mess. I didn't even talk to the little girl or offer my name. Shit, he was right not to respond to my Tinder match. He must think I'm awful. Mel wouldn't have had that issue. She would have that little girl laughing and the father already eating out of the palm of her hand.

The doctor finally makes his appearance up the hallway, and I walk to meet him in the middle. "Three-year-old girl with severe asthma has had four attacks tonight. Arrived struggling for breath with an oxygen reading of less than 92. I administered a dosage of corticosteroid."

"Excellent. What's the condition of the child now?" he questions as we near the room.

"Good. Stable," I reply.

"As efficient as ever, Gigi," he says before whipping back the curtain and walking in to check on her.

I follow him in just in case he needs anything. "Hi, I'm Dr. Richards," he says as he offers the father his hand.

"Hey, I'm Sean," he says, reaching out to shake the doctor's hand before indicating his little girl, "and this little terror is Georgia."

You're kidding? I share a name with the guy's kid. Could this situation be any more coincidental?

"I understand your daughter has been suffering severe asthma attacks?" the doctor goes on.

"Yes, that's correct," Sean says, clutching Georgia's hand as if the two of them are all they have in the world. "She had three at home that were manageable with her inhaler. That's when I brought her here. The fourth attack started in the parking lot and then, umm," he says, waving a hand toward me with a cringe, realizing he doesn't know my name.

"Gigi," the doctor supplies before I get a chance to respond.

Sean's brows furrow at the name, but he continues as a lump gets caught in my throat, realizing he might recognize me after all. "Thanks. Gigi gave her an injection and she was able to breathe again."

"Good," Dr. Richards says before stepping up to little Georgia and pressing his stethoscope to her chest. The room falls into silence as the doctor concentrates, and I watch the way Georgia so effortlessly knows just what to do, as if this isn't her first mad dash to the hospital. "Alright," he says to Sean. "I think it's best we get her admitted and keep her overnight for observation."

Sean nods while the doctor turns to me and hands me her chart. "Can you get them sorted?"

"Of course," I smile before he disappears.

With Sean occupied by his upset child, I exit the room and head back to the waiting room, trying to figure out exactly where we can put her. I get her everything she'll need to get admitted, and after a quick call to the pediatric ward upstairs, I find a private room for little Georgia.

Just as I go to head back to let them know what's going on, Sue hands me the clipboard with all the paperwork Sean is going to have to fill out, giving me a knowing smile. "I figured you'd need this."

"Unfortunately, I do," I say with a yawn as I take the clipboard and head back to Sean and his daughter. I hand Sean the paperwork and a pen, and he starts scrawling out his details as I get little Georgia ready to be transferred to the ward.

Ten minutes later, she's settled with the best doctors and nurses Denver has to offer.

I go about grabbing extra pillows and blankets from the supply closet, figuring Sean will most likely ignore hospital policy and climb right into bed with his daughter. She's so small, and compared to her, the bed is massive. There's more than enough space for the two of them to be comfortable.

Then certain they have everything they'll need, I let the ward nurses take over as I scram and get my ass out of there. I'm halfway up the hall when his deep, velvety voice calls after me. "Um, Gigi, is it?"

Fuck.

Turning around to face the most delicious man I've ever laid eyes on, I try my hardest to be professional, hating how obvious I am. "Yes?" I smile, my heart pounding in my chest. "Is there something you need?"

"No, umm. We're fine. It's just that . . ." he cringes as he rubs the back of his neck, and I can't help but notice the way his biceps bulge with the movement and his shirt rides up at his hip to show off the most mouth-watering sliver of tanned skin. I force my gaze to remain locked on him, which is when I realize that it's the dead of night and he isn't wearing a coat. The poor guy didn't even get a second to grab a coat before racing out of the house with his sick baby, and here he is, not even a hint that he's thinking about his own needs. "Have we met?

I mean, I know your face from somewhere."

Fuck me, this is not happening.

"Umm, no," I smile, feeling awkward as fuck. "I don't think so."

"I'm sure of it," he insists as the embarrassment really starts to set in. "Sorry. I'm usually really good at this shit. If it wasn't for everything going down with Georgie, I'd probably be able to figure it out."

"It's fine. I understand. Besides, I'm certain, we've never *met* before."

He gives me a curious stare that tells me he thinks I'm wrong, and the way he narrows his eyes, truly trying to figure it out, has me desperate to run away like a little bitch. For him to recognize my face means he has checked his Tinder account, probably even searched my profile as well, but he still didn't respond.

"Anyway, unless you need anything for your daughter, I should really get going," I tell him. "We've got a busy ER tonight."

"Oh, of course," he says, taking a hesitant step back, clearly knowing I'm lying. After all, his daughter was the only patient when he walked in. "I won't hold you up."

With that, he gives me a forced smile, and I find myself wondering what a real smile would look like from him, but knowing I can't get carried away, I quickly excuse myself and turn on my heel, all but running back down the hall. I take a risk and peek back over my shoulder to see him still looking after me, trying to figure it out, and as he catches my stare, my cheeks flush a bright shade of red.

Shit. What is wrong with me?

Scurrying away, I get my ass back down to the ER, and seeing that everything is calm and under control, I deem it safe to finally take my break. The second I finish annihilating my food, I pull my phone out and hash out a text as I relax back in the nurses' break room, counting down the hours until I can get out of here.

Gigi – Dude. The Tinder guy is here. He's fucking dreamy. What are the fucking chances?

Her reply comes through almost instantly, and I realize she must be playing on her phone, probably swiping through Tinder looking for tonight's sausage. There's no stopping this girl when she's hungry for dick.

Mel – Take him to the on-call room and fuck him sideways.

I practically snort my lemonade all over the table while trying not to laugh like a damn hyena.

Gigi – Sorry, I'm not a slutty whore like you.

Mel – You only wish you were. Go talk to him. Get his number.

Gigi – No, he's got his kid with him. She's absolutely gorgeous by the way. And besides, he didn't respond to the whole Tinder thing. He's not interested.

Mel – Of course he has a gorgeous kid, she has his DNA. Believe me, any guy would be stupid not to be interested in you. But before you start hitting that, make sure there's no ring on his finger. Where there are kids, there's usually baby-momma drama.

Gigi – Ughhhhhh. I didn't even think about that. Just my fucking luck, right?

Mel –I mean . . . I'd still hit it.

I'm about to respond when a new patient comes through the ER doors, and I shove my head out the break room door to see what's going on. Realizing I'm going to be needed, I drop my phone into my pocket and get back to work. After all, helping people is what I love to do. I just wish my newest patient wasn't struggling with a gastro bug.

I busily get on with my duties as another three gastro patients come through the door, and I realize tonight will be longer than I ever anticipated. A gastro outbreak is exactly what we need floating around here.

Four hours later, my shift is over, and despite knowing Georgia is being carefully cared for upstairs, I find myself wandering back up to check on her one last time. Georgia's chest needs to be listened to and we need to make sure she doesn't go spiraling into her fifth asthma attack for the night, or maybe I'm just making excuses to see Sean one last time.

Stepping into her room, I find Sean sitting up in the bed, wide awake with Georgia wrapped in his arms. I take in the exhausted little girl in his arms and it breaks my heart. Her little eyes flutter, and she moans in her broken sleep, trying to snuggle even closer to her daddy, and for some reason, I find myself growing attached to this beautiful little girl that I only met a few hours ago.

I give Sean a tight smile. "How's she doing?" I ask, picking up her chart and double-checking that she's getting everything she needs.

"Better now," he murmurs, his voice so low I can almost feel the vibrations right through my chest. "Thanks to you."

He holds my stare, and I fumble for a moment, forgetting what the hell I'm supposed to be doing. "I, umm . . . I was just doing my job," I tell him. Hooking the chart back over the end of Georgia's bed, I glance up and meet that intense stare. "I'm just finishing my shift for the night, but I'm glad your little girl is doing better."

With that, I hightail it out of there, exiting the room while wishing there was something more I could do for this little girl, but it's not like there's a magical cure for asthma. It's just something she'll have to struggle with throughout her life.

Twenty minutes later, I'm utterly exhausted as I push through the door of my apartment. After dropping my shit on the ground, I trudge down the hallway before pausing at the bathroom door, glancing in and looking longingly at the shower. Letting out a sigh, I debate my need to scrub any gastro germs off me over my need to sleep, when Mel's voice sails down the hallway. "Is that you, Gi?" she asks from her room.

"Yeah, just me," I reply, stripping out of my clothes as I groggily make my way down past her room and into my own, already naked by the time I hit the bed, more than prepared to risk the gastro germs in my need to sleep. I'll just be sure to change my sheets first thing in the morning.

"Did you fuck Mr. Dreamy?" she questions through the wall.

"No," I groan.

"Frigid bitch."

"Fuck you, whore," I say with a yawn. "Go and nurse your STDs."

"Mmkay," she says before promptly falling back asleep.

Snuggling into my bed, I try to sleep, but I find myself thinking back to Sean and Georgia. I know I'll never see them again, but I can't help but feel torn about it.

I feel so helpless.

Every now and then, you'll come across a patient who tears your heart out, and Georgia was one of them for me. She doesn't deserve to suffer like this. I can only imagine how terrifying it must be for both her and Sean.

I just wish there was something more I could do for her, something that could at least put a smile on her face. But come tomorrow, she'll have Mel looking after her in the pediatric ward, and soon enough, Dr. Richards is going to discharge her and she'll be back to living her normal happy life.

Despite how much I want to see them again, for Georgia's sake, I hope I don't have to. So, somebody please tell me why the hell that hurts so bad.

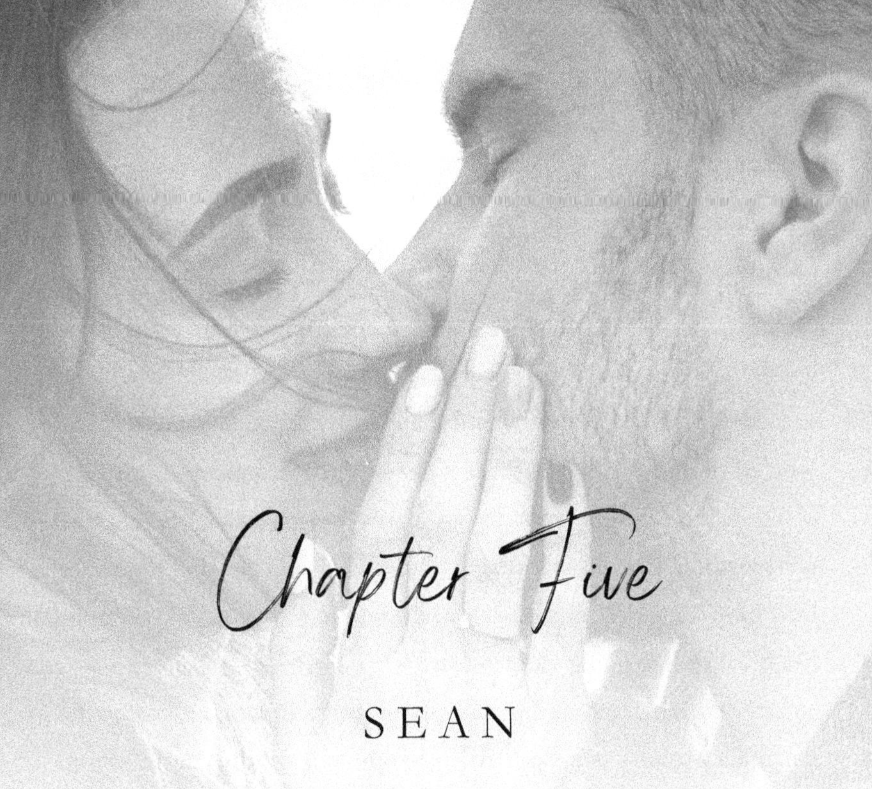

Chapter Five

SEAN

What a shit night.

My arms are stiff from holding onto Georgie all night, but every time I would try to wriggle out from under her, she'd wake. Then the nurses would come in and wake her, then the doctor would come and wake her, the only person who didn't want to poke and prod at her was Gigi.

The whole thing fucking sucked. I just want to take her home.

I've never been so terrified in my life. Georgie had an awful night with her asthma—the worst one so far. She had three attacks at home and after not being able to breathe properly after the third, I buckled her straight into my truck and got her ass to the hospital. But when that fourth one hit in the hospital parking lot . . . fuck.

She didn't want to be out of my arms, so the second I strapped her into her car seat she screamed. She was so tired and exhausted, all she wanted to do was sleep.

I raced to the hospital knowing the screaming wasn't going to be good for her lungs. We'd just pulled into the parking lot when she gasped for breath and my world stopped. I turned around, and the look of terror on her face will forever stay with me. My little girl couldn't breathe. She kept trying, desperately needing the oxygen, grasping onto her throat as she tried to suck in a breath, but no matter how hard she tried, she couldn't. Her eyes were wide, and I could see her wordlessly begging me to make it stop.

I think I had parked my truck up on the curb right in front of the emergency room door. I can't even be sure if I cut the engine or not. All I know is that I had to get my baby help.

I ripped her out of her car seat before running into the emergency room and screaming for help. Some woman, Gigi, came and took her from my arms, and I had to stop myself from holding on longer.

Gigi raced and nearly threw her down on the bed in her rush to get her breathing. She looked her over, asked a few questions that I can't for the life of me remember, then gave her the injection that saved her life.

I could have kissed the woman right then and there. She'd saved my baby girl, and I don't know how I'll ever repay her. Come to think of it, I don't even know if I said thank you to her. I was so caught up with everything that was going on with Georgie that I don't even know if I was a pleasant human being.

Probably not. Since Sara passed, I've been known to be a moody old bastard.

Dr. Richards strides through the door, bringing me back to the present, and I watch as he checks over Georgia before finally telling me that she's doing much better and that with a new Ventolin prescription and dosage, she'll be discharged this morning.

"Thank goodness, Georgie Girl," I say to my little girl, giving her a squeeze. "We get to go home soon."

She smiles up at me in relief as the nurse with the breakfast cart comes and pokes her head through the door and offers Georgie a plate. She greedily accepts and is busy chowing down before the nurse has even left the room.

The hours slowly tick by, and despite being told that we'll be discharged this morning, I realize it could still be a very long wait. I sit impatiently waiting at the end of Georgie's bed, desperate to get out of here and get my little girl home. Looking down at my watch, I groan. I need to be in court in three hours, and despite how badly I want to stay right here beside my little girl, I don't exactly have the kind of job that offers me freedom.

I pull my phone out and bring up Logan's number before pressing it against my ear. It rings three times before his too-cheery voice sails through the line. "Yo, what's up?"

"You got any plans today?" I ask with a cringe. It's the beginning of a new hockey season, and since he has his first game at the end of the week, he should be back in training. I'm hoping like fuck today is a rest day for him.

"Just have a team meeting this morning, then free as a bird," he tells me. "Why? What's up?"

Relief fills my veins, and I let out a heavy sigh. "Do you think you guys could watch Georgie for a few hours? I've got to head into court."

"Sure, but it's Monday. Doesn't Georgie usually go to preschool today?" he questions.

"Usually, yeah," I explain, letting him hear the exhaustion in my tone, not needing to mask it with my family. "We had a shit night. By the fourth asthma attack, she ended up in the hospital unable to breathe. We've been here all night."

"Fuck," Logan curses, cutting off my explanation of our horrendous night, sounding as though he's getting up and racing around his home, his keys already in hand. "Is she okay? We're coming down."

"No, don't come down. She'll be discharged soon. She's doing much better, but I need her to be with someone I can trust, especially today. I've got the Sanchez case, and I can't afford to be distracted. I know the school is good and on the ball with her asthma, but there are fifty other kids there for them to worry about. I can't have anything slipping through the cracks, not today."

"Yeah, I get it," he says. "Sure thing, man. Just bring her around whenever you need. I can Zoom the team meeting. Management will understand."

"Thanks, bro," I tell him. "We'll be there in roughly an hour, depending how quickly Georgie gets discharged."

I end the call and am delighted when a nurse comes in and gives me all the discharge papers, but no one is more delighted than Georgie. I get straight to work and sign everything that needs to be signed before collecting Georgie and finally leaving the room.

Georgie chatters away, and we're halfway down the hall when I find myself pausing and doubling back to the nurses' station. A young nurse, maybe twenty-five or so is sitting at the table, her head and shoulder practically glued together as she holds the phone between them, clearly bored while waiting on hold.

She looks up at me as I approach, and I give her an awkward smile, not really knowing what I'm doing. "Hi, uhh . . . Mel," I say, glancing down to read her name badge.

She gives me a welcoming smile, and her eyes sparkle as though she knows something she shouldn't—something I see way too often with the guilty pricks I face in the courtroom. "Hi there," she says politely, though something tells me she's anything but. "How can I help you?"

"I know this is probably a long shot, but I was wondering if the nurse who took care of my daughter was here. I'd like to thank her."

"Really?" she questions, looking as though she's about to burst. "That wouldn't be Gigi, would it? Petite brunette, super cute with a killer smile and an ass—" She cuts herself off, glancing at Georgie in my arms before correcting herself, "booty to die for?"

"Yeah, that's her," I say, feeling a little odd agreeing to those things, but she's not wrong. "Is she around?"

"No, actually. She isn't," she says with a cringe before quickly glancing up and down the hall. I can practically see the lightbulb go off in her mind, and not a second later, she pulls her phone out of her scrubs and writes something down on a pink Post-it note. "Here," she says a moment later, handing me the little piece of scrap paper. "That's Gigi's number, but don't tell anyone you got it from me."

"Thanks," I smile gratefully as I look down at the pink paper and see Gigi's number scrawled in black marker, unsure why the paper seems to be burning in the palm of my hand. Glancing down at Georgie, I give her a nudge. "What do you say?"

"Fank you for looking after me," Georgie says in that beautiful little voice.

Mel's eyes flick to my little girl and take her in, clearly adoring her just as much as everyone else Georgie meets does. "My, oh my. You certainly are gorgeous, aren't you?"

Georgie giggles at the compliment, and I say a quick goodbye to the woman before heading out to the parking lot, only to see my truck is no longer blocking the entryway and I cringe, realizing it must have been towed. "Shit," I mutter, trying to figure out how we're going to deal with this while also making it into court on time.

"Hey," a man says to my right, and I turn to find a paramedic, creeping toward us. "You looking for your truck?"

"Yeah, you know where it is?" I say, needing to tighten my hold on Georgie when she sees the ambulance and nearly loses her shit.

He digs into his pockets and pulls out a very familiar set of car keys and tosses them my way. "I parked it round back," he tells me, hooking his thumb in the right direction.

Relief pounds through my veins, and I let out a heavy breath. "Fuck, thanks, man. I thought it might have been towed. I'm sorry to have left it there like that," I tell him.

"It's no problem. It happens more than you'd think," he says before giving Georgie a fond smile. "Anyone who parks their truck like that . . . Well, shit. I've been doing this long enough to know when it's an emergency. Just keep her healthy."

"Will do," I say, feeling overwhelmed by his kindness.

He turns away to get back to work, and as I take off around back to look for my truck, I make a mental note to buy the guy a case of beer. He could have easily had my truck towed. Hell, he should have, considering the way I was parked, but he had my back and showed kindness to a complete stranger who was having a shitty night.

The world needs more men like that.

Needing to get on my way, I drive us home, this time without breaking any laws, and before I know it, I'm dressed in my suit and stopping by Logan's ridiculously massive home.

Georgie jumps out of my truck and makes her way up the stairs as I follow behind with her bag, double-checking I have all her medications and spare inhalers just in case. She motions for me to pick her up so she can reach the doorbell and then proceeds to press it over and over again until Uncle Logan appears at the door.

She squeals in delight when she sees him and throws herself out of my arms. Luckily for Georgie, Logan's reflexes are lightning fast, and he scoops her out of the air. "How's my girl?" he asks as she squishes her face into his chest and wipes snot all over the shirt he probably needs to wear during his Zoom meeting.

"Goowd," she says in her little baby voice. "I went to hopital again."

"Oh, dear," Logan says with wide eyes, putting on a show for her. "Did the doctor make you all better?"

Georgie shakes her head. "No. Da prwitty gurl did."

"Really? The pretty girl?" he questions, his gaze flicking to mine as he arches a brow, but I'm not having it. I'm not falling into his trap.

"Uh-huh," Georgie says with a smile. "She helwped me breathe."

"That's good," Logan says before placing her down and letting her race into his home to run amok and probably force little Lilly into a toy stroller.

Logan and I follow her in, and as I dump all of her things on the kitchen counter, Logan looks at me with fierce concern flashing in his eyes. "She's really alright?" he asks.

"Yeah, she's doing much better," I tell him as I let out a breath of relief, needing him not to drill me on this right now, not sure how much longer I can hold it together. "But that reminds me," I say as I pull the pink Post-it note from my pocket with Gigi's number. "I've got the nurse's number. I want to call her."

Logan's eyes widen in surprise, gaping at me as though I just told him I was trying out for the national ballet. "You're going to call her?" he questions, his eyes only getting wider.

I pull my phone out and start dialing Gigi's number. "Calm down, moron. I'm just calling to thank her for everything she did for Georgie.

Nothing else."

"Oh . . . Okay, then," Logan says as he takes a seat at the kitchen table, clearly very disappointed that he wasn't about to witness the stars aligning for me to fall madly in love with some random chick I just met. I fucking love my brother, but he's a cup-half-full kind of guy, and his optimism is an illness.

The phone rings, and as a strange nervousness settles deep into my gut, I have to turn away, unable to meet Logan's eye.

"Hello," her voice croaks into the phone, something about the soft tone making a strange flutter start in my stomach.

"Shit, you were sleeping," I mutter. I should have thought this out. The woman just worked a night shift. Of course she'd be sleeping. How fucking stupid could I be? I wanted to thank the woman and now I've managed to wake her from the sleep she desperately needs.

"Huh? Who is this?" she questions.

Fuck, I've made a fool of myself. *Abort.* I should just end the call and pretend it never happened.

"Hi. Sorry. It's Sean. You looked after my daughter last night," I say, hoping I don't sound like some kind of fucked-up stalker who did questionable things to get her number.

"Umm, yeah," she says hesitantly. "How'd you get my number?"

"One of the nurses gave it to me," I admit with a cringe, hoping I'm not getting the woman in any kind of trouble. After all, she helped me out. I wouldn't want to return the favor by dumping her in a pile of steaming shit.

Gigi lets out a sigh and I can practically hear the wheels turning in her mind. "That nurse wouldn't have been Mel, was it?" she asks, a smile in her tone that makes my hands shake.

"Yeah," I say as Logan gets up and walks around the counter, trying to catch my eye as if wanting to coach me through this. "I hope that's okay."

"It's fine. She's my best friend."

Thank fuck.

"Right, so, I was just calling because I wanted to say thank you for last night," I say as Logan starts trying to mimic me asking her out for dinner. I try to wave him away, but the bastard is persistent. "I don't know how I'm ever going to repay you. You saved my daughter's life. Without you, I don't know what would have happened."

"Oh, no," she replies, bashfully. "It's fine. I was just doing my job."

I'm just about to tell her that it's so much more than that, and while it's just her job, it means the absolute world to me, when the phone is plucked out of my hand. Logan backs up a few steps and with his training, I know it's not even worth trying to get it back from him. He could run for hours on end.

Logan lifts my phone to his ear and grins at me. "Hey, are you the chick who saved my niece?" he questions.

I give him a scathing glare and he brings the phone down and hits speaker. "Yeah, I guess I am," she says.

"Then you need to come out with us on Saturday," he tells her.

What the fuck is this asshole doing? I shoot daggers at Logan, but he cheerfully ignores me.

"I'm sorry?" Gigi questions.

"You heard me," Logan says, too fucking gleeful for his own good. He lifts his gaze to mine with a secretive smile, making it very clear what the fucker is doing, and I know he's only doing it because he knows damn well I never would. "We're going riding and you're coming."

Huh? Riding? This is the first I'm hearing of it, but apparently, it's in the cards for this weekend. I haven't taken Georgie riding yet and there's no doubt in my mind that she'll absolutely love it. You know, as long as I get her all the proper safety gear and more. I don't think I could handle her falling off.

Hmm, I wonder if I could get them all in pink. Georgie would love that. There are so many things I'm going to have to get her, but I suppose I should start with her own dirt bike. On second thought, that's too dangerous. Sara would have never allowed it. Perhaps a four-wheeler.

"Riding?" Gigi grunts, breaking me out of my inner thoughts.

"Yeah, you know, dirt bike riding," Logan informs her.

"Okay . . . umm, thanks," she says, "but I don't know the first thing about riding. It was nice of you to offer, but I don't think so."

"I'm sorry, but you have no choice in the matter," Logan tells her, his eyes sparkling with mischief. "You saved my niece's life, and now it's your duty to text Sean your address so he can pick you up on Saturday morning and thank you properly."

Gigi laughs, clearly amused by my brother's tactics, and I hate how much I like the sound. "And if I decline?" she questions.

"Then, I promise you that I won't stop bugging you until you agree, and if you knew me, you'd know just how much of a threat that really is."

Oh geez, laying it on thick, Logan.

There's silence on the other end of the line, and I wonder if she's had enough and ended the call until that soft tone flows through the speakers again. "You're telling me there's absolutely no way of backing out of this, huh?"

"That would be correct," Logan tells her.

Gigi lets out a heavy sigh, but something tells me it's not because she's annoyed. "Damn, I guess I'll be tagging along. But be warned, my ass is not getting on a dirt bike. And . . . there better be snacks. I don't go anywhere without snacks."

Logan scoffs. "Trust me, there are always snacks," he says. "And as for getting on a bike, unfortunately, that's not your call to make. But don't worry, Sean's a great teacher. He'll have you performing backflips in no time."

I go to snatch the phone out of Logan's hand, desperate for him to shut the fuck up. I mean, it's clearly obvious he's trying to throw this girl in my face, but we don't know a damn thing about her. She probably has a boyfriend and isn't interested in falling victim to one of Logan's fucked-up games. He knows I'm not fucking ready for this shit, so I don't know why he's pushing it. All he's doing is setting us both up, and at some point, I'm gonna have to push her away and hurt her, which isn't fair to her.

Logan pulls his hand out of my way and joyously continues his conversation with Gigi.

"Oh, geez," she laughs in the sweetest tone, making me wonder what kind of person she is. Though, judging from the way she jumped straight to Georgie's rescue and is happily chatting away with a complete stranger, I feel as though she's the kind of woman I wouldn't mind Georgie spending time with.

Damn it. I'll go through with this ridiculous trip, but that's it. Logan's right . . . again. I owe this girl the world. The least I can do is show her just how thankful I am. Besides, it will give me a chance to get Georgie on a dirt bike for the first time.

"Text your address to this number and Sean will pick you up at nine."

"Nine?" she gasps, cutting off Logan's instructions.

"Yes, nine. We don't want to lose any daylight."

"Fuck me," she mutters. "Daylight? Are you sure the sun is even out of bed before nine?"

Logan laughs then finally lets her go, hopefully to get some more rest after working the night shift. But he doesn't let her go until making her promise to send her address, threatening that if she doesn't, he's going to call her non-stop until she does.

He gingerly hands me my phone with a wicked sparkle in his eyes, and we both look down at the stupid thing as a text message comes through. I open the message to find her address, and I can't help but smirk at the proud look on Logan's face.

"Looks like you got yourself a date, brother," he says as he claps me on the back.

"It's not a date," I say, barely managing to resist punching the fucker right in the face. "I'm just doing this to say thank you for saving my daughter's life."

"Whatever helps you sleep at night, bro."

I narrow my eyes at the dickhead before looking down at my watch. "Shit, I've got to go," I tell him. "Tell Georgie I love her, and don't let her run around too much. I can't have her back in the hospital again."

"Don't worry about her. We've got it handled," he says. "Go nail the bastard."

"I always do," I grin, referring to my conviction rate in the courthouse.

With that, I race out the door, determined not to be late for one of the biggest cases of the year.

Chapter Six

GIGI

What the fuck just happened?

It's one thing to call a girl and tell her thanks, but it's a whole other thing for that girl to agree to go dirt bike riding. What the hell is wrong with me? I don't wanna do that. But there's no denying Sean's friend . . . or brother . . . or . . . I don't know. Whoever he is, he's a conniving little manipulator in the best kind of way. I don't know how it happened, but he laid on the charm and had me eating out of the palm of his hand. Hell, at one point, I could have sworn it might have even been my idea.

I was fast asleep and had been for the past five hours when the call came in, so maybe that's why I agreed. I clearly wasn't awake enough for that shit. Though, they seem fun, and I find myself oddly excited to see Sean again. Apart from the fact that I have absolutely no idea how to ride a dirt bike. But I'm cool to just watch. I'm sure it will be fun all the same. I really hate stepping outside of my comfort zone, but it should be interesting.

Clenching my eyes together, I try to will myself to fall back asleep, but it's not going to happen. I have no idea if it's because I got to speak with Sean again or because of my impending doom of inevitably embarrassing myself come Saturday.

Then realizing I haven't bitched out a certain roommate yet, I grab my phone and hash out a quick text.

Gigi – You're dead.

Mel – Don't know what you're talking about.

God, she's the worst liar.

With a groan, I sit up in bed and swivel around until my feet are firmly on the ground, pushing into my oversized bunny slippers. Realizing today is going to be sponsored by caffeine, I get up and trudge down the hallway before making my way into the kitchen and searching for a mug.

As I get into a fight with the coffee machine, I turn on a little background music before finally making the stupid thing work. With my mug firmly in my hand, I scoop my Kindle off the counter and flop down onto the couch, opening up some book about a secret society reverse harem called Boys of Winter.

Bringing my mug to my lips, I take a sip, and the scalding liquid instantly burns my tongue and throat. My eyes widen in horror, and I throw myself off the couch, trying not to spill it all over myself. "Holy mother of sweet baby Jesus," I shriek before rushing to the kitchen.

Heading straight for the sink, I turn on the tap and shove my head right under the cold water with my tongue hanging out, desperately trying to soothe the wicked burn.

Holy crap. That sucked, like really fucking bad. It was like drinking molten lava fresh out of the volcano. Though one thing is for sure, Mel and I need to invest in a new coffee machine.

When my throat stops burning, I head back to the couch and pick up my discarded Kindle, finding myself consumed by the pages until I forget the world around me.

When there are no more pages, I toss up the pros and cons of starting the second book in the series and putting my mind at ease after that wicked cliffhanger, but I figure I should probably do a few house chores first.

Cranking up the music, I start by cleaning the apartment and singing along as I go. The apartment starts looking like a fucking landlord's wet dream when I decide it's the best idea to master the art of baking today.

After destroying the kitchen, I hover by the oven, waiting for the timer to go off, and the second it does, I all but dive into it to pull out my cake. After waiting no less than three seconds for it to cool, I cut myself a hefty slice before promptly throwing the whole thing in the trash.

What the hell is wrong with me? It shouldn't be this hard to follow a packet mix. Toddlers could do a better job than me. Hell, this is what takeout is for.

Hearing the keys jingling in the front door, I turn and look up just in time to watch Mel walk through the door, and I go to offer her a smile when I remember this whole Sean situation is her fault. My smile turns into a glare, and she bursts into laughter as she dumps dinner on the kitchen counter. "He called, didn't he?"

"Yes," I grumble as I get up to help her dish it out.

She holds my stare, her brows bouncing with anticipation. "And?" she prompts.

"And now I'm going dirt bike riding on Saturday."

"Oh shit," she laughs, doubling over and slapping her thigh, unable to reel it in. "That's hilarious."

"It's not even a little bit hilarious," I mutter under my breath as I take my dinner back to the couch and get comfortable, trying to put the whole dirt bike riding thing to the back of my head. "How was work?"

"Not great," she says, trying to hold it together, but when she looks across at me, she breaks and tears start welling in her eyes. "We lost one of our kids. He's been battling leukemia for a few years and his little body decided it was time."

"Shit," I sigh, putting my plate down and pulling Mel into my arms. She folds into me, her face in the curve of my neck as she lets it all out. Unfortunately, death is just a part of the job. One really shitty part, but it's something we all have to deal with. Each of us handles it differently. Some are able to switch off, but Mel feels it right down in her soul. Those little dudes in the pediatric ward are often there for so long, they become her family, and when the worst happens, she feels it all, which is one of the reasons I love her so much.

The first patient I lost was traumatic. I'd been covering a shift in the cancer ward, which was hard enough as it is. Her name was Kristina and she was a mother of three little boys. I'll never forget them. She had been fighting breast cancer and after going into remission a few years before, it came back with a vengeance. It just happened that I was there on her final day. She passed with her boys in her arms and her husband by her side. Still to this day, the memory tears my heart to shreds.

I hold Mel for a few minutes as her tears run their course, and as she dries the last of them off her face, she finally pulls back and gives me a tight smile. "Sorry," she murmurs.

"Don't be sorry," I tell her, squeezing her hand. "We've all been there."

And with that, she picks up her plate and tries to get on with her night, the heaviness lingering on both our shoulders.

I wake on Saturday morning an absolute nervous wreck.

Sean is supposedly picking me up today for our dirt bike riding adventure, and I haven't heard from him or his brother since the phone call. Clearly, he isn't coming. It was probably some big joke, and while the thought shouldn't upset me, it somehow hits me right where it hurts. This guy is no one to me, just some random man I found on Tinder. Sure, I saved his little girl, but nothing more. I was doing my job and I would have done exactly the same thing had it been anyone else.

"What the hell is going on in here?" Mel demands, storming into my room and flopping down on my bed before pulling the blankets right up to her chin. "It's way too early for all this noise."

"I have this stupid riding thing today, no thanks to you," I mutter, rolling my eyes as I continue yanking clothes out of my closet and trying to figure out something that will be suitable for today.

"Quit stressing," she says on a yawn. "You'll be fine. And if by any luck, you'll be screaming his name all night."

"Ugh," I groan, pulling out a top before tossing it straight back in. "Shut up. I'm not screwing him, despite how much I might want to. It's not like that."

After another few minutes of searching, I give up and drop down on the end of my bed, unsure why I feel so deflated. "What the hell am I doing?"

"You're overthinking it is what you're doing," she tells me. "You're having fun. It's dirt bike riding. No one expects you to be the belle of the ball. They're a bunch of hopefully nice people who just want to take you out to say thank you for saving the little girl."

"Then why am I so nervous about this?"

"I don't know," she grunts. "Maybe because you actually like him and have been masturbating all week to the thought of him giving you the best dick you've ever had."

"I have not been doing that."

Mel laughs, a stupid smirk stretching across her lips. "Girl, we have paper-thin walls. I know exactly how often you've been thinking about him. I can even count just how many times the imaginary version of Sean got you off."

Fuck.

My cheeks flush, and I thank my lucky stars that Mel is not the type of girl to get offended by a little bean flicking. Hell, she's practically the poster girl for that shit. Glancing away before the embarrassment consumes me, I let out a heavy sigh. "I hardly know the guy."

Mel sits up and reaches down the bed to squeeze my shoulder, and as I meet her gaze, I find a warm smile playing on her full lips. "You might not know him on a deep, spiritual level, but you *do* know him," she insists. "You know he's a great father. You know he's kind. You know you're attracted to him, and you know the thought of spending the day with him is making your stomach twist and turn with somersaults. You're just nervous, and you have every right to be, but I don't think you *need* to be."

My stare hardens and I let out a huff. "I really hate it when you're right."

"Anyone would think you'd be used to it by now," she tells me. "Now, get your ass off the bed and get yourself dressed. Otherwise, lover-boy is going to show up and you'll still be in your underwear."

Shit.

"Fine," I groan, getting up and making sure to jostle around as much as possible, knowing how it gets under her skin. Then after doing a deep dive through my closet, I find a pair of jeans and a black tank before holding them out to her. "What about this?"

"Cute," she smiles. "But grab the other tank. It shows more cleavage."

I roll my eyes but, nonetheless, I grab the other tank and make my way up to the bathroom. "Don't forget to shave your kitty. Lord knows no one has ventured through that jungle for months," Mel teases as I close the bathroom door behind me.

Taking my time in the shower, I make sure every inch of my skin is looking flawless because you never know, I might just end up in his bed tonight. Well, here's to hoping anyway. Though, considering he has a kid, the chances of that actually happening are slim to nothing.

Mel finally drags her ass out of bed and starts working on breakfast as I get dressed and ready for my riding adventure, making sure to put just a little extra effort into my hair and makeup.

An hour later, I'm fed and ready to go, but goddamn, I'm nervous.

A knock sounds at the door and my eyes widen, my heart instantly getting caught in my throat and making it almost impossible to breathe. "Oooh, he's here," Mel teases as she walks out of the bathroom with her toothbrush sticking out of her mouth.

I narrow my eyes at her before double-checking my reflection in the hallway mirror and reminding myself that this isn't a date, it's just a thank you for saving his little girl. Confident I'm as ready as I'm ever going to be, I let out a breath and turn toward the door.

It's now or never.

Striding across my small apartment, I curl my hand around the handle and pull the door open, only for my knees to go weak as I find a very relaxed Sean with his daughter in his arms. He looks delicious.

Shit. I can't go there. This is not a date.

My gaze quickly sails over him, taking in his dark jeans and white shirt that leaves nothing to the imagination about what he's got hiding underneath. "Hi," I say, giving him a tight smile, feeling slightly awkward. It's certainly a strange situation I've managed to get myself into.

"Hey," he says, just as awkwardly as Georgia turns in his arms to get a good look at me. "You ready to go?"

"Yeah," I say with a cringe, hesitating in the doorway as I meet his dark stare before giving him one last chance to bow out. "You know, you don't need to do this, right?"

"Ahh, but I do," he smiles, blowing me the fuck away. "Besides, you and I both know my brother would be right here on your doorstep if I even thought of showing up without you."

Damn it. He's got a good point.

Sean takes a step back and sweeps his arm around to gesture down the hallway, and I can just imagine what must be going through Mel's head right now. "Trust me," Sean continues. "It's in your best interest if you play by Logan's rules."

I can't help but smile as a soft flutter makes its way through my stomach. "Okay," I laugh, way too taken by this perfect stranger. "I'll just grab my bag."

I turn around and dash into the kitchen to grab my handbag off the table to find Mel hiding around the corner, her hands up and making a string of inappropriate gestures like some kind of guidebook to how she thinks this is going to go.

"Stop it," I hiss under my breath.

"Have fun," she grins.

I roll my eyes and get my ass out of there before she manages to embarrass me, and with my handbag under my arm, I pull the door closed behind me and join Sean and Georgia in the hallway. "You ever ride a dirt bike before?" Sean asks as we start up the hallway.

"Ha. No," I scoff. "And honestly, I have no intention of even trying today. I wasn't built for that kind of thing."

"Bullshit," he laughs.

Georgia squeals, her eyes going wide. "Oh, Daddy said a nawty word," she gasps as she watches her daddy in horror.

Sean looks at his daughter, laughter sparkling in her dark eyes. "Uh oh," he says.

"You're in big trowble, Mister," Georgia scolds.

Sean nods his head, accepting whatever will be with his daughter before looking back at me. "Look, I'm not about to be that guy who's going to force you to do something you don't wanna do. But my brothers have a . . . different sense of morality, and I can honestly tell you now, you're not leaving today without at least giving it a go."

The nerves start building deep in my stomach, but not for the same reasons they were earlier. The thought of my ass on a dirt bike terrifies me, and I'm certain I'll be making a fool of myself today. "Really?" I question, having seen one too many people come through the ER doors from tragic accidents caused by dirt bikes.

"Don't worry, you'll be fine," he tells me. "It's not like we're just going to give you a helmet and leave you to figure it out yourself. You'll be safe."

Yeah right!

"Okay," I swallow, nervously.

Sean opens the door to the building and ushers me outside like a perfect gentleman, which is when I see a beast of a truck with a dirt bike loaded up in the back and a little pink four-wheeled thingy beside it. I can't help but smile at the sight. I never realized they make such small ones. Though, I couldn't imagine many kids being allowed to do this sort of thing.

"You're not going to put Georgia on that, are you?"

"Yeah," he grins as we near the truck. "She's going to kill it. There's no stopping this kid. She's a bit of a daredevil."

My eyes widen with fear for the little girl, but I only see excitement shining through hers. "That's my bike," she tells me as she points to the four-wheeled monstrosity, and I instantly realize I was wrong to doubt it.

She's not my child, and I have no idea of her limits. I've never done this before, so I really shouldn't have an opinion on the topic. Besides, after seeing how Sean cared for his daughter the other day in the hospital, I'm sure he's not about to go and put her in harm's way. Whatever Georgia does today will be done in a controlled environment.

Sean goes to the backseat and gets busy buckling Georgia into her car seat, so I take the leap and pull myself up into his truck, having to reach up and grip the handlebar to haul my ass off the ground.

Crap, there's no going back now.

The second the door closes, I'm smacked in the face with a smell that makes my insides quiver and my thighs clench, and I realize it's all him. Georgia sings in the backseat as Sean climbs into the driver's seat. He spares me a quick smile as if trying to put me at ease, and with that, he starts the truck.

He pulls out of the parking spot and turns to me with curiosity in his deep eyes. "So," he starts, pulling out into the traffic. "Tell me about yourself, Gigi."

Chapter Seven

SEAN

"Tell me about yourself, Gigi," I ask as the overwhelming need to know this girl comes over me and starts fucking with my head. She pulled open the door in jeans and a black top that shows just a bit of cleavage, and I nearly fell over.

The woman is fine, like really fucking fine. I know I saw her in the hospital the other night, but she was in her scrubs and I was a fucking mess. This though, it feels different. It's almost as though I'm only just seeing her now.

Her brunette locks are tied back in a loose braid with little wispy bits framing her face, and it's fucking beautiful. She has just a touch of lip gloss on her lips, making them look juicy as fuck, and I find myself wanting a taste before quickly dismissing the thought.

Fuck.

My wife is six feet under, and I'm thinking about what it would be like to kiss this woman. What the fuck is wrong with me?

There's no denying it's strange though. I've never had a reaction like that to any other woman apart from Sara, and to be honest, it scares the shit out of me.

I need to stick to the plan and ignore my traitorous thoughts. This is strictly platonic. I walked her out of the apartment like any gentleman should and went out of my way to avoid helping her up into my truck. It was a dick move, but I don't want her to get the wrong impression here. We're just two people spending the day together with the rest of my family. Nothing more to it.

It'll be fine. We'll all have a great time. I'll thank her for everything she did for Georgie and take her home afterward, never to see her again. It's as simple as that.

"What do you want to know?" Gigi questions before turning around in her seat and giggling at the way Georgie gets the words wrong to *Heads, Shoulders, Knees and Toes.*

I find myself gazing at her, taking in the way she watches Georgie with adoration in her green eyes, and I'm completely thrown off before I remember I'm driving a big motherfucking truck and force my stare back to the road.

Shit. What was her question? Right, what do I want to know about her?

Pft . . . everything.

"Umm, you're a nurse?" I question, making myself look like a complete twat. Of course, she's a fucking nurse. That's why we're all here, dumbass.

"Midwife," she says with a wide smile, blowing me the fuck away as she meets my lingering gaze.

"How long have you been doing that?"

"Uhh, nursing for a few years, and then I did the extra training to become a midwife and have been doing that for about three years now," she tells me, clearly letting on that she loves what she does. I can't blame her. It would be a rewarding job. Though, I don't doubt it comes with its dark days.

I pull up at a red light and turn to her. "So, you don't always work in the emergency room then?"

"No, not usually. I was just covering a shift when you were there," she explains as the light turns green and I creep out into the intersection. "I started in the ER and after being thrown in front of a woman during childbirth, I studied a little more and went into midwifery."

"Wow, really?" I question, finding myself completely intrigued by this woman while trying to mask the way the topic of delivering babies makes my chest ache. Despite my hang-ups about childbirth, there's no denying that this woman is impressive.

"Yeah, I love it," she tells me, her eyes lighting up like Christmas morning. "Helping a baby come into the world is just so . . . I don't know. I want to say rewarding, but I feel that doesn't do it justice."

"I get it," I tell her, thinking of Georgie and how overwhelmed by love I was the day she was born . . . you know, before that was overshadowed by my wife's death. "It sounds incredible. Only a handful of people would have the guts to be able to do a job like that."

"Yeah, I guess," she says proudly. "What about you? What keeps you busy?"

"Apart from Georgie?" I grin, exhausted just thinking about how much work she can be. "I'm a criminal lawyer. I've got my own firm."

"Woah," she says with wide eyes, side-eyeing me as if impressed. "I don't think I've met anyone as badass as you."

"Bullshit," I grunt, trying not to let that go to my head. I mean, sure. I might already be the top attorney in the country, but I don't need the ego that comes along with it. "I'm sure you've had your fair share of badasses come through the hospital doors."

"True," she tells me. "We had a stab victim come in on Monday night."

Crap, this sounds awfully familiar to me, right now. "It wasn't a blonde dude with tattoos, was it?"

"Yeah?" she asks.

Shit.

Glancing back at her, I catch her eyes. "You didn't work on him by any chance, did you?"

Say no. Say no. Say no. Please, say no. On second thought, perhaps this would be easier if she said yes.

Gigi shakes her head. "No, I wanted to, though," she says with a heavy sigh, clearly irritated by whatever went down that night. "Why?"

Oh, thank God.

"Conflict of interest, is all," I explain. "He's not a good guy. I'm defending the man he shot two minutes before. Had you worked on him, it wouldn't be right for me to be spending time with you."

"Seriously?" she questions, her brows arched. "Sounds like you really know what you're talking about."

I laugh and nod. "I hope so. Otherwise, there's a bunch of really shitty people I've locked up who are gonna come for my throat."

"Stoooop," she says, wide-eyed again as she swivels in her seat, trying to face me front on. "You're out here locking people up? So, you're doing the real criminal stuff, not just petty things like stealing a car?"

"That's right."

She looks at me with a smile in her eyes. "You any good?" she teases.

I can't help the cocky smirk that stretches across my face. So much for the fucking ego. "The best," I confirm, not a hint of deceit in my tone. "Why? You go and get yourself in trouble?"

Her cheeks flush and something tells me she's in more trouble right now than she can handle. "I'll have you know that I'm a law-abiding citizen. It's my best friend I'm worried about. Maybe it'll be handy to know a criminal lawyer. Who knows what kind of trouble she'll get herself into one day," she laughs before narrowing her gaze at me. "Hold up. When you say you're *the best*, is that your ego talking?"

"No, really," I laugh, forcing myself to look back at the road. "I've got the highest conviction rate in the country."

"My daddy is a wockstar," Georgie boasts from the backseat.

A wide grin stretches across my face, and I glance back at my little girl, holding out my fist and watching as she beams back at me, bumping her fist with mine. "Damn straight, Georgie Girl!"

Gigi gapes at me, clearly realizing she's in the presence of a courtroom God. "Holy shit," she gasps, a slow smile spreading across her face. "That's . . . wow. I'm impressed."

"Thanks," I say proudly, glad my years at law school and the killer hours I put in are able to impress someone. My brothers and Cassie think it's cool, of course, but impressive? I'm not sure they'd go that far. They stopped being impressed with my ability to argue a point when we were kids. Georgie on the other hand thinks it's fucking incredible. And hell, so do I.

Veering off the road, I turn into the vacant acreage my brothers and I own and start down the long dirt road. Gigi sits forward in her seat, her brows furrowed as she peers out at the property. "Uhhhhmmm . . . please tell me you haven't brought me out here to, you know," she says with a cringe before dragging her thumb across her throat.

A laugh rumbles through my chest as I glance out at the big, empty property. It's clear to see why she might think that. After all, we're complete strangers. She doesn't know a damn thing about me or my family. Hell, on second thought, what woman in her right mind would have accepted Logan's invitation?

"Chill out. This is where my brothers and I come to ride. We bought it off this old guy a few years ago who was struggling to maintain it. We've come out here every few weeks since."

"Wow," she whispers as she takes it all in. "How big is it?"

"About a hundred acres," I tell her. "Give or take."

"Shit. You could have awesome parties out here and no one would have a clue," she says as we come into the clearing where I see both my brothers' trucks and Jax's parked under the shade of a massive tree.

"Before all the kids came along, that's exactly what we did," I tell her, remembering it so clearly.

The girls are busy setting up an area for the kids to play safely as the guys grab chairs and coolers out of their trucks. I pull up beside them, and as Gigi gasps from beside me, I know exactly what she's seeing.

A smirk pulls across my face when I notice the way her eyes flick between Logan and Carter, then back to me before starting all over again.

This shit never gets old.

In three.

Two.

One.

"You're triplets!" she shrieks.

I laugh, glancing at my brothers, trying to see it through new eyes. But when I realize that we're all pretty much dressed exactly the same, I know it only makes it harder to spot the differences. "Yeah, we are."

"Wow, that's awesome," she says as she opens the door and hops down from the truck. "You know, I had a woman give birth to triplets a few weeks ago, and let me tell you, all's good and well after the first comes out, but by the time the third is knocking on the door, there's nothing pretty about it."

"I really could have done without that information," I tell her as I go around and unstrap Georgie before walking with Gigi to meet the others, each one of their stares already locked on us. "Hey guys, this is Gigi," I introduce as I place Georgie down with her cousins.

I go around the circle and let her know all their names and her face instantly brightens as I point out Brianna.

"You . . . were you my midwife?" Brianna says before Gigi gets a chance to say it herself, a little unsure of the connection.

"Indeed, I was," Gigi smiles. "You had twins. Umm . . . Nate and Parker?"

It all becomes clear. The other night in the hospital I had recognized her face, but I couldn't figure out why, but now it finally makes sense. She's the midwife who brought Georgie a crib and blanket while we waited during Bri's labor. But that was a little over two years ago now. I'm floored that she remembers.

"You remember?" Bri asks, proudly.

"How could I forget?" she laughs, her mouth opening in shock as she glances up at me. "You guys were getting high and sleeping in the bathtub."

"Hold up a second. That was not me," I say, pointing to my dickhead brothers. "They're the culprits right there."

"Oh, my god," Bri says, her face flushing with embarrassment. "I'm so sorry."

Gigi laughs and the girls fall into easy conversation about the kids, and I get the strange feeling that Gigi is going to be well-loved among my family. Not that it matters. Today is a one-off. After I drop her home, that's it.

With the girls happy, I head around the back of my truck and start unloading my dirt bike. "Ahh shit," Carter grunts as he appears at the back of my truck and gets a good look at Georgie's four-wheeler. I look at him in confusion. "What are the chances? I just bought Georgie the same fucking four-wheeler."

"No, shit?" I laugh. "Even with the pink plastics?"

"Yep," he says, shaking his head as he jumps up into the tray to start releasing the safety straps from my bike. "Looks like Lilly has a new four-wheeler."

"Dude, she's like six months old," I laugh. "Elle will kill you if you even suggest it."

"Nah, it'll be fine. She'll grow into it," he says as we get the dirt bike down before starting on Georgie's four-wheeler.

I help the boys with the other dirt bikes, and before we know it, the clearing is filled with them. We get back to the group, and I drop into the chair beside Gigi. "So, Gigi's never ridden before," I inform the girls.

"I don't blame her," Elle grunts. "If I had my way, I would never have tried it either."

"Were you forced into it, too?" Gigi questions.

"Yes," she scoffs, clearly still very sore about the topic. But I can't blame her. Logan left her traumatized after he took her out only to have the engine catch fire.

"Babe," Logan interjects. "*Forced* is a bit of a strong word for it."

"You're shitting me, right?" Elle laughs. "You put me over your shoulder, kicking and screaming, and physically put me on the stupid thing. Not to mention, the bike caught on fire."

"Come on," he grins. "It wasn't that bad."

"Ahh, yeah, it was," I agree as Gigi's eyes widen in fear.

His response is cut off by the sound of Jax kick starting his bike. The noise scares the shit out of all of the babies and makes the little ones burst into tears, apart from Georgie. She's used to the sound and giggles, more than ready for her turn.

Jax takes off and soon enough, Cassie is jumping to her feet and kickstarting her bike to race after him, a trick that took her far too long to master, but I can't hold it against her. Kick starting these fuckers takes a lot of skill and strength, but she was too fucking stubborn to buy a bike with a push-button start.

"Wow, they're good," Gigi murmurs beside me as Hudson crawls to her legs, demanding to be picked up. She scoops him into her arms and he grins up at her with his big toothless smile.

"Yeah, apart from Bri and Elle, the rest of us have been riding since we were kids."

"So, you're all that good?" she grins.

"Pretty much."

"Is there anything you can't do?" she questions.

Logan scoffs, being the smartass he is, and arches a brow in challenge. "Trust me, there's plenty of things this fucker can't do. I can make a list if you'd like."

"Watch it, asshole," I throw back at him. "Otherwise, I'll be forced to tell Gigi all about the broken dick incident."

Gigi looks at Logan, trying her hardest to hold back a grin. "Broken dick incident?" she questions.

Logan shoots daggers at me, shaking his head. "Low blow, man. Low blow," he says before glancing back at Gigi. "And for the record, it wasn't a broken dick. My dick was fine. It could do all the things it was supposed to do."

Elle smirks at her husband. "You keep telling yourself that."

Logan turns on his wife, shaking his head. "Oh yeah?" he challenges. "You wanna see how unbroken my dick really is?"

Elle squeals as Logan barrels into her and hoists her over his shoulder, carrying her away with a hand on her ass. Gigi laughs and looks back at me. "Do I even wanna know?"

"Definitely not," I murmur before nodding out toward Jax and Cassie as they fly across the property together. Carter's twins watch them with wide eyes, making me wonder if they're going to ditch ice hockey for riding. "You do anything like this as a kid?"

"Not really," she says. "I'm an only child with two workaholic parents. My childhood consisted of my nanny screaming at me and making sure my homework was done before my parents got home."

"Oh, I'm sorry," I say, unsure why it bothers me so much.

Georgie cuts off our conversation as she gets up and grabs her bag of riding gear and starts trying to haul it toward us. The bag is practically three times as big as she is. My lips pull into a smirk, and I watch as she gets tired and stops in front of Bri to pull all the contents out. Bri gets the hint and starts getting her ready, so I do what any other parent would do and get her four-wheeler warmed up, knowing it better be ready before she is, otherwise, we're going to have problems.

With all her safety gear on, Georgie rushes across the grass and instantly jumps on her four-wheeler, putting her hands on the handlebars and pretending to rev the engine, making sure to spit all over me as she mimics the noise of a dirt bike.

Gigi gets up with her phone to record her first ride, and I'm thankful. This is a moment with my daughter I'd like to remember and show her when she's older. Hell, I've gotten used to taking lots of photos and videos after realizing that I didn't have nearly enough memories recorded of Sara. Though the ones I do have are plastered across my home for Georgie to soak up.

I go through all the instructions with Georgie, making sure she knows the stop from the start, and watch as she takes off like a bat out of hell, the four-wheeler sending a wave of dirt spitting up behind her.

Georgie darts across the property, and my heart falls right out of my fucking ass.

Shit.

I race after her, my phone, wallet, and keys all falling out of my pockets as I go. "Slow down," I scream at her giggling back, but of course she's having too much fun.

Jax races up on his bike beside her, keeping close in case we need him, as I all but lunge for Georgie, forcing her to ease up on the accelerator, and when she finally stops, she beams up at me. "Fun, Daddy," she laughs.

"Yeah, fun isn't a word I would use to describe that, kid," I say before quickly adjusting the accelerator so she can't go quite so fast. With my heart firmly back in my chest and covered head to toe in dirt, I give Georgie another lecture. "Alright, Missy, you good?" I ask.

"Yep," she smiles.

"Show me the stop."

She points it out.

"Show me the start."

Again, she does as she's told, knowing damn well she won't get away with pushing the limits twice.

"Alright," I say before pointing out a big tree. "If you go past that tree, I'll have to turn it off, okay? You need to stay where Daddy can see you."

"Yes, Daddy," she says before taking off again, this time at a speed that doesn't send me to an early grave. Heading back to the girls, I pick up all my things out of the grass and dust myself off as I watch Georgie puttering around the property.

"She's doing great for her first time," Elle says, proudly rocking the messy sex hair, making me wonder if I took longer with Georgie than I thought . . . or perhaps Logan has really mastered the quickie and doesn't know how to appropriately satisfy his woman. Though judging by her flushed cheeks, she's more than satisfied.

"She sure is," I say. "She's too confident, though. I don't want her getting ahead of herself."

"She'll be fine," Bri says. "Besides, if she hurts herself, we have a nurse here to patch her up." I find myself looking over to Gigi and seeing the wide smile on her face, I can't help but feel at peace, knowing she's enjoying herself. And for some reason, it scares the shit out of me.

Keeping my eye on Georgie, I dump everything out of my pockets and head over to my dirt bike and get it started, unable to resist heading out there to ride with her. Hitting the accelerator, I speed up the dirt road to catch her before slowing to her pace. I can practically hear her giggles over the sound of the engines, and it fills my heart with pride.

She's so amazing.

A lot of kids would be too scared to even try it, yet here my Georgie is absolutely rocking it. Maybe I could put her in competitions. I can only imagine what Sara would have thought about that. Fuck, she'd have my balls churning through a meat grinder in seconds.

I ride with Georgie for a while before Logan and Carter come racing up behind us. Cass and Jax come back from their ride, and it soon turns into a pissing contest with Logan refusing to give in until he wins.

We pass a massive puddle, and I point it out to Georgie, telling her to be careful not to end up in it. Only in true Georgie fashion, she doesn't listen. Instead, she speeds up and flies right through it, sending a wave of mud up all around her, absolutely soaking Jax and Logan.

I put my hand out, indicating for her to stop, but she zooms right past me, high-fiving my outstretched hand with her evil little chuckle following behind, and honestly, I can't blame her. Jax and Logan won't hesitate to get her back and she knows it.

"Holy shit," Carter laughs as he takes in the boys drenched in muddy water. "That was fucking hilarious."

"That kid's going to get it," Logan says before racing after Georgie.

"I second that," Jax grunts before joining them.

Georgie turns back with a smug grin, thinking she's gotten away with it, but seeing them coming for her, her eyes widen and she squeals. Reaching the big tree she's not allowed to ride past, she jumps off, leaving the bike running, and takes off on foot. Logan and Jax come to a stop and take off after her to make it a fair fight, and I thank my lucky stars when Logan takes a moment out of his revenge to grab Georgie's four-wheeler that's rolling dangerously close to a hill. He cuts the engine and takes off at a sprint to catch up.

Going after the four-wheeler, knowing Georgie isn't going to run all the way back to get it, I bring it back over to our group when I turn to find Georgie thrown over Logan's shoulder while he tickles her. She screams and begs to be put down, but I know the boys won't stop until they have their sweet revenge, and I can't help but mentally prepare for her inhaler, knowing this is a bit much, but where the fuck do I draw the line? The kid has to have enjoyment in her life, otherwise, what's the fucking point?

Since her hospital stay last weekend, she's been doing great, but I head over to her bag and grab the inhaler anyway. All this screaming and running couldn't be great for her lungs.

Realizing they're taking her right back to the muddy puddle, I groan, knowing damn well I left her change of clothes on her bed. And not a moment later, I stand back, shaking my head as I watch the two grown-ass men having a mud fight with my toddler.

Ten minutes later, all three of them are covered from head to toe in mud, and when Jax whispers in her ear and her gaze snaps to me with an adorable evil grin, I realize I'm fucked.

Shit. There's no way I'm getting out of this unscathed.

She races toward me, and I have no choice but to welcome her right into my arms. She launches through the air, and I catch the little she-devil as she bursts with laughter, covering me in mud, making sure to use my shirt as a mop to wipe off her face.

"Thanks, kid," I grunt as I put her down on the grass and get started stripping her out of her muddy clothes.

Jax and Logan do the same while Cass and Elle start swooning over their men, though, it doesn't go unnoticed when Gigi's eyes begin to stray their way, with a light flush on her cheeks. I grin to myself as I grab the packet of baby wipes and get started cleaning up this kid, wondering if Bri brought spare clothes for the twins. They're roughly the same size.

My best friend, Tom, shows up shortly after, and Georgie loses her tiny mind, running up to him, and throwing herself in his arms. I introduce him to Gigi, and I can instantly tell that he's on edge about her. It wouldn't be clear to Gigi, but it's certainly clear to me. I see it all over his face and make a mental note to talk with him about it later because now really isn't the time.

Though, I can't for the life of me work out what it is he doesn't like. She's pretty much perfect. She's beautiful, she's kind, she's friendly, not to mention, she's responsible for saving Georgie's life. I have no idea why he's acting this way, and what's more, I can't figure out why the hell I care so much.

We get lunch done and out of the way before I turn and face Gigi with a wide smirk, knowing damn well she's been avoiding this all morning. "Alright, Gigi, you're up," I grin and watch with undeniable pleasure as her face falls and she promptly loses her mind.

Chapter Eight

GIGI

"You're kidding, right?" I question as I look at Sean, my mouth hanging wide open. "Like hell. I'm not getting on that death trap."

Sean begins stalking me, and I realize all that fun I've been having today is well and truly over.

I've been having such a great day so far, and now Sean is about to ruin it. I didn't realize just how good it was going to be hanging out with a bunch of strangers, but now that I'm here, I certainly don't regret it. The only downfall is when Sean's friend showed up. He seems like a bit of a buzzkill.

He arches a brow in challenge. "You can either do it yourself, or I'll be forced to take a page out of Logan's book and do it for you."

I cringe as I look over at the beast of a dirt bike. The thing looks scary as hell, but if Georgie can figure out a four-wheeler, then surely I can do this, right? "Are you sure? I mean, I'm fine just sitting here and watching."

"Nope, sorry, Gigi. You're going to learn to ride a dirt bike today, whether you like it or not."

"Damn it," I groan as I get up, my hands starting to shake.

I stand next to the stupid dirt bike, and being this close, I realize the damn thing is practically bigger than me. Sean joins me and starts going over all the basics I'll need to know. "Can you drive a stick?" he questions as I get completely overwhelmed by his explanation.

"Do I look like the kind of girl who knows how to drive a stick?" I grin.

He gives me a once-over, clearly having his answer. "Well, that explains a lot," he teases before giving me a crash course on the functions of a clutch and why I need one.

"I think I've got it," I tell him after his third explanation of the gears. I mean, if I can learn the names of complicated medications, then surely I can get the hang of this.

"Alright, get on," he says as he holds the bike still.

My stomach clenches with nerves, and I look at the bike like it's some kind of challenge. Doing my best to climb on the damn thing, I hold onto his big shoulder to balance and am barely able to touch the ground with my tippy toes.

"Are you sure this is safe?" I question as he grabs a helmet and pulls it down over my head, making sure to smack the top of it for good luck. And honestly, I need all the luck in the world.

"Probably not," he grins before kickstarting the dirt bike.

My eyes widen, but the sound of the engine drowns out what he's saying. Did he say this isn't safe? "Holy shit," I curse as the nerves take over me. The bike rumbles under me, the sound deafening as I feel the vibration right through the seat, forcing me to adjust myself before I unintentionally get off on his bike.

Wowza. That, I was not expecting.

"Okay, remember, slowly release the clutch and give it a little go," he instructs, talking to me the same way he had spoken to Georgie when teaching her how to ride her four-wheeler. But honestly, I appreciate the extra effort. I need all the help I can get.

I concentrate as hard as possible before slowly releasing the clutch and hitting the accelerator, trying to get the timing just right. The bike jolts forward before instantly stalling, sending me rocking forward toward the handlebars. "Shit," I screech as I grip onto them for dear life.

"You're fine," Sean laughs as he quickly grabs the dirt bike to stop me from falling to my death. "You released the clutch too fast." He moves in close, one hand on the handle beside mine, the other on the seat behind me before kick starting the bike again. "Give it another try."

"Ahh, fuck, fuck, fuck, fuck," I mutter under my breath as I try my hardest, ignoring the vibration under my lady taco and concentrating on the stupid clutch. I slowly release it and somehow manage to coordinate myself enough to twist the accelerator. The bike lurches forward, putting across the property, and as I move away from Sean, I find myself completely on my own with panic soaring through my chest, despite going slower than a snail.

Shit. I'm riding a fucking dirt bike.

My hands clench around the handlebars, scared for my life as I try to navigate through the grass and dodge the rocks and ditches. Keeping my gaze locked on the path ahead, I see the stupid mud puddle and instantly freak out.

I'm not ready for this shit.

I try to turn to avoid it, but it's too late, I go straight through, but with my speed so slow, the bike doesn't find traction and slides through the mud like a fucking Slip-N-Slide, throwing me off balance. I quickly lose control of the bike and fall to the side, having to throw myself right in the mud to avoid the bike coming down on top of me.

"FUCK," Sean roars, already in a sprint to get to me. He comes straight for me, not having a single care for the bike I just dropped. "Are you okay?" he questions, his eyes wide as they scan over me from head to toe.

"Yeah, I think so," I tell him as he offers me a hand to help me up, but realizing I can't touch him without covering him in mud again, I wave him off and get to my feet. Chunks of mud drop off me as I notice the scratches across my palms. "The mud softened my landing, so it's nothing but a bruised ego and a few scratches."

"Shit," he curses, glancing down at the mud covering me. "I

brought you here to try and thank you, not to kill you."

"I'm fine. Despite the mud, I'm actually having a really good time," I tell him as he picks his bike up off the ground. "Sorry," I say, waving toward the muddy bike. "I hope I didn't scratch it."

"Don't worry," he smirks. "This bike has seen worse falls than that." He kickstarts it again and indicates for me to get back on. "Are you going to give it another try?"

I cringe and really don't want to, but at the same time, I don't want him to think I'm not the girl who can get back up and shake it off. "Okay," I sigh as I throw a leg over and get comfortable, hoping I haven't lost my magic touch.

Grabbing hold of the handlebars, I gasp as pain shoots through my palms.

"What's wrong?" he asks as I pull my hands back.

I flip them over and study the scratches on my palms before trying to rub the lingering mud onto my pants. "Nothing. They just sting when I hold the handles," I explain.

"Shit," he sighs before pressing his lips together as if deep in thought. "Move forward."

My brows furrow, but I do as I'm told before mentally freaking out when he climbs on the bike behind me—his wide chest pressing up against my back as I feel his thick thighs resting beside mine. Hell, don't even get me started on what I feel against my ass.

My, oh, my. Maybe dreams really do come true.

Sean reaches around me to grasp the handlebars, and the strangest feeling flutters through me as my heart starts to race. "Hold on," he murmurs, his warm breath tickling the back of my neck and sending goosebumps soaring across my skin.

Before I can get control of my emotions, the dirt bike shoots forward, and I scream out as my hands launch forward to grip the handlebars. I suddenly don't care about the stinging in my hands or the feel of his strong body pressed up against mine; I'm positive I'm about to die. I focus on the sound of Sean's laughter to keep from thinking about my imminent death, despite knowing his laughter only exists out of my fear.

He zooms past his family and down the dirt road that quickly disappears into the grass. "Relax," he tells me. "I won't let you get hurt."

His words soothe me, and I relax against him, taking absolute pleasure in the way his body feels pressed so tightly against mine. Hell, apart from Mel, it's the closest human contact I've had in months.

Instead of freaking out, I take in my surroundings and find myself in awe. The property is beautiful, despite being a bit rough around the edges.

Sean rides for about ten minutes, showing me the land before pointing out a small creek that runs right through the center of the property. He brings the bike to a stop beside it and climbs off before offering me his hand and helping me down.

"I wasn't expecting this," I tell him as I take it all in and listen to the sound of the running water. I step right up to the creek and look down into the crystal-clear water to see the pebbles beneath. "Wow, it's beautiful."

Unable to help myself, I bend down and stick my hands into the freezing water and quickly rinse off as much mud as possible before scooping out a perfectly smooth pebble. I straighten out to find Sean right by my side and wonder if this is classified as a date yet.

"I kind of like it here," he tells me as I rub the pebble between my fingers. "We actually had no idea the creek was here the first few times we came, but once we found it, I find myself coming down here every time."

Holy cow. I don't even know how to respond to that, but I don't really care, I could die a happy woman just listening to him talk. "It's very peaceful down here," I muse. "Like the rest of the world and all the bullshit that comes along with it doesn't exist."

"Exactly."

I feel there's more to the story about why he comes down here, but I don't want to pry. Instead, I decide it's finally time to come clean. "So, umm, I have something to tell you," I say, surprising myself with the set of steel balls I just happened to grow between my legs.

He looks at me curiously, clearly wondering what the hell I could possibly have to tell him when we were perfect strangers not five hours ago. "What's up?" he questions, keeping his eyes on mine.

"I, ahh . . . shit, this is embarrassing."

His curiosity quickly turns to interest, and I search for the balls of steel that I must have just dropped somewhere. "Go on," he encourages.

Shit, rip it off like a Band-Aid.

"So, last Friday night," I start before cringing again. "Mel and I were having a few too many glasses of Moscato and we found you on Tinder, so naturally she forced me to swipe right on you."

Booming laughter rips out of his body as the embarrassment washes up and consumes me. "I knew I recognized you," he grins. "Fuck. That's so funny."

Well . . . I certainly didn't think so.

Sean pulls his phone out of his pocket and dread fills every part of me. I start shaking my head, knowing exactly where this is going. "No, no, please don't," I practically beg, but there's no stopping him now.

He finds his Tinder app and brings up my profile. "There you are," he laughs, turning his phone to point me out as if I didn't know how humiliating my profile is.

I narrow my eyes and cross my arms over my chest, waiting for his laughter to run its course. "Are you done mocking me yet?"

"Not quite, but I'll stop," he grins, dropping his phone back into his pocket. "Why didn't you say something in the hospital?"

I give him a blank look. Isn't it obvious? "I was embarrassed," I admit.

"Why?" he questions. "Because I didn't message you or do whatever the fuck I was supposed to do after you matched?"

"Uhh . . . yeah."

"Don't be. Logan put the app on my phone. I had no intention of using it, but I'm flattered," he says with a wink that melts my panties right off my body.

I resist the urge to groan. Seriously? Would it have killed him to confirm if he would have actually messaged me or not? I spent days waiting on that. Perhaps leaving me hanging is becoming a hobby for him.

Sean looks down at me, a smile playing on his lips as my heart races. His smile begins to fade as a seriousness creeps into his eyes, and I suck in a breath, watching as his dark eyes become hooded and drop to my lips.

Oh, please, God. He's got me all the way out here, covered in mud. Just close the gap and kiss me. If I was a brave woman like Mel, I would do it myself. I'd throw myself into his strong arms and melt into him as I push up onto my toes and claim everything I want.

He starts to lean, and I find myself holding my breath, only he doesn't come any further, and a wave of devastation pounds through my chest. His gaze flicks away, and as deep regret flashes in his dark eyes, his lips pull into a tight line. "We should go," he says, crushing my hopes and dreams. "Georgie worries when I'm gone too long."

I try to school my features and pretend like I'm not dying inside.

"Oh, sure," I say.

So. Fucking. Close.

I walk back over to the dirt bike while pocketing the smooth, white rock and climb on the death machine, wondering what it is about me that repulses men. With disappointment heavy in my chest, Sean throws his leg over to straddle the dirt bike before kick starting it. He gets comfortable behind me and takes off at the speed of light, both of us in a very awkward silence.

We get back to the rest of his family, and I hop off the dirt bike, feeling uneasy. Walking over to where the kids are playing on the ground, I worry my lip, deep in thought when I feel someone watching me. Glancing up, I find Tom's inquisitive stare flicking between me and Sean, the distaste in his eyes clear as day, making me wonder what the hell I did to make him not like me.

I join the kids on the ground and enjoy watching them play while everyone else sits around laughing at Sean's recap of me falling right into the mud. I laugh along, trying to pretend as though I'm okay as we all enjoy the afternoon in the beautiful Denver sunshine, knowing it won't be long until winter truly sets in.

My phone chimes beside me, and I scoop it up, finding a new text from Mel.

Mel – Have you been thoroughly screwed yet?

I roll my eyes, but I'm not really feeling it right now, usually, she'd have me in stitches, but all I can think about is the almost kiss.

Gigi – If you mean screwed over, then yes! The only action I've got is from the dirt bike between my legs.

Mel – Shit, that bad?

Gigi – Yeah, I thought it might have been going great, but I was wrong.

Georgie demands my attention, and I toss my phone to the ground to give the little angel whatever it is she desires, wondering why I'm still hanging around. I mean, sure. I'm still kind of having a good time, but I'd prefer to be back at home, wallowing in self-doubt.

It's not long before Sean comes and bends down to speak to Georgie, his gaze quickly flicking to mine before focusing on his little girl. "Daddy's going for a ride with the boys, okay?"

"Okay, Daddy," she says.

"Be a good girl."

She ignores his comments and continues with her game, and I have to grin at the scowl she manages to put on her father's face, kinda wishing I could put one there myself.

With the boys gone, I grab my phone off the ground and join the girls. "So," Elle smiles the second the boys disappear out of sight, making me realize I'm about to be drilled. "Is something going on between you two?"

"I don't know," I sigh, honestly. "I thought maybe he liked me and that's why he invited me out here. I mean, I get wanting to say thank you for helping Georgie last weekend, but inviting a random girl out to a family thing is a lot, right? I think I got my hopes up, but he's not interested."

"You don't think?" Cassie questions.

I shrug my shoulders. "You guys know him better than I do, but I don't know. Maybe he thought he was interested, but I was standing right there and he backed off," I confirm.

A strange look flutters through the girls' eyes and I can't help but feel as though I'm missing something. They share a glance between themselves before Bri looks back at me with a curious stare. "And how do you feel?"

Despite the confusion overwhelming my every thought, I can't keep the smile that spreads across my lips, and just like that, my answer is given way before I've said a single word. "I'm not going to lie," I say, no point in hiding the truth now. "He's drop-dead gorgeous, and the way he is with Georgie . . . there's no denying there's something there, but I don't really know him well enough to make up my mind."

"He's a great guy," Cassie confirms, making both Elle and Bri agree eagerly. "Like honestly, the best. I'll even go as far to say that out of all the boys, my husband included, Sean is the one with the purest heart. He only ever wants what's best for everyone."

"Yeah, I see that," I sigh as I hit the home button for my phone to check the time, only I'm not looking at my phone—it's Sean's in my hand and I don't fucking like what I'm seeing.

My eyes widen, taking in the home screen image—the happiest fucking couple I've ever seen on their wedding day.

I'm a fucking fool. How could I fall for this shit? The guy is married, and I'm here acting like a lovesick puppy and completely embarrassing myself in front of his family. Is this some kind of joke?

What am I doing? I need to get out of here.

Getting up, I quickly search around for my phone and find it right where I was sitting before and realize that Sean's phone must have fallen out of his pocket when he was talking to Georgie, and I picked up the wrong one.

Turning back to the girls with a cringe, I pull out my best acting skills, making a show of looking at my phone as though reading a message. "I'm so sorry," I say. "I hate to do this to you guys, but would it be possible for someone to give me a lift back to my apartment? I'm being called into work."

"Oh, of course," Cassie says, jumping to her feet. "Is everything alright?"

"I don't know," I cringe, feeling like a backstabbing bitch, lying to the nicest girls I've met in a long time. "Usually when I'm called in like this there's been some kind of accident."

"Oh, shit. Yeah, sure," she says before turning to Elle and Brianna. "Can you guys watch Hudson? I shouldn't be too long."

"No problem," Brianna says.

Cassie and I pile into Jax's truck and she turns to me with a grin. "I know this is a bad situation for you, but I've been desperate for an excuse to drive this truck."

"I'm glad I could be of service," I smile.

With a wicked grin, Cassie starts up the truck and gets me out of there. Then fifteen minutes later, I direct her to my apartment and she brings the truck to a stop. "Hope your shift isn't too chaotic," she says.

"Thanks, Cassie. I've had a great day. You truly have an amazing family," I tell her.

She gives me a proud smile, and as I step back to close the door, she waves to me through the window. The second I step back from the curb, she takes off like Lightning McQueen.

I let out a sigh, and the moment she disappears around the corner, I let the heaviness consume me. I trudge up to my apartment and push my way through the door, finding Mel sitting on the floor with her iPad braced on the coffee table and her makeup kit scattered around the living room floor.

She looks up at me, and I see the questions in her eyes before she even gets a chance to speak them, then saving her the hassle, I jut out my bottom lip and give it to her straight. "He's married," I cry.

"Oh, that fucking rat bastard," she mutters, knowing just how hard this one has hit me. "I'll get the wine while you get your makeup. I'm just about to hit play on a winged eyeliner tutorial."

"Okay," I sigh.

I go about the apartment, taking my sweet-ass time, and return to the living room to find a glass of Moscato right beside me and the bottle in the center of the coffee table, ready and waiting to be annihilated.

"Thank you," I tell her, the heaviness refusing to lift.

"Don't worry about it. There'll be others out there."

"He was kinda perfect though." I give her a tight smile before turning to her iPad, ready to master the winged eyeliner, and half an hour later, Mel and I look like rabid raccoons. I don't get it. We did everything right, and the chick in the video made it look so easy. No one tells you just how hard this shit is. I guess it's going to be plain old mascara and eye shadow for me.

A text comes through on my phone, vibrating loudly on the table and scaring the shit out of both of us. Then grabbing my phone, I open the text, only to have the floodgates open wide.

Sean – Cassie said you had an emergency. I hope everything's okay. Thanks for coming today.

With a sigh, I hit delete on the message, trying to hold back the tears.

This chick will not be a pawn in some random guy's game ever again. That'll teach me to get my hopes up and try to put myself out there. Taking my glass, I throw back what's left before flicking to the next video, determined to master the art of false lashes.

Chapter Nine

SEAN

I trudge up the stairs with an exhausted Georgie slumped over my shoulder, gently snoring. It was a massive day for her after all the riding, the running around, and the games with her cousins and uncles. Not to mention, she insisted on helping me wash her four-wheeler before bailing when it was time to clean my dirt bike.

Pushing through to her bedroom, I lay her down in her bed and switch on the baby monitor before kissing her forehead and heading back downstairs. I grab two beers out of the fridge and hand one to Tom before dropping down onto the opposite couch, utterly exhausted.

Tom watches me with a curious stare, the same one he's been

giving me all day, but doesn't say a word, and it's driving me insane. I know exactly what this is about, and I'm almost daring him to bring it up. "Dude, what the fuck?" I question, ready to have this out.

His lips pull into a thin line, and I can see him debating if he actually wants to ask me what's on his mind. Then with a breath, the bastard lets me have it. "What's the deal with this chick?"

"You mean Gigi?" I ask, knowing damn well that's who he's referring to.

"Yeah, her," he grunts with distaste, making it clear he doesn't approve of her, though I have no fucking idea why. She was great with my family, not that there's anything to approve of in the first place. "Is there something going on between you two?"

"No," I scoff. "Logan invited her out so we could thank her. I told you what she did for Georgie. It's called being nice, something you could learn from."

He rolls his eyes and it has me itching to drop him. "So, there's nothing going on then?"

"Nope," I lie, knowing that after a lifetime of friendship, he can see right through me.

"Get fucked. Stop lying," he grunts, getting worked up. "You doubled with her on your bike. You pissed off for half an hour. You looked like someone kicked your fucking dog when she left. And then you watched your phone all afternoon, hoping she'd text you back."

I shake my head, ready to deny it until I'm blue in the face. "It's not like that," I say, realizing for a fucking top-notch lawyer, I'm a shitty liar. I should probably work on that.

"That's fucking bullshit and you know it," he says, "Then tell me, what's it like?"

"I don't know, she's a cool chick." I shrug. "What's your fucking problem?"

"Really?" he questions, not buying my casual attitude.

"Really," I confirm. "She's just . . . I don't know. She's cool, a breath of fresh air. And for the first time in ages, I wasn't sitting there today, watching my family being in love with their partners and feeling like a fucking third wheel to them all. I'm not with Gigi if that's what you're asking, but it was fucking nice having company for a change."

"Okay," he scoffs, giving in and leaning back into the couch, clearly not on board with a damn thing I'm saying. Tom was great friends with Sara, they loved each other like siblings, so it's damn clear where all this bullshit is coming from. Hell, I fucking get it myself. I've struggled with the guilt all day.

Leaning forward, I rest my elbows on my knees and look down at the floor, not wanting to meet his eye. "Relax, alright. Yes, I think Gigi is fucking awesome. Yes, I might be attracted to her, and yes, she's the first girl to make me smile in a long time, but that doesn't mean I've forgotten about Sara. I'm not replacing her, and I never will."

"Better not," he grunts under his breath.

"Look," I say, deciding it's best to be upfront with him. "Logan's been talking about me starting to date again, and I think it's not a bad idea. It's not an easy pill to swallow, but he's right."

A scowl settles across Tom's face, and I hate that I've put it there. "You've got to be shitting me," he says with a shake of his head. "So, because Logan thinks it's a good idea, you're just going to go along with it?"

"Don't give me that shit," I snap. Logan and Tom have been thorns in my side since we were teenagers, and the two of them have constantly butted heads. "This isn't fucking easy for me, Tom. You lost a friend, but I lost my fucking wife, the mother of my child. She was the only woman I've ever loved, and in the blink of an eye, she was gone. I didn't even get to say goodbye. It fucking kills me to even think about starting to move on, but I have to for me and Georgia," I say. "But just because you're holding on to the past doesn't mean I shouldn't try to find some semblance of happiness. Or would you prefer I just stayed this way, fucking miserable and pining for someone who's never coming back?"

"That's not what I mean," he says. "Of course I want you to be happy again. I guess, I feel like you're forgetting about Sara. The idea of you being with someone else makes me feel like you're replacing her."

"You're fucked in the head if you think for even a second that I could forget Sara," I tell him. "Even now, three years later, she consumes my every thought. I could never replace her, but I need to make room in my life for something more. She's a ghost, man. I've gotta stop hoping that one day she'll come back to me. It's never going to happen."

Tom lets out a heavy sigh and lifts his beer to his lips, taking a long drink before putting the empty bottle on the coffee table. "It's just . . . it's hard watching you with someone else. I guess it's just going to take a little adjustment on my part."

I nod, getting where he's coming from. "Is that why you were giving Gigi dirty looks all day?" I ask.

"Yeah," he sighs, looking a little embarrassed.

"For fuck's sake," I grin, shaking my head at my best friend. "I'm not gonna lie, I've been struggling with it all day. The thought of being with someone else is terrifying. It feels like I'm betraying Sara in some way, even though I know she'd want me to try."

Tom nods and gives me a tight smile. "She would want that, wouldn't she?"

"Yeah, but it doesn't matter anyway. I don't think it's going to be happening anytime soon. I'm pretty sure I've already fucked things up with Gigi."

His brows furrow, looking at me in concern. "What do you mean?"

I let out a sigh, and give him the truth, realizing that after twelve years of only ever being with one woman, I have no fucking idea what to do when it comes to dating. "Well, she made it clear that she was interested, and I basically freaked out and shut it down."

"How so?"

"When I took her riding, we went down to the creek and were talking. Then one thing led to another and I was gonna kiss her. But she was looking up at me with those big eyes, just daring me to do it, and I fucking bailed. I left her hanging and came up with some bullshit about needing to get back to Georgie. I could tell she was confused. She didn't really say much after that and then I came back from my ride with you guys and she was gone."

"Dude," he laughs. "You used to have so much game in high school. What the fuck happened to you?"

I give him a hard stare. We both know exactly what happened to me.

"Shut up," I mutter. "This shit is hard. I'm not some fucking manwhore like you and my brothers. I don't have years of practice hitting on women. I fell in love with the first girl I dated."

"I know, man," he says, his lips pulling into an amused smirk. "Look, I'll get the boys together and we could give you some pointers," he suggests. "I know they're a little rusty now they're locked down and all, but I'm sure they'll be able to offer something worthwhile."

Fucking hell. I could only imagine the type of shit they would come up with. Not to mention, I'd never be able to live down asking my brothers for help in that way. "I'll pass."

"So, why didn't you kiss her?" Tom asks, getting up and grabbing us another round of beers. "Were you thinking about Sara?"

I cringe, not wanting to admit to it, but knowing he'll only keep pestering me until I do. "Yes and no," I tell him. "At first it was Sara holding me back until I remembered that she's gone and there's no reason for me not to try. So I was all for it . . . until I realized that apart from Sara, I haven't kissed another woman since I was sixteen . . . and I kind of panicked."

Tom falls into a fit of laughter, barely able to hand me my beer. "Fuck, that's hilarious," he says, dropping down on the couch as my gaze shoots over to the baby monitor, hoping his booming laughter doesn't wake Georgie. I'm just about to start laughing with him, trying to find the amusement in it, when his next comments have my teeth grinding together. "Dude, you got to find yourself a pair of balls and man the fuck up."

The fuck?

"Look who's talking, dickhead."

"Whatever," he scoffs. "I have no issues getting laid."

"Exactly, it's about time you manned up and created a life with one of them," I tell him. "Look at you. You're fucking thirty and stuck in the same old routine, letting life pass you by. This whole playboy thing is just a ruse because you're terrified of commitment, same shit as Carter three years ago, and look how happy he is now."

He looks as though he's truly thinking it over, but I know it's going to take a lot more than that to get through to him. "Nah," he says, shaking it off. "If it ain't broke, don't try to fix it. Besides, why mess with a good thing?"

I roll my eyes. The only thing that's ever going to help him see the light is when he finally finds the perfect woman, only to lose her because he was too fucking scared to realize what's important in life. I can't wait for that day to come. It'll be magical.

An hour later, he pushes himself up off the couch, scooping up the empty beer bottles and dropping them in the trash. "I better get out of here," he tells me before pressing a few buttons on his phone and flipping it around to show me a picture of a half-naked chick. "Got a date with this little vixen."

Jesus. Some things never change. "Alright, man. I'll see you around."

Before I know it, Tom is out the door, and I'm kicked back on my couch with my feet up. I put on the replay of Logan's game from last week and pull out my phone to check if Gigi ended up responding. Cassie mentioned that she was pulled into work to cover a shift, which is why she had to leave, and I sent her a text, but that was hours ago.

I was sure she was into me. Her gaze constantly met mine, seeking me out and lighting up every time I talked to her. Hell, she practically stopped breathing when I got on the back of the dirt bike with her. And I'm not gonna lie, it was nice. It's the closest I've been to a woman in three years.

I had to resist wrapping my arms around her waist and pulling her tighter against me. Then when I hit the accelerator and the bike took off, I was smacked in the face with the smell of her fruity shampoo, and I couldn't resist breathing her in. I don't know what it is, but there's something about this girl.

Since the day Sara died, I've only ever found peace in Georgie, but standing at that creek with Gigi, I got that same feeling. All I wanted to do was pull her into my arms and feel her lips on mine. I could see she wanted me to, but I don't know why. What woman would want to be with someone as screwed up as me? I'm a broken man with a kid. I'm not exactly winning any *Bachelor of the Year* awards.

When I pulled away, I could see the disappointment flooding her, and I felt like a fucking prick. What kind of man does that? Leads a woman on and then leaves her hanging? The last thing I wanted to do was hurt her feelings, and now . . . well, fuck. Who knows?

I get it, it's my fault. She put herself out there, and I shut it down.

She came across really shy, so I wouldn't be surprised if she's feeling embarrassed, but she shouldn't. She's beautiful and interesting, and honestly, I'm surprised she hasn't found some guy that's swept her off her feet yet.

I'm a fucking idiot.

Pulling up Gigi's Tinder profile, I open her picture, and as her wide smile greets me, I can't help but feel like a fool.

I let a perfectly good woman slip through my fingers because I'm scared I'm going to hurt Sara in some nonexistent way, despite knowing how she would want this for me. Like I said, I'm a fucking idiot.

Putting my phone away, I get up off the couch and turn off the game. I'm just going to have to face the fact that I've screwed this one up. Maybe I'll wait another year or two and try again. Surely, I'll eventually find someone to help fill the void. Until then, it's just me and Georgie, and I'm okay with that.

I trudge back up the stairs with the baby monitor in my hand, and I peek into Georgie's room, hovering for a while as I listen to the steady rhythm of her chest rising and falling, knowing tonight is going to be a good one. There will be no gasping for breath, no horrendous attacks, or desperate sprints to the emergency room. Hell, I might actually be able to get a full night's sleep tonight.

After the crazy day, I step into my bathroom and get myself showered, finding mud in places no man should ever have to scrub mud from. Before I know it, I'm in bed, struggling to find sleep and thinking about the timing of Gigi's shift.

Considering she was probably feeling down, the timing seems a little convenient. Was she actually asked to come into work or was she faking it so she could hightail it out of there and not have to deal with me after I royally fucked up? Yeah, knowing my luck, that would be it.

Damn it.

Unable to help myself, I reach for my phone before pulling my hand back. She has my number. If she wanted to talk to me, she would have messaged or called. She clearly isn't interested in wasting her time on me, nor should she. After hurting her today, she probably needs space before she'll even give me the time of day to apologize.

A yawn rips through me, and I try to settle my thoughts. I need to forget about her. I'm obviously not ready to enter the dating world. I should cut my losses before I completely embarrass myself.

My eyes grow heavy, and I find myself beginning to fall into unconsciousness when my eyes fly open, hearing the familiar cry coming through the baby monitor. "Daddy."

Fuck.

I get up out of bed and head into Georgie's room to find her little blue eyes filled with tears, and it kills me. Dropping to my knees beside her bed, I brush my fingers through her hair, trying to soothe her. "What's wrong, baby? Did you have a bad dream?"

Her lower lip pouts out and she nods her little head.

With a sigh, I climb into her bed and start singing *Twinkle, Twinkle, Little Star* as I run my fingers through her hair. I guess tonight isn't going to be as easy as I'd thought.

Chapter Ten

GIGI

It's a new day and a new me. Kind of. Okay, not really. Moral of the story, Sean no longer exists to me. From here on out, it's just me and Mel, living our best lives. Well, I suppose Mel will be living her best life seeing as though she's getting dicked down every night. Me on the other hand, I've recently invested in a new vibrator, but the jury is still out on that.

We drive down the highway early in the morning for our shift at the hospital. I've always been a morning person, but Mel, on the other hand, not so much. She needs a little kick up the ass each morning to get started, hence why the music is blasting and we each have an extra-large coffee in our hands—a coffee we had to stop to get, seeing as though our coffee machine is still being an asshole.

We sing along to the songs, shouting the lyrics at the top of our lungs as our raw throats beg us to stop. I zoom down the highway, completely lost in the song when red and blue lights start flashing in my rearview mirror. "Ahh, fuck," I mutter as my gaze flashes down to my speedometer.

Yep, definitely speeding.

I study the police car behind me. Maybe he's after someone else. I mean, there are a lot of cars on the road this morning. Maybe he's about to change lanes and get the guy beside me.

"What's going on?" Mel questions as I begin turning the music down and pulling off to the side.

"Cops," I grunt.

"Were you speeding?" she questions.

I let out a heavy sigh. "Definitely."

Sure enough, the cop veers off the side of the road and pulls up behind me. Just fucking great. That's exactly what I need on a Monday morning.

The door opens and the policeman gets out of his car, and I watch through my side mirror as he makes his way toward me. Lowering my window, I begin searching for my license and registration, knowing he's bound to ask.

I turn to face the man who hovers in my window and gasp as the recognition hits me. "Great," I grumble under my breath as Sean's douchebag best friend stares back at me, a twisted grin stretching across his stupid face.

"Well, if it isn't Gigi," he says, looking more than excited that he's about to bust my ass.

I give him a fake smile, but there's no hiding the disdain in my tone. "Tom."

"Tom?" Mel questions from beside me and practically leans over into my lap so she can get a good look at the guy. "Tom? As in Sean's best friend?"

"The one and only," he says with a nod, his cocky attitude having me wonder just how much jail time I'd get for assaulting an officer on duty. I suppose it's a good thing I now have the best criminal lawyer in the country owing me a favor after he tried to turn me into a skanky homewrecking side chick. Though considering he didn't have the balls to even kiss me, it leaves me wondering what kind of balls he could possibly have in a courtroom.

Oh well, it's old news now. It's in the past. Besides, I don't think I need to be involving myself with a man who was so ready to cheat on his wife in the presence of his baby. Like what the fuck was that about?

Despite my frustrations with the asshole cop, Mel can't possibly skip the opportunity to feast her eyes upon the guy. There's no doubt he's hot. He's exactly her type. Hot? Check. Uniform? Check. Manwhore? Double check. "Well, hello, Tom," she purrs as she reaches over me to offer him her hand. "I'm Mel."

Tom winks and takes her hand right in front of my face. "Pleasure to meet you, Mel."

"For fuck's sake," I groan, knowing exactly where this is going and wishing they would just get on with it and fuck in the backseat so I can get my ass to work.

Mel looks up at me, practically in my lap. "I don't know what you're talking about, Gi," she says, her gaze flicking back to Tom's. "He seems perfectly perfect."

"Ugh," I mutter, the frustration burning me up. She was more than happy to bitch about him all day yesterday before she realized he has a jaw that could cut through glass and eyes that have women's legs opening all over the world. "You couldn't be more wrong."

Tom cuts into our conversation. "Are you aware you were speeding, Gigi?" he questions.

Yes.

"No, I wasn't, actually," I say, glancing up at him. "I was certain I was going the speed limit. Do you have proof that I was speeding?"

"I do."

"And you're positive your equipment isn't faulty?" I ask, momentarily saying a prayer for Logan's broken equipment. Though from the sound of it, Elle certainly had no complaints.

Tom sighs, clearly knowing I'm more than prepared to give him a hard time, especially after spending all of Saturday with him glaring daggers at me for no apparent reason. Though to be fair, he probably thought I was helping Sean cheat on his wife. "Are you aware that speeding is an offense?" he questions further.

Well duh. I have to stop myself from rolling my eyes as I turn to the man who so clearly despises me. "Look, Tom, you and I both know that I'm not driving away without a ticket. You made it very clear that's just the kind of man you are. So can we get on with it? Unlike you who would prefer to spend his morning pulling over random girls on the highway, we have actual lives to save."

His lips press into a tight line. "I don't like you, Gigi," he states.

"No shit," I grunt. "You made that perfectly clear on Saturday. But you know what? I don't care. You decided you didn't want to like me before you even gave me a chance, and that's your loss because I'm fucking awesome."

"She really is," Mel cuts in.

"Besides, it speaks volumes about the kind of person you are. And honestly, that's really not the kind of person I care to have taking up room in my life."

"You don't know a damn thing about the kind of person I am."

"I'm more than happy to keep it that way," I tell him, probably digging myself a deeper hole, but what does it matter? It's not like I'm ever going to see him again. Though, I can only imagine what this ticket is going to look like. "Can we get this shit wrapped up?"

Tom smirks at me before holding his hand out. "License and registration."

Jackass.

I hand over what he needs and after taking his sweet time, he shoves them back through the window before slowly turning on his heel and dawdling back to his cruiser, getting on my last nerve. I probably deserve it. I'm being a complete bitch, but it's not as though he's being the poster boy for kindness. He started this shit on Saturday. I'm only finishing it. Though, I don't exactly know how I'm going to finish it seeing as he's the one who'll get the last word when he hands me the ticket.

Tom takes his sweet time, preparing my ticket before appearing back at my window. His eyes meet Mel's across the car and he sends her a wink that any girl would fall for. She eats it up, and I realize he'll be in my apartment tonight. Fucking perfect. Looks like I'll be going out.

He reaches across me, not giving a shit about my personal space, and hands Mel a piece of paper before thrusting my ticket in my face. "Keep away from Sean. He doesn't need this shit."

"No fucking problem," I scoff.

Tom struts away like he's king shit, and I look down at my ticket. Fuck, two hundred and sixty dollars. Great.

I throw the ticket in the backseat to get lost among the other shit in my car and get back on the highway. "Don't you dare call that jerk," I warn Mel, who's already programming his number into her phone.

"Jesus, woman. What's crawled up your ass this morning? You were a complete bitch. Do you have your period?"

"No," I snap, wondering if I should take offense to that. "He was a jerk on Saturday and besides, he deserved it with his little arrogant attitude and smirk. I woke up this morning with a promise that this whole Sean bullshit was in the past, and BAM, there's his best friend pulling me over. It's like the universe is laughing in my face."

"Chill out," she laughs. "This whole Sean thing is really getting to you, isn't it?"

"No," I grunt.

"Liar."

I roll my eyes as I concentrate on the road. She's right. I'm a mess. I haven't stopped thinking about that almost kiss with him since the moment it happened. Apart from the whole hot wife, he's the perfect guy. He was funny, charming, successful, and a great father. Not to mention, he was the female equivalent of a wet dream. What is that, by the way? A moist nap? A slick snooze?

I just can't wrap my head around what he was thinking. Did he not expect me to find out? I suppose he never actually clarified if it was a date. Maybe he meant it when he said he just wanted to take me out to thank me for saving his little girl, but then, you'd think his wife would have been there. It's her little girl too. And what gives with the girls? Why didn't one of them feel the need to mention it? I mean, what happened to pussy power and all that? Chicks before dicks. Not one of them had my back.

Hell, maybe almost kissing me was a spur-of-the-moment kind of thing, and I'm the idiot who got hurt feelings in the process.

Clearly they're still together. Otherwise, he wouldn't have their wedding photo as his background on his phone. God, I'm an idiot and he's a cheater . . . Well, I guess he can't be labeled a cheater as he didn't actually kiss me, but the intention was there and, in my book, it counts.

"Earth to Gigi," Mel practically shouts at me. "Stop thinking about it. What happened to all this 'new day, new me' bullshit you were spouting this morning?"

I let out a breath. "You're right," I tell her. "I shouldn't be getting caught up on it."

"There's nothing to get caught up on. The guy is married. End of story. No matter how many fucked-up family dates he tries to take you on, he's off-limits. You need to steer clear of that one."

Indeed, I do.

Pulling up at the hospital, we grab our bags and rush through the door after Tom's slimy ass nearly made us late for our shift. But seriously, how inconsiderate. I've gotten tickets before, and I know that shit doesn't take that long. He knows we're nurses, and if he didn't then he's fucking blind since we're both completely decked out in scrubs. We have important jobs. Being late isn't an option in the work we do, it's the difference between life and death. Hell, as a cop, he should understand that.

Making our way into the nurses' lounge, we quickly sign in for our shift before dumping our bags in our lockers. "Try to have lunch together today?" Mel questions as she hovers in the doorway.

"We'll try. I have a few inductions today. It'll be busy," I tell her.

"Okay," she says. "Go with the flow then?"

"Sounds good," I say before she disappears out the door.

I head up to the nurses' station on the maternity ward and find Sue still here after working the night shift. "Jesus, cutting it close," she grins as she looks down at her watch and puts on a show of being disappointed in my tardiness.

"I know," I sigh as I double-check what's going on today. "I got pulled over for speeding again."

"Again?" she gasps. "My god! Gigi, you need to slow down. Why do you think half the patients in the ER are here?"

"I know," I mumble, too afraid to roll my eyes at this woman. We've had this exact conversation a million times before, and I know exactly how it will end—my ear clutched between her fingers as she drags me through the ER, giving me prime examples of why speeding is wrong. Hell, I've started to realize she does it for everything. Just the slight mention of my dirt bike riding had her taking me on a tour of the trauma ward and visiting a guy who'd come off his Harley and was missing half his skull. "I'll slow down."

"I'll believe it when I see it," she says under her breath.

I go to say a quick goodbye when she tells me she's doing a double and will be in and out for the day, and I smile before heading down the hallway to my first patient of the day. I push through the door and find a beautiful young woman, five centimeters dilated and completely freaking out. It's her first baby, and she's ridiculously underprepared for what she's about to do today. After calming her down and giving her a quick run-through of what the day should mostly look like, I show her husband a few things he can do to help her with her pain management.

I go up and down the halls checking on the patients, and I have to deliver a little baby boy after the doctor was called into an emergency cesarean. The rush reminds me just how much I love my job.

There's nothing better than this.

Studies show that people will change their careers a few times over their lifetime, but not me. I'm set. This is exactly where I want to be and no possible situation could change that. I've seen it all.

It's well after midday when I finally get to take a break, and I head into the nurses' lounge and grab my bag. I drop down on the couch to respond to a text from Mom that came through hours ago when Mel comes barreling through the door covered in vomit.

"I think I'm going to skip eating today," she says with a cringe as she grabs a new set of scrubs and heads for the bathroom. She begins stripping out in the hallway before jumping in the shower to hopefully scrub the vomit off every crevice of her body.

I grin as I listen to her performance, pleased she's finally getting the payback she deserves after laughing when I got drenched in pee. "Are you still going to come to lunch with me, though?" I call, hoping she can hear me over the shower.

"Yeah," she says. "Maybe I could eat once this shit is off me and I get the smell out of my hair."

Perfect.

Ten minutes later, she comes out dressed and ready, so we head down to the cafeteria before taking way too long to decide what to eat. After finally settling on a chicken salad, we bypass the seating area and find an on-call room to get just a little peace and quiet. Mel instantly falls to the ground and stretches out her legs while I flop onto the bed and dig into my lunch, my stomach gurgling after only having my coffee this morning. "My feet are killing me today," she whines.

"Me too," I tell her. "I delivered a little boy solo today."

Her face lights up with excitement. "Really?" she questions. "You're so lucky to be a midwife. I bet you don't get covered in vomit nearly as much as I do."

"True, but I get covered in shit and amniotic fluid instead."

We both fall into uncontrollable fits of laughter, only stopping when my cheeks begin to hurt. I finish off my lunch, and with ten minutes remaining before we have to head back, I stretch out on the bed and close my eyes.

I listen to the sound of Mel typing away on her phone, and I don't doubt she's messaging Tom, more than happy to still fuck the dude despite my hang-ups and the shitty way he treated me this morning . . . not that I'm particularly innocent in that one. "Do I need to go out tonight?" I question.

"Ahh, yeah," she confirms, a smile in her voice.

"This better be just a one-time thing," I warn her, really not wanting my best friend with a guy like Tom. She can definitely find someone better than that.

"Ha," she scoffs, "Isn't it always?"

"Good point," I laugh.

By the end of the day, I'm utterly exhausted, and if I can't be at home, then there's only one other place I'd rather be.

I push through the door to my parents' place and instantly fall onto their couch. "Oh, hi, honey. What are you doing here?" my mother asks as she drops her laundry basket at her feet and reaches over the top of the couch to give me a welcoming cuddle.

"Mel has a friend over," I explain.

"Oh," she says, her face scrunching with distaste, knowing exactly what it is I mean by *friend.*

"Do you mind if I crash for dinner?" I ask as she picks her laundry basket back up off the floor and shuffles over to the drying rack, getting busy hanging the wet clothes.

"Of course, honey," she says.

"You know, washing is a lot easier with a clothes dryer," I tell her, getting up off the couch and giving her a hand.

"I know," she says with a heavy sigh, rolling her eyes, and clearly not wanting to revisit the old argument. "How was work?"

"Good," I say before a wide smile tears across my face, and I launch into the rundown of my day, making sure to tell her all about the vomit Mel decided to go dancing in. The clothes are hung in no time and before I know it, Mom puts me to work in the kitchen, giving me the easy jobs, knowing that cooking really isn't my forte.

An hour later, my dad strides through the door and instantly pulls me into a warm hug. "How have you been, pumpkin?" he asks, refusing to let me go.

I'm an only child, and I must admit, I absolutely love it that way. My parents spoil me like you wouldn't believe, and I soak that shit right up. It's fantastic. Growing up, we weren't that well off, but my parents did everything in their power to make sure I never went without. Though, that also meant I was alone a lot while they both worked demanding jobs.

I've made myself a promise that one day I'm going to spoil them right back, whether that be paying off their mortgage or sending them around the world, I don't know. All I do know is that they deserve it and so much more.

I'm sure things have gotten easier for them financially since I moved out a few years ago, but I still want them to have everything they've ever dreamed of. After all, they brought me into the world and showed me unconditional love each and every day.

I sit down to dinner with my parents, and they boast about how great I am, and naturally, I let them. "So, how's everything going?" Dad asks, always worried about my welfare.

"Good," I smile.

My mom narrows her eyes at my answer. She's always been able to see right through me. "What do you mean *good?* What aren't you telling us?"

"Nothing," I grumble.

"Georgia," she scolds.

I let out a huff as I look up at my mom, and unable to help myself, my bottom lip pouts out. "It's a boy."

"What boy?" my father demands, hating the idea that I'm a grown-ass woman.

"His name is Sean. I met him in the ER and helped his daughter. Then I somehow got roped into going dirt bike riding, and just when I thought he was perfect, I found out the guy is married."

Dad scoffs, which brings on a string of grumbled curses under his breath.

"Don't worry, love. You can't let it get you down. I dated hundreds of clowns before I met your father," my mother says before giving me an encouraging smile. "And you know what? He's a clown, too."

"What are you saying, Mom?" I smirk, playing with her and enjoying the reaction I know I'm going to get. "You want me to settle for a clown?"

She gives me a blank stare. "You know exactly what I mean."

"I know," I smile. "You want me to date hundreds of men."

"Georgia," she scolds.

"Gee," Dad sighs. "Don't do that to your poor mom."

A wicked satisfaction fires through my chest. There's nothing I love more than teasing these two, and there's nothing they love more than calling me out on it. "Sorry," I murmur.

"Gee," Dad reprimands as if I'm still a child. "What have I told you about apologizing?"

I force myself to not roll my eyes at him. "Only do it if you truly mean it," I say, reciting the memorized phrase from my childhood.

"Good, now quit talking about boys and eat your dinner. You need more meat on your bones."

With that, we dig into our food, and twenty minutes later, we wash up and eventually find our way to the couch. Dad flicks through the channels while I cuddle up to my mother and enjoy being a child again, forgetting about life, forgetting about responsibilities, and forgetting about Sean.

Chapter Eleven

SEAN

Striding through the door of Georgie's preschool, I grab her bag and watch as she plays with the other kids, a wide smile resting on my lips. She spins around, laughing with her friends, and spots me almost immediately. Her little face lights up. "Daddy!" she booms, barreling into me with open arms.

After giving her a quick cuddle and checking on her day, I squeeze my arms through her little school bag and grab her around the waist to hoist her up on my shoulders.

I unlatch the safety gate and slip through, making sure to not let any of the other rugrats out. "Say bye, Georgie," I tell her as she giggles, showing off to her friends that she's on her daddy's shoulders.

"Bye, bye, Miss Beccy," Georgie says.

The preschool teacher turns around and gives my girl a beaming smile. "See you next week, Georgie," she tells her before training a flirty stare on me. "See you later, Sean."

"Bye Bec," I say, doing my best to avoid eye contact as I turn on my heel and walk up the hallway. Ever since Sara passed, I've grown used to the way random women look at me like a challenge, but I'm fucking over it.

Walking out the door and into the parking lot, I hold onto Georgie's ankles so she doesn't fall. "Were you a good girl today?" I ask, reaching my truck and pulling her down.

"No," she grins, her eyes sparkling with mischief as I open the door and start buckling her in.

I stop what I'm doing and look up at the little monkey. "Why?" I question, knowing this could go anywhere.

Her eyes meet mine and she gives me big puppy dog eyes as though that's going to save her. "Well . . ." she starts, glancing away. "Sammy was pwaying wif Gemma, but I wanted to pway wif her, so I pushed him down and he cried like baby Hudson."

"Georgia," I scold, wondering why the hell her teachers didn't bring this up with me. I mean, it's not like this is normal for her. She's never intentionally hurt another child before.

A million questions fly through my mind. Why did she do it? Has she forgotten her manners or is something bigger going on? Did Sammy do something to piss her off, or is this just a new phase? And more importantly, where the hell is Sara when I need her? "Why did you do that?" I question, desperate for answers.

"I wanted to pway," she tells me as if it's an acceptable answer.

"Are you allowed to push your friends down?" I question.

"Sammy not my fwend," she says with a shake of her head.

"Oh, and that makes it alright, does it?" I ask, still a little in shock. She looks at me with those big, beautiful eyes and nods her head. "Georgia," I scold. "No, it's not okay. You hurt Sammy and made him sad."

She pouts her bottom lip out and hits me with those beautiful puppy dog eyes again, making me turn away to avoid caving like a fucking bitch. "What happened after that?" I ask. "Did you get in trouble?"

"No," she says with a wide smile. "I pwayed wif Gemma."

Ahh shit.

Maybe it's nothing and she has blatantly forgotten that hurting other people is not okay. No, that couldn't be it. She knows better. Damn. What the hell am I going to do with her?

I let out a heavy sigh and close her door before walking around to the driver's side and getting in. This is a conversation for another time. Maybe I should speak with Brianna about this. She's a grade school teacher and will most likely have some advice on how to handle it.

Starting up my truck, I pull out of the parking lot while Georgie chats away to herself and points out every yard that has a garden out front. The game gets old quickly, but I *ooh* and *ahh* every damn time.

We're just pulling into my driveway when a call comes through

Bluetooth. "Hey, what's up?" I question, seeing Logan's name across my screen.

Logan's booming laughter instantly fills my truck. "Yo," he says, trying his hardest to gain control of himself. Georgie giggles in the background, and I have to strain to make out his words. "We were playing football and Carter broke his leg on—"

"What?" I cut in.

"—Cassie's face. There's blood everywhere, man. You should see it."

"Fuck," I curse as Georgie gasps, her eyes wide with fear, hating the thought of her favorite aunty in pain, though clearly not sparing a second thought for Carter's leg. "Why are you laughing? Is Cass hurt?"

"I don't mean to laugh," he says, "But you should have seen it, man. They both went down. It was amazing."

"Are they okay?" I question.

"Nah, definitely not," he says, finally sobering up. "We're on our way to the hospital. Carter's leg is broken and Cassie's nose . . . Look, it's not good. Jax is pissed and Bri is raging. Pretty sure the two of them are about to get into a fistfight soon, and I don't know, man. I'm worried for Jax. Bri's a feisty little thing when she's defending Carter."

"Shit," I say as I turn around at the bottom of the driveway and head straight back out. "Is Cass upset?"

"Oh yeah," he mutters. "But not about her nose. She's pissed that she didn't win the fucking game, but I think she's still in shock. It'll hit her when the bruising comes out tomorrow and she looks like a raccoon."

"I bet," I grunt. "We're on our way."

"Alright, man. We'll see you soon," he says. "Just be on the lookout for Jax. He's not happy she got hurt."

"I can only imagine," I say, picturing it so clearly. "But surely he knows that Carter wouldn't have done it on purpose."

"Yep, he knows, but there's no stopping Jax where Cassie is concerned. He'll calm down eventually."

"Alright," I murmur as I rush down the all too familiar road. "We'll be there in a sec."

Logan ends the call and Georgie instantly jumps into action. "What happened to Cass? Why is she bweeding? Where are we going?"

"Aunty Cassie and Uncle Carter had a little accident," I explain.

"What kind of accident?" her curious little mind questions.

"They were playing silly games and bumped into each other. Uncle Carter's leg is very sore and Cassie's nose has a little ouch. They just need to visit the doctor to get all fixed up."

"Oh no," she says as dramatically as possible before dismissing the topic entirely and focusing out the window, singing *one, two, three, four, five. Once I caught a fish alive.*

I concentrate on the road until I'm pulling up next to Logan's truck and rushing inside with Georgie in my arms. I find my misfit family all squished into a room, and they instantly turn to me with horrified looks as if I'm the parent, but I guess I kind of am.

"What the hell is going on here?" I scold them all.

I look at Carter first, sitting on the bed with his leg propped up and a doctor examining it. "I swear, it was an accident," he says with his hands up, immediately jumping on the defense.

Jax scoffs and draws my attention to the other side of the room where he sits with Cassie in his lap, and I can't help but take in the massive handful of bloodied tissues glued to her face. She looks fucking miserable. I guess the shock has worn off and the pain has set in.

Jax jumps straight into his recap of their afternoon while Carter argues the whole time. After thirty minutes, the only thing I've gotten from them is a headache. "Shut up," I yell over the top of their voices, my heart slowing back to normal realizing they're all going to be just fine. "You're all fucking idiots. I don't care anymore. Just get yourselves fixed."

With that, they finally settle down and another doctor comes in to see Cass. I stride over with Georgie, listening intently as he tells Cassie that her nose is going to have to be set, then watch as my little sister promptly starts freaking out about how this is going to affect her singing. Carter is then told the same thing, only he's going to have to be knocked out for it.

Realizing this is going to be a long night, I take Georgie out to the waiting room and sit down with Logan and Elle as they watch over all the kids. I only just get comfortable when Georgie pipes up with those big puppy dog eyes. "I hungwy," she tells me, holding her belly as though it might explode if she doesn't get food into it soon.

I look down at her with a smile. "Of course, you are."

Logan and Elle get up beside me and together we somehow manage to get all five kids to the cafeteria, and as I go over to order, Logan does his best to wrestle the kids into the cheap hospital highchairs. I return a few moments later with my arms full of food and crash into the seat beside Georgie.

We're halfway through our meal when Elle focuses on something behind me. "Hey, is that Gigi?" she questions with a mouthful of her hamburger.

My heart lurches in my chest and my head whips around to find the woman that I haven't been able to get out of my mind for the past two weeks. She stands with another nurse, happily chatting away as they study the salad selections. The need to go to her runs through me, but I hold back. I'd give anything to feel that sense of ease I get when I'm with her, but I get the feeling she wouldn't want me to. She never replied to my text, and I haven't heard from her since.

"Dude, what are you waiting for?" Logan says as he watches me studying her. "You're clearly into her. Why don't you go talk to her?"

"Nah," I grunt. "If she wanted to talk, she would have reached out."

"I don't know," Elle pipes up. "She seemed shy to me. Maybe she's too nervous to put herself out there. Maybe you'll need to break that barrier instead."

Crap. I look down at Georgie and realize she hasn't heard a word we're talking about. "What do you think, Georgie? Should I say hi to Gigi?"

"Gigi?" she questions, turning around and searching the cafeteria with sauce smeared all over her face. Her eyes light up as she spots her across the room, and without giving me a second to stop her, she jumps on top of the table and screams at the top of her tiny lungs. "GIGI!"

Ahh, fuck me.

What the hell are children even for if they're not embarrassing you? "Thanks a lot, kid," I groan as Gigi spins on her heel and searches out the voice. Her eyes land on our table and she cringes, making me feel like absolute shit, but I guess I deserve it. She gives Georgie a bright smile and reluctantly makes her way across the cafeteria, looking as though she would prefer to be anywhere but here.

"Dude, she does not look excited about coming over here," Logan mutters under his breath.

"No shit," I murmur as I get to my feet and force a smile across my face, wanting to fucking die inside.

"Hey guys," she smiles, doing everything she can to avoid my stare before stepping up in front of Georgie, gently pinching her chin, and giving her the most dazzling smile. "What are you doing here?"

Logan pipes up with a grin. "There was a little accident at my place involving Carter's leg and Cassie's nose."

Gigi's hands fly to her mouth, gasping in horror as her eyes widen. "Oh shit. Are they okay?" she asks, finally meeting my eyes for only a short second before flicking them back to Logan's.

"Yeah," he laughs. "They'll be fine. They're getting fixed up now."

"Oh, good. I'll go down and check on them, make sure they have everything they need," she says before glancing down at Georgie. "How are you, miss? Are you keeping out of trouble?"

"No," Georgie grins as she looks up at her, making me jealous over how easily she can talk to the woman.

"Oh, dear," Gigi laughs. She looks back up at me awkwardly before averting her gaze to Logan and Elle and giving them a tight smile. "Well, I better run," she says. "It's been a crazy shift, but it was nice seeing you again."

She turns on her heel to leave, clearly ready to bail on this awkward as fuck encounter, and though I don't recall moving, I find myself rushing after her. It can't end this way. "Gigi," I call, gaining her attention.

She turns around, and the disinterest and hurt in her eyes has me on edge. "What's up?" she asks, very clearly wanting to be anywhere but here.

"I, umm," I start, my hand hooking around the back of my neck, feeling like I'm going to be sick with nerves. "Shit, I don't know why I'm being so fucking awkward about this, but I was wondering if you'd maybe want to grab dinner with me?"

She stares at me, the silence killing me. "Seriously?" she finally grunts in surprise, but judging by her tone, I don't think this is going to go as well as I'd hoped.

"Yeah."

She cringes. I see the rejection in her eyes before she even gets a chance to say a word, and I will the ground to open up beneath my feet and swallow me whole. "I don't think that's such a great idea, Sean," she tells me. "I can't get myself involved in all of this."

My brows furrow. What the hell is she talking about? "Involved in what?" I question.

She lets out a heavy sigh and shakes her head, that same hurt from earlier shining brighter now than ever. "Sorry," she says before turning away and disappearing out the door with the other nurse.

I stand there dumbfounded, and quite honestly, I feel like an absolute dickhead. I've never been rejected before. Well, actually, I've never put myself out there to be rejected. Things with Sara happened so quickly and naturally, I've never had to do this whole asking a chick out bullshit. It's fucking awful.

With a sigh, I turn back to my family and realize that I'm a shitload closer than I thought, and judging by the look on Logan's face, they heard every fucking word. Logan grins at me, embarrassment in his eyes as he shakes his head. "Dude, what the fuck was that?" he asks, looking truly appalled.

"It was nothing," I defend.

"No, that was not nothing," he says. "That was a whole lot of something, but I have no idea what the something was."

"Leave him alone," Elle cuts in. "He's trying. He's new to this."

"Nah, this shit needs to be dealt with now before we unleash him on the world. I don't know if you know this, babe, but us Waters' boys have a reputation to uphold, and Sean . . . he's gonna go right ahead and fuck it all up."

"What do you care about the Waters' manwhore reputation? Both you and Carter are married!"

I roll my eyes as the rest of our meal consists of Logan going over all his old pick-up techniques while Elle scoffs and shakes her head. Apparently, she thinks those girls were after the glory of being able to claim they slept with Logan Waters, the NHL star, rather than falling victim to his so-called game.

I ignore every damn word Logan has to say and finish my meal, feeling completely dejected. I know I should probably listen to some of his bullshit to better myself in the future, but for now, I'm content sitting here and wallowing in the sting of Gigi's rejection.

Half an hour later, we get comfortable in the waiting room and settle in for a long night. Georgie falls asleep in the chair next to me while Logan, Elle, and I do our best to keep up with the rest of the kids.

The doctor finally comes out a few hours later, and I've never been so happy to see him. He lets us know that all broken bones have been set and that we can sit in the room with them while the drugs wear off. Though, I'm sure they're just saying this so they can get rid of all the upset kids in their waiting room.

We pick up all the babies, and I struggle to balance a sleeping Georgie and a screaming Nate in each hand. When I finally stride into the room, I dump the kids onto Carter's bed and collapse into a chair, completely exhausted.

Chapter Twelve

GIGI

Why does he have to be here? I mean, I'm not working tomorrow. Cassie and Carter could have decided to break each other's bones then. That would have worked wonders for my schedule.

Instead, he had to go and flash that handsome face that I can't have and ruin the rest of my shift. I have hardly been able to concentrate, and it's honestly pissing me off. Why am I finding it so damn hard to move on from this? The guy is fucking married. It's not that hard. He's taken and I need to move on.

And, where the hell does he get off asking me to go for dinner?

What the fuck is up with that? He's got to be kidding himself if he thinks I'm going to date him. He's crazy. Does he think I'm stupid or is he just a nasty guy? His poor wife.

I need a fucking drink.

Glancing up at the clock, I realize I only have twenty minutes of my shift left before I can finally get out of here and stop fearing that I'll accidentally run into him in the hallways. I mean, why does he keep showing up in my life? This is torture.

"Gigi," I hear from Sue behind me. I turn to find her walking toward me with a bunch of paperwork in her hand, so I move to meet her in the middle.

"What can I help you with?"

Glancing at her watch, she checks the time before looking back up at me. "You're just about finished, right?" she asks.

"Sure am," I say, hoping like fuck she's not about to ask me to do a double.

"Have you finished all your patient reports?"

"Just about. I have one more patient to check on and then I'm all good."

"Excellent," she says as she hands me her paperwork. "Would you be able to drop these reports downstairs? Then you can leave. Everything is under control here."

Relief pounds through my veins. "Sure thing."

She shuffles off, and I find myself so lucky to have such an awesome supervisor. She's so chill and it makes for such a nice work environment.

I pop the paperwork down with my things and quickly check on my last patient. Then before I know it, I'm down in the locker room, grabbing my bag. I pull out my phone to check how Mel is doing and find a text already waiting.

Mel – I'm gonna be a while. I'll make my own way home. Have a good night xxx.

Damn. There goes my plans for the night. I quickly hash out a reply, kind of relieved that I can get out of here early. If not, I would have been waiting around for Mel to finish, and I'd definitely prefer to be home right now with a glass of wine.

Gigi – Okay, sure. I'll see you in the morning.

Picking up the stack of paperwork, I gingerly make my way downstairs and make sure Sue's paperwork ends up in the right hands before saying goodnight to everyone and getting on my way.

I walk up the hallway and a little girl wandering out of the supply closet all by herself catches my eye. "Georgie?" I question, instantly recognizing the little girl.

She freezes, clearly thinking she's just been caught doing something she shouldn't be, and as her gaze settles on me, those big blue eyes light up. "Gigi," she smiles, before dropping the pillow in the middle of the hallway and racing toward me.

She jumps so I quickly bend down and catch her in my arms.

"What are you doing out here?" I question. "Where's your mommy and daddy?"

"Daddy sweeping," she tells me, making me realize she's just escaped without anyone being wiser.

"He's sleeping, is he?" I question, the thought of a sleeping Sean intriguing me more than it ever should.

Georgie gives me a beaming smile and nods her head as I walk over to the nurses' station and check which room her family is in. "And what about your mommy?" I ask as I scan the room numbers, needing to put Georgie up on the counter so I can get this shit done faster.

"Mommy's in heben with Grandma and Grandpa," she tells me, those big blue eyes drawing me in.

Horror slams through my chest, and my jaw slackens, unable to steal my gaze away from the little girl. "Heben?" I ask with a racing heart, hoping I'm not hearing this correctly. "Do you mean heaven? Your mommy's in heaven?"

Please say no. Please say no.

"Yep, heben."

Shit. My heart breaks for this little girl. Her mommy is gone. How could I not know this? I jumped to conclusions, assuming Sean was a cheating bastard when in reality, he's actually the furthest thing from it, probably just trying to get by and put himself out there.

Fuck.

I'm such a fucking bitch. He must think I'm a monster.

I can't imagine what it would be like to lose your partner like that. I mean, when the hell did it happen? Does Georgie remember her and miss her every single day? The poor guy has been a single dad to a little girl who suffers from severe asthma attacks. I can't even begin to imagine how hard it must be. Shit, so many questions are going through my mind, but all I want to do is throw myself at him and take the pain away. But I've fucked this up way too much for that.

Hell, the guy asked me out to dinner for God's sake, and I turned him down. How am I supposed to come back from that?

Georgie's movement pulls me out of my head, and I look down at the angel who's currently pointing to her lady bits. "This is my jiney," she says before moving her hand to her tiny ass. "And this is my hiney."

Oh, sweet baby Jesus. "Yes, honey, it is," I smile, trying not to laugh.

"Do you have a jiney?" she questions.

Fuck me! How did our conversation take this turn? "Yes," I laugh. "I do have a jiney."

Realizing she's only just getting started and is bound to tell me more about the human anatomy, I scoop her off the counter and put an end to it before she asks where babies come from. We head down the hallway, and I stop to grab the discarded pillow along the way.

I stand with Georgie outside the door, needing a minute to compose myself before walking in there and seeing the man I've most likely hurt after he's already suffered so much.

I take a deep breath and slowly blow it out before stepping through the door. As I take in the scene before me, I smile to myself. Every single adult in the room is fast asleep. Cassie and Carter lay in beds with the dividing curtain pulled right back. They both look awful, especially Cassie who has deep bruising around her eyes. Jax is curled up beside her with Hudson asleep between them.

Brianna sits in the chair right beside Carter, asleep with her head lolled to the side while Logan is sprawled out on the floor beside the twins and Lilly, who are all quietly playing while Elle lays right by him, using his ass as a pillow.

Then there's Sean. *Fucking beautiful Sean.* He's laid back on the couch with his legs propped up over the side. He has a space beside him reserved for Georgie, and it's clear how she was so easily able to escape.

I lightly knock on the door, hating that I need to wake them, and I watch as everyone's eyes spring open. Sean immediately flies to his feet as he realizes his daughter is no longer safely tucked in his arms, but calms when he sees us by the door.

"Hi," I cringe in the doorway as they all look at me. "I found this one wandering around in the supply room," I explain as I hold up the pillow.

"Shit," Sean mutters, instantly crossing the room and scooping Georgie out of my arms. His fingers brush against my skin, sending goosebumps sailing over me, and I never want to leave this moment, but it's not like I can hold onto him without making a fool of myself.

"Thank you," he whispers with his eyes on mine, clearly wanting to say something else, but leaving the topic alone. He glances away and focuses his attention on his daughter. "What were you doing?"

"I needed a piwow," she tells him.

He lets out a frustrated sigh before placing her down on the couch, probably getting ready for the lecture of the year about wandering away in strange places. Then wanting to give them the privacy they deserve, I give the room a tight smile before making my move to leave.

"Um, Gigi," I hear.

Ahh, fuck. What now?

I turn around to find Jax sitting up and looking over at me. "What's up?"

"Do you think we could get some more painkillers for Cass?" he asks, glancing at his wife, clearly seeing how uncomfortable she is.

Cassie instantly objects. "No, Jax. I'm fine. I just want this shit to wear off so we can go home."

I walk deeper into the room and pick up her chart, glancing over it with a frown as I take it all in. "You should have been able to go home ages ago," I murmur.

"You're kidding right?" Jax grunts.

"Not at all," I say, moving across to Carter's bed and checking his, and sure enough, he should have been out of here too. Realizing they've been overlooked by the night shift, anger starts bubbling through my veins, but I bury it down and smile at them. "I'll go find the doctor and get you guys out of here."

"Thanks," Jax says, relief flashing in his eyes.

Still desperate to get home, I quickly scurry around the ward and find the doctor, and after a quick rundown and explaining how they've been looked over, he promises to see them next. Pleased I've been able to help them in some little way, I make my way out the door.

Getting in my car, I can't seem to get Sean out of my head. I owe him an apology, big time. My only issue is that I'm almost positive he wouldn't want to hear from me.

With a sigh, I get myself home and run a bath. Without Mel here, I'm as free as a bird and strut around the apartment in my underwear, not that Mel stops me from doing it in the first place. I make myself dinner before grabbing my Kindle, and the only thing missing is my glass of wine, so I get that shit sorted as well.

After an hour of still not being able to get him off my mind, I pull up a new message and sit on my couch, staring at it, wondering what the hell I'm going to say.

Why does this have to be so hard?

Then deciding to give it to him straight, I start typing.

Gigi – Hey Sean, I know I'm probably the last person you want to hear from, but I need to apologize. On Saturday, I picked up your phone thinking it was mine, and seeing your background image, realized you were married. I kinda thought there was something between us and I was hurt, which is why I left. Then when I found Georgie in the supply closet, I asked her where her mommy and daddy were, and she told me that her mommy was in heaven. I feel like such a fool. I jumped to conclusions and assumed the worst of you. I was awful to you today and you didn't deserve that. I'm so sorry. I really hope you don't think I'm an awful person.

I hit send and instantly throw my phone away.

Crap. I did it. I reached out to a guy. Jesus Christ. This is worse than the whole Tinder thing.

I find myself watching my phone on the coffee table, waiting for him to respond. Ten minutes pass, then twenty and thirty. Then just as I'm coming to the conclusion that it's over and that I've completely fucked this up, my phone lights up.

My heart races and I stare at it, too nervous to actually check the message. *Crap, come on Gigi, where are those steel balls you had while dirt bike riding?* He's either going to say, *That's okay, Gigi. I forgive you. Come and fall madly in love with me* or, *Get fucked, Gigi. You're a rotten asshole.*

Ahh, shit. Shit. Shit. Shit.

I let out a nervous breath and will the butterflies in my stomach to settle. Then needing to get this over and done with before I drive myself crazy, I fly forward and grab the phone before I convince myself to burn it.

Sean – I don't really know what to say to you. I feel like this could have been avoided had you talked to me.

Shit, well that leaves me confused. Is this a bad thing? I have no fucking clue. That wasn't how he was supposed to respond. Where's the offer to come and fall in love with him? Where's the angry get fucked message? I can deal with those, but this? Shit.

Pulling up my big girl panties, I swallow my pride and hit reply.

Gigi – You're completely right. I'm sorry. Talking to new people isn't exactly easy for me, especially ones that look like you.

Send. Fuckkkkkk, I went there.

Sean – I know what you mean, but yeah, my wife is gone. Sara died three years ago during childbirth. It was the hardest thing I've ever gone through and it left me broken. I was with Sara since high school, and you're the first . . . I don't know how to do this . . . thing with you.

A new message comes through before I even get a chance to finish reading the first.

Sean – I wasn't intentionally trying to hide it from you, just didn't know how or when the right time is to drop a bomb like that, especially when I had no idea where we stand with each other.

Woah.

That, I was not expecting. I read and reread his words over and over again, so much to unpack there. But his main message is that his wife died during childbirth, so he's been doing this whole single-parenting thing since Georgie was a newborn, and I realize he's a lot stronger than I could ever have imagined.

He called whatever's going on here a *thing* and honestly, I don't think I could possibly come up with a more appropriate word for it. It is a *thing.* It's not *nothing* but it also hasn't graduated to being *something.* We obviously have an attraction to each other—me clearly a lot more than he does.

A million things run through my mind as I try to figure out how to respond. Deciding to keep it simple since we've both said a lot already

. . .

Gigi – Can we start over?

Sean – Dinner?

Holy shit.

Gigi – I'd love to.

Chapter Thirteen

SEAN

My eyes remain locked on the door as I sit at the bar of the nicest restaurant in town, feeling sick to my stomach. I can't believe I'm about to do this. It's my first date since Sara, and I've never been so nervous in my life.

I still can't believe it's even happening. When that text from Gigi came through, I must have sat there, dumbfounded, looking at the screen for ages trying to figure out what the hell to say.

The fact that she knows about Sara seems to make things easier. Maybe it will help her to understand why I'm so standoffish when it comes to this shit. I told her that I was broken, but she still agreed to go to dinner with me, so maybe I didn't completely screw things up.

All I know is that right now, she's giving me a second chance, and I couldn't be more grateful.

I really like her, and that thought alone scares the shit out of me. I don't want to screw this up with her. I have to do this right, especially when I have Georgie to think about. Though Gigi seems like the kind of woman who just gets it.

The restaurant door opens, and I hold my breath as a woman walks in, but realizing it's not her, I exhale deeply, my heart thundering erratically in my chest. Shit, why the fuck am I being such a little bitch about this? I'm a grown-ass man. I can handle this.

I order a beer and force myself to relax. She's just a woman. An amazing woman. A woman who has saved my child's life and then brought her back to me when she wandered away, even though she thought I was a cheating prick at the time.

The idea that Gigi thought I was the kind of man to cheat on my wife nearly killed me. But I suppose I can't hold it against her. She had only just met me, and the evidence was staring her in the face. How the hell was she supposed to know that my wife died? It's not like I was forthcoming about the topic. But when the hell is it appropriate to tell a woman you like that your wife is dead?

The door opens again, and this time my heart stops. She's fucking beautiful.

Gigi walks in wearing an oversized sweater that falls off her shoulder with a short black skirt barely visible beneath. Her toned legs peek out below, and I can't help but follow them down to the knee-high boots that blow me the fuck away.

I stand, watching as her gaze scans the room and stops on mine, and the second they do, something fucking clutches my chest and refuses to let go. A beaming smile spreads over her face, and just like I knew with Sara, I fucking know now.

This woman is going to be my world.

Contentment settles through me, and the nerves instantly fade away, knowing that no matter what happens, this is going to be okay. I just hope she's alright with slow.

She makes her way to me, and from the way her soft gaze drops and her cheeks flush, it's perfectly clear that she's nervous. She has every right to be. It's not like we've had a normal start. "Hi," she smiles.

I can't help myself and step right into her, my hand on her waist as I lean in and press a kiss to her cheek. "How are you?" I ask, reluctantly pulling back as I offer her the seat beside mine and signal for the bartender to come take her order.

Her gaze lifts to mine, and my fingers itch to reach out to her again. "Honestly, I'm kind of freaking out," she says.

"Don't freak out," I tell her, my gaze sailing over her again, determined not to fuck this up. "You look beautiful, by the way."

Her cheeks flush, and I fucking love it. "Thank you," she smiles. "You don't look too bad yourself."

The bartender steps up in front of us, and I meet her stare. "What can I get you to drink?"

"Moscato please," she says.

The bartender gets straight to it and quickly places her glass down in front of her, which she happily accepts. She takes a sip, tilting her chin up and showing off the beautiful column of her neck.

She really is radiant. With the Denver sunset shining through the window and hitting her back, I could almost swear she was wearing a halo.

The restaurant hostess appears beside us, and I watch as her eyes greedily travel up and down Gigi's body with appreciation, and I can't help but feel a kinship, because fuck . . . same. "Your table is ready," she announces.

At that, Gigi and I stand, and I place my hand on her lower back as we follow the hostess, electricity shooting through my fingertips. I help Gigi into her seat, and I can't help but feel as though we're getting off to a flying start. I know it's only just begun, but I feel like it couldn't be going any better.

Gigi takes another sip of her wine, and I watch as she finally starts to relax. She's comfortable here with me, just as I am with her. In fact, I'm more than comfortable with her. *She helps me breathe again.*

We look over the menu, and I realize this shit is a little fancier than I thought. I honestly don't understand what the fuck is on this menu. I look up at Gigi and see the crease between her eyebrows as she studies the menu, trying to figure it out. "Do you have any idea what the hell this shit is?" I question.

She looks up from her menu and a guilty grin tears across her face. "No clue," she admits.

I nod toward the exit. "You want to go get pizza?"

Her grin turns into a beaming smile. "Would that be too rude?"

"Hell no," I say as I push back out of my chair and come around to her side. I offer her my hand, and she greedily finishes what's left of her Moscato before placing her hand in mine. And the moment we touch, the fire burns between us. She looks up at me, our eyes meeting over the table as my future becomes set in stone.

I'm fucking breathless as I help her out of her chair, and I find myself holding onto her hand a second longer than necessary. I put cash down on the table for their troubles and lead Gigi out of the restaurant.

We cross the street and once again, I find my hand resting on her lower back, though it's begging to wrap around her waist. But she doesn't dare shrug away from my touch.

We walk straight into the pizza place and put in our order before making our way over to the liquor store to grab a bottle of wine. And judging by the way Gigi so easily navigates her way around the store, I'd dare say she's a frequent flyer to this particular place of business.

By the time we get back to grab our pizza, it's ready to go. When we take our order and step out into the street, an idea hits me, and I find myself sliding my hand into hers, leading her away.

"Do you have a coat?" I ask as an afterthought, pausing in the street.

"Yeah," she says, pointing across the road. "It's in my car."

Quickly crossing the road, she dives into her bag and finds her keys before unlocking the car and scrambling through it for her coat. Then with one hand in hers and the other balancing the pizza, we walk five minutes down the road to the deserted park, and I lead her to one of the picnic tables that sits right under a lamppost.

As I set the pizza down on the table, she smiles and takes a seat, unzipping her heeled boots and kicking them off. She crosses her legs under her and makes herself comfortable, and I love that she's this carefree. "The heels aren't you?" I question as I pop the cork out of the wine bottle.

She thinks about her answer for just a moment. "Sort of," she finally says. "I love heels. I have quite an impressive collection, but I actually hate wearing them."

"Hurt your feet?"

"Yep," she smiles. "It's like dudes who collect expensive watches and have them lined up in their closet like a fancy display, but every morning, they still pick out the same old cheap watch they got as a graduation present a million years ago. I think I just like to look at them."

I laugh, never having felt more called out in my life, and as we get stuck into our pizza, I can see it so perfectly—me and Gigi having a night in together, completely at ease with each other as Georgie runs amuck.

She eyes the bottle of wine before that same crease from earlier appears between her eyebrows. "What's wrong?" I ask.

"How am I supposed to drink that? We have no glasses."

Shit. I knew I was forgetting something. "You're not opposed to drinking out of the bottle, are you?"

"No," she laughs. "I just didn't want to look like a slob on a first date."

"You're good." And with that, she surprises me and picks the bottle straight up to take a drink.

We fall into easy conversation, and I'm having the best fucking time. She's always got something to say, and there hasn't been a single awkward moment between us. We've just about finished the pizza when she looks up at me with hesitation brimming in her bright eyes. "Can I ask you a question?"

"Sure," I say, wondering where this is going.

"Can you tell me about Sara?"

Oh shit. My heart stops.

Can I tell this woman about her without completely breaking down? I don't fucking know. I'm going to have to tell her about Sara at some point, she's a massive part of both mine and Georgie's life, and if this is going to go anywhere, I have to be open and honest about everything. Gigi deserves no less.

My hands start to shake, and a part of me feels as though I need to keep this all to myself, but not sharing with Gigi how amazing Sara was would be a tragedy. "Sara was my high school sweetheart," I tell her, finding the words coming out much easier than I ever thought. "She transferred to my high school when I was sixteen, and the second I saw her, I had to have her. She was this blonde goddess and she blew me away. I'd never met a girl like that before. Naturally, she refused to go out with me because she wanted to settle into the school, but I wasn't taking no for an answer."

"I can imagine," Gigi says, listening to my story intently.

"I have to admit, I was a bit of a ladies' man back in high school, so she caved pretty quickly, and the rest is history. I married her as soon as I could, and two years later, she fell pregnant."

"Then you had Georgie," she says.

"And then we had Georgie."

"Your message said that she passed during childbirth?" she questions.

I let out a breath as the memory of that day hits me. "Yeah, Georgie was stuck and going into distress, so Sara had to have an emergency C-section. Georgie was born and placed on Sara's chest, and she instantly fell in love with her. It was honestly the best moment of my life." A smile settles across my lips, remembering the feeling like it was yesterday. "It happened so quickly. One second, she was being stitched up, the next, Sara was unresponsive and bleeding out. She'd hemorrhaged and they couldn't stop the bleeding."

I finish off my story and look up at her, only her eyes are down and that crease between her eyebrow is there once again. "What hospital was this at?" she questions.

"Yours," I tell her.

Her eyes close and she looks broken. "Sara Waters," she breathes, as if realizing something I can't quite figure out.

"Yeah."

"Shit," she curses under her breath.

"What's going on, Gigi?" I ask, already dreading her answer.

She looks up at me with tears in her big eyes and her heart on her sleeve. She tries to blink them away, but all that does is make them fall down her cheeks. "I remember it. I was working that day," she whispers. "Sara wasn't one of my patients, but I was there at the end."

Fuck.

I don't know what to say. The woman I want to date was present for the worst moment in my life. She was there when I fell to my knees and screamed for my wife. She was there when I broke down into tears. She was there when I refused to look at my daughter.

I feel fucking sick.

I bring my elbows up on the table and rest my head in my hands. I honestly have no idea how to feel about this. She witnessed it all. How am I supposed to move forward from this? Would something like this make a relationship stronger, or should I just back out now before I start pushing her away?

"Are you okay?" her soft voice asks from across the table, her hand dropping to my arm.

I raise my head out of my hands and look at her. "I, ahh . . . don't know," I tell her honestly. "I think that's going to take a second to process."

"Okay," she says, tightening her lips and pushing herself up from the table. She makes her way around and takes a seat next to me, sitting as close as possible without actually touching me, and I find it somehow puts me at ease. "I'm sorry I said anything. I just thought it would be best to be upfront and honest rather than having you find out later."

"No," I say. "I'm glad you told me. I was just blindsided by it. I wasn't expecting that."

"Me either," she says.

"I should have known it could be a possibility," I tell her. "You work exactly where it happened, same ward and everything. I was stupid not to consider it."

"No, you weren't," she murmurs quietly beside me, a sadness in her eyes. "Do you need me to go?"

My eyes flick up to her, and I realize that's the last thing I want. I turn my body to face her and reach out. I pull her hand into both of mine and look down at them connected. Her hand is soft and welcoming in mine, and I find I really like it there.

"No," I tell her and then decide if she can be upfront with me then I need to do the same for her. "I like you, Gigi, and I'm not about to pretend that dating again after Sara is easy because it's really not."

She nods as she takes it in. "This might be a little presumptuous here, but in case you haven't figured it out, I kind of like you, too, and I feel like something is starting here," she tells me as she indicates the space between us. "Maybe we could take it slow?"

I study her for a moment before releasing her hand and reaching forward. My fingers twine around the back of her neck as hers drop to my thigh, sending sparks shooting through me. I gently pull her toward me, taking it slow to give her a chance to pull away if she needs, and as her face inches closer, my heart starts to race.

Unable to wait another second, I close the gap, pressing my lips to hers and kissing her gently, and she instantly melts into me, her lips so soft and warm. She kisses me back, and something settles in my chest, knowing that this is right, that this is exactly where I'm supposed to be.

Gigi's hand rises to my chest, gently pressing against my heart, and as I find myself getting lost in our kiss, the ugliness of betrayal pulses through my veins like poison. I know Sara is gone, and I'm not doing anything wrong, but I guess it's just going to take a little while.

Pulling back from Gigi, I keep her close, my hand coming around to the side of her face as my thumb stretches out and brushes over her full lips. "Slow," I tell her.

"Slow," she repeats, her lips moving against my thumb.

We sit for another hour getting to know each other, and I tell her all about my parents and how we lost them, which has her tearing up again, and I pull her into my arms the very way I've been craving all night.

Gigi tells me about her childhood and how she became such good friends with Mel. Then goes on to tell me about her run-in with Tom and how Mel has been sleeping with him every night this week.

Honestly, the fact that he was sleeping with her friend doesn't surprise me. That's just Tom, but the fact that he's gone back for seconds or even thirds blows me the fuck away. I'll have to figure out what's going on there.

A deathly chill seeps into the air, and when Gigi's teeth begin to chatter, disappointment spreads through me, realizing it's time to bring tonight to an end. "Can I take you home?" I ask as I grab the pizza box and jam it into the trash.

She's right in the middle of taking a sip from the wine bottle when she nearly spurts it out, her eyes going wide. "I thought we were taking it slow?"

"Huh?" I grunt before realizing exactly where her mind has gone. "Oh," I laugh. "I meant, can I drive you home?"

Her cheeks flush with embarrassment, and I can't resist brushing the backs of my fingers over them as she looks up at me. "I have my car here," she reminds me.

Right, I knew that. "Can I walk you to it?"

"I'd love that," she smiles up at me.

Gigi slips her knee-high boots back on before taking my hand, and being the perfect gentleman, I walk her back to her car. But that's as far as my gentleman tendencies go when I crowd her against the side of her car, my hands gripping her waist as I step into her, pinning her with my body. She gasps, her eyes flicking up to meet mine just as I bring my lips down on hers and kiss her deeply.

Gigi melts into me, her hands creeping up around the back of my neck and holding me close.

Betrayal still stings like a knife through my chest, but I fear that's something that may never go away. So, I test the waters and deepen our kiss, so fucking aware of how good she tastes. Gigi moans into me, her fingers moving up into the back of my hair, putting me right on the edge, desperate for more.

Fuck this whole going slow thing.

I know it's what I truly need to help me feel at peace with welcoming another woman into my world, and when it comes down to it, I probably won't be able to take it that far, but there's no denying that Gigi is one hell of a sexy vixen.

Before I get carried away, I pull back and force myself to open her car door. She smiles up at me, everything she's feeling shining in her blazing green eyes.

I tuck her safely into her car before I bend her over the hood and show the world what I'm dying to do to her, and after flashing me with one more breathtaking smile, she takes off, leaving me standing in the street, unable to wait to see where the hell this new road takes me.

Chapter Fourteen

SEAN

My glass shatters on the floor as I take in my daughter in her bed, desperately gasping for breath. "GEORGIE," I cry, racing to her.

This can't be happening, not again.

I scoop her into my arms and grab her inhaler, trying to sit her up at the same time, my heart pounding so fucking fast, my hands shake. I put the inhaler to her lips and instantly puff the Ventolin into her mouth, only she can't get a deep enough breath to send the medicine down her throat. I try again, but it's no use.

My baby can't fucking breathe.

Fear grips hold of me as I pull her to my chest and race out of her bedroom, flying down the stairs two at a time. I need to find a phone. I need a fucking ambulance. Now

"You're going to be okay," I promise her, frantically searching for my phone, knowing every last second counts. Hell, if I don't get her help soon, it will be too late. I can't fucking lose her. I won't.

Finding my phone by the oven, I dial 911 and hit speakerphone, quickly telling them what's going down, and as the ambulance is dispatched and the operator remains on the phone, I focus all of my attention on my baby girl.

She needs to calm down. The more she panics, the worse it's going to get. That includes crying. If she bursts into tears right now, it could be over.

I try my hardest to soothe her, but she can sense the panic deep within me, and it only makes her fret. "It's okay, my sweet Georgie. It's going to be okay," I murmur, desperately wishing I could believe my own words. "Slow breaths. Help is nearly here."

I mentally prepare myself in case I need to breathe for her or perform CPR. With Georgie still in my arms, I move to stand right by the open door, hitting the button for the gate and watching for the moment when paramedics arrive.

Putting Georgie down, I get her into the best position, the one I've watched the paramedics use too many fucking times to count. I drop to my knees beside her and see in her eyes that she's begging me not to let her go, but I need to be smart here. I can't be in the way.

I consider running her up to the front gate but I'm sure the frosty night air is not going to help her right now.

Hearing the sirens in the distance, I thank God that they're nearly here. I can't fucking stand myself right now. I had to go and get a glass of fucking water. I was gone for all of two seconds, and those two seconds nearly cost me my daughter.

I grip hold of my baby, willing the paramedics to hurry up. *Please, Sara. Don't take her from me. I know you miss her, but I'm not ready yet. Is this punishment for thinking of another woman? Punishment for needing to be happy without you? Needing to move on? Please, baby. Don't take her from me.*

The paramedics storm through the door with the shot ready, and I watch as the woman does all the same shit that Gigi had done a few weeks ago. And the second the shot is administered, the woman pulls back and watches Georgie through a tight, fearful stare.

And the moment Georgie takes a gasping breath, I fucking crumble.

Georgie's throat quickly begins opening up again, and her breathing deepens. Her gasps are still shallow and not enough, but it's the oxygen her little body so desperately needs.

Georgie tries to get up off the ground, desperately trying to fight her way into my arms, but the paramedics hold her down to ensure she's stable before letting her go anywhere.

Reaching past the paramedic, I grip Georgie's hand as she starts sobbing, calling for me. "Just one more second, baby," I tell her, wishing she couldn't see the tears in my eyes. I need to be strong for her.

That was too fucking close.

The paramedics finish what they're doing and go to put her on the gurney, but she refuses, and I carry her out to the ambulance instead, holding her to my chest, unable to even think about letting her go. We all climb into the back of the ambulance and Georgie allows them to strap her into the gurney as I sit across from her, clutching her hand.

She spends the whole ride in the ambulance with her eyes trained on mine, fear flooding her gaze. I try my best to soothe her, but until she's settled in the hospital, that's not going to happen.

We get to the hospital in record time, and she's wheeled inside before being transferred onto a bed. As her breathing has returned to normal and her airways are cleared and open, it takes a while for the doctor to come in.

While we wait, I take my chance to pull her into my arms, burying my face into her hair as she glues herself to my chest. "I don't know what I would have done without you," I whisper as she cries silent tears that soak into my shirt.

The doctor finally comes in and checks her over before demanding she stays for observation, and at this point, I'll sell my fucking house and move in permanently. We discuss her long-term asthma plan as it's clearly not working for her anymore, but the thought of putting her on stronger medication kills me, but if it means it will save her life then I'll take it.

My little girl is never going to have a normal life.

She's going to be battling this until her final days, in and out of doctor's offices and seeking out the best specialists in the country. It will get easier as she grows and will be able to recognize the symptoms, but for now, I have to do everything in my power to be there for her as much as humanly possible.

The doctor says we'll discuss the options once he's assessed her after the twenty-four-hour observation period, and with that, he's out the door. A nurse comes waltzing in and within minutes, we're transferred up to the pediatric ward, and once Georgie is comfortable, she's attached to a monitor that will keep track of her breathing. I watch as the nurse double-checks the stock in the room for all asthma medications and feel reassured by her attention to detail.

After leaving my phone at home, I haven't got much in the way of entertainment, so I climb into the bed beside Georgie and turn on the tiny television in the corner of the room. I turn the volume down so she can get some proper rest and make myself at home, knowing I won't get a wink of sleep tonight.

After one of the longest nights of my life, the sun finally shines through the window of Georgie's hospital room. With the morning comes the nurses' shift change, and I'm surprised when Gigi's best friend, Mel, comes waltzing in with a wide smile.

She takes one look at Georgie before turning to me with wide eyes. "Oh, hi," she says, a little surprised to see me here.

I give her a tight smile as she walks deeper into the room and checks Georgie's chart. "Hey, Mel. How are you?" I question, feeling as though my eyes are falling out of my head.

The sound of my voice has Georgie stirring in her bed. "I'm

good," she says. "Yourself?"

"Could be better," I say as she puts the chart back and comes around to Georgie's side to check her monitor.

"I bet," she murmurs before looking down at Georgie. "And how are you, sweet cheeks?"

"Goowd," she says with a beaming smile. "I went in ambuwance."

"Oh, really?" Mel gasps, making Georgie smile wide and nod her head. Mel looks back up at me with furrowed eyebrows. "Gi didn't mention you were taking up residence in my ward."

"Yeah, no," I say. "It was a rush getting out of the house, I left my phone at home. Hell, I left my whole fucking house wide open. I haven't been able to call my family or Gigi. I'll have to call my secretary at some point, too."

"Oh, here," she says, digging into her pocket and pulling out her phone. She launches it across the bed, and I pluck it out of the air. "Just make sure you give it back. There is shit in there that nobody needs to see!"

"Are you sure?" I question, shaking my head, not wanting to even imagine what kind of shit she has on her phone. If she's the kind of girl to keep Tom interested, then she must be down for some nasty shit.

"Yeah," she says.

"Is this because you're still seeing Tom and you want to be placed firmly in my good book?"

"No," she says, a slight blush coming over her cheeks. "I don't need to get in your good book. I'm already there."

"Really?" I question. "How so?"

"I'm the woman looking after your little girl today, and I'm in charge of your discharge papers. Not to mention, you've been dating my best friend for the past two weeks. So technically, you should be busting your balls to get into *my* good book," she gives me a wide smile before waltzing out of the room, and I can't fault her. She's right.

Not wanting to hold onto Mel's phone any longer than necessary, I get on with it and try to remember Cassie's number. It rings twice before my sister's voice comes through the line. "Hello," she answers with a question in her tone.

"Cass, it's me," I say.

"Oh, what's up? Where's your phone?"

"At home," I grunt. "Listen, Georgie's in the hospital again," I start. She gasps but I cut off her question. "We're here for the day. Do you reckon you guys could drop off some clothes, maybe lock my fucking door behind you?"

"Of course," she says. "Is Georgie okay?"

"She is now," I say, letting her hear the seriousness in my tone. "It was close. Real fucking close. But she's good. She's just here for observation now."

"Fuck," she breathes, her voice shaky. "Okay. We'll come straight down."

"How's your face?"

"Fine," she grumbles, clearly not fine at all. "I'll give the boys a call and let them know what's going on."

"Thanks, kid."

"No problem," she says. "We'll be there soon."

She ends the call and I dial my secretary next. I let her know about Georgie's condition and ask her to reschedule all of my appointments for later in the week. And as soon as that's out of the way, I head out to the nurses' station and hand Mel her phone. "Thank you so much," I tell her, relieved to have that over and done with.

Once I'm back in Georgie's room, I turn the television to the kid's channel for her, and after such a long night, we settle in for an even longer day.

Cassie and her bruised face come and go, and the theme song to *Sesame Street* gets stuck in my head. When lunch comes around, Georgie and I choke down the awful hospital food, and by afternoon, the sound of Georgie's monitor beeping away has given me one hell of a nasty headache.

Today couldn't be any worse, but I'll take it a million times over having Georgie not able to breathe.

The doctor comes and goes but gives me nothing in the way of actually helping my daughter. Though at this stage, there isn't a lot we can do. She's been on every type of medication. We're just going to have to wait out the winter and hope it sorts itself out.

It all changes the second Gigi appears in the doorway. Seeing her leaning against the door with that beautiful smile is like seeing a ray of sunshine in the deepest pits of hell. "Hi," she whispers as she takes in Georgie fast asleep in her bed. "Mel let me know you were here."

I pat the space beside me on the couch and she instantly comes over and falls in next to me. "You doing okay?" she asks as I put my arm over her shoulder and pull her into me.

I shrug my shoulders. "Exhausted," I tell her honestly. "Sorry I didn't tell you we were here."

"That's fine. I get it," she says. "Do you mind if I check her chart?"

"Go for it."

Gigi gets up and crosses the room to Georgie's bed, and I can't help but watch her, my eyes trained on her ass in her scrubs. She grabs the chart and starts looking it over, her lips pressing into a hard line as she takes it all in.

"I left her to get a glass of water," I tell her. "I was gone for two fucking seconds, and it nearly cost me my daughter."

Gigi hooks the chart back onto the end of Georgie's bed and makes her way over to me, her hand on my thigh as she sits down beside me. "You can't blame yourself for this, Sean," she tells me, adjusting herself on the couch to look at me. "How could you have possibly seen that coming?"

"She was having asthma attacks all night. She'd already had three."

"Stop. You're an amazing father. Anyone can see that, especially Georgie. You need to give yourself some room to breathe. You're not Superman, Sean. You're a regular human, just like the rest of us, only you allow yourself to bear the weight of the world on your shoulders."

I let out a sigh and think it over. I know deep down that she's right, but it's going to take a while to come to terms with it. If I hadn't left to get a drink, I could have avoided it. I would have heard the change in her breathing and gotten her medication before the attack could progress. Instead, my baby was left struggling in her bed while I took my fucking time pouring a glass of water.

Seeing my resignation, Gigi starts to relax. "You're just here for observation now?" she questions before getting up and checking Georgie's monitor.

"Yeah," I tell her. "How's she looking?"

"Looks good," she says. "You'll be out of here before you know it."

"Thank God," I sigh. "Are you on your break?"

"Yeah."

Shit, I'm sure she doesn't want to spend her break in a hospital room. She spends her whole day in them. She deserves to get out and rest. "Why don't you go enjoy your break?" I say, getting up and moving in behind her, my hands resting on her shoulders.

She shakes her head and turns, those big eyes coming up to mine. "Why don't you go have one? I'm almost positive you haven't eaten properly. I'll stay with Georgie, and besides," she adds with a sparkle in her eyes. "I *am* enjoying my break."

I grin at her comment, but it's the earlier one that puts me on edge. "I can't leave her, and I can't do that to you."

"You can and you will," she says. "I've already eaten and you look like you're about to fall asleep on your feet. I've got forty-five minutes before I need to be back, so go and get something decent to eat. Mel is about to go on her break, so I'll have company. I promise you, I won't leave this room. Georgie will be safe with me."

I desperately want to take her up on her offer, even if it's only for ten minutes so I could run down to the cafeteria and grab something to eat, but the thought of walking out of this room without Georgie right by my side is terrifying.

"Sean," Gigi scolds as she sees the indecision on my face. "You need to take a break. If you don't, you're going to be exhausted when you get her home tonight. And correct me if I'm wrong, but I'm almost certain you're going to be sitting up all night with her, and you can't do that if you're falling asleep."

Shit.

"Damn it, Gigi," I groan with a sigh. "I don't like that you're right."

"Get used to it," she says, her hands finding mine. "Go."

Letting out a sigh, I look back at Georgie. "Are you sure?" I question one last time.

Gigi places her hand on my chest and splays her fingers. "I'm positive," she tells me as she looks up at me, those lips begging to be kissed.

Unable to help myself, I lean into her and gently press my lips against hers, and she soaks it up like it's her only lifeline. "I'll be back in no time," I tell her. Every day, my feelings for her only get stronger.

I step back from her and watch as she drops down onto the couch, crossing her legs under her and pulling out her phone, making a show of getting comfortable. And I know with complete certainty that my daughter will be safe in her capable hands. I'm only going to be gone for a few moments, and I completely trust Gigi when she says that she won't leave the room.

With that, I walk to the door just in time to see Mel walking in with her lunch. She takes a seat next to Gigi and together they relax on the couch, taking absolute pleasure in the few moments of peace that they get each day.

Chapter Fifteen

GIGI

"I'm so tired," Mel yawns as she puts her feet up on my lap and relaxes back onto the couch. "It's been such a long shift. The little boy in the next room is having such a hard day. I have to go in there every fifteen minutes."

"Oh, really?" I ask as I flick my eyes back to Georgia to check she's still sound asleep. "What's he in for?"

"His appendix burst. The poor kid is in so much pain. He has allergies to most painkillers, so he's pretty much having to tough it out," she explains with a sad smile.

"Oh, no," I frown with a heavy heart. "The poor little guy."

"Yeah, it's horrible, but he's being so strong. His mother is a complete wreck, and I can tell he wants to break down into tears, but he's being brave for her."

I let out a sigh. "He's going to be a heartbreaker when he's older."

"No doubt about it," Mel smiles as she takes a sip of her water.

Georgie makes a noise and both our heads snap toward her, watching to see what she does next. We hold our breaths, not wanting to make a single noise to wake her, especially after the night she had. Georgie rolls over and squishes her face into the pillow before calming into her sleep, and I let out a breath.

She's had an awful night, and I bet she's absolutely wrecked. I can't even begin to imagine how scary that would have been for her. Being unable to breathe and having paramedics crashing into your house in the middle of the night and carrying you away. Shit, it has me desperate to hold onto her and never let go, but Sean's got that job well under control.

"So," I say, fixing my stare on Mel and bringing up the one thing I haven't wanted to talk about. "How's Tom doing?"

Mel shrugs her shoulders, averting her stare. "How would I know?"

"Because you're still sleeping with him," I grunt.

"I am not," she argues.

I continue as if she didn't just blatantly lie to my face. "You've snuck out of your bedroom nearly every night, except for last night when he snuck into our place and rocked your world while you screamed out his name," I tell her. "But I can't work it out. You spend your day cursing him and then climb in bed with him at night. What's it going to be? Do you love him or do you hate him?"

"What?" she questions, panic in her eyes. "Neither. I mean, of course I hate him. He's a jackass. Not to mention, he still hasn't done anything about your ticket despite you dating his best friend."

"You like him," I say, not happy about it.

"No, really," she argues, "I don't. He drives me insane. Plus he's got an ego on him. I just enjoy fucking him. That's all."

"The sooner you face it the better. He drives you insane because you can't stop thinking about him, and it freaks you out that you keep going back to him because that might just mean that you're developing feelings for him. Though I can't for the life of me figure out why. His dick must be huge."

She presses her lips together in a tight line. "Can we not talk about this anymore?"

"Only if you admit that I'm right," I practically sing.

"You're dead wrong."

I grin as I look over at her and place my hand on her thigh, waiting until I have her undivided attention. "It's okay, Smelly Melly," I say, digging deep to find my most condescending tone. "You're going through this thing we call denial. It's a strong emotion, and I get it. It's like a cloud of fog covering your thoughts, but don't stress, my slutty friend, the fog will soon clear and the denial will fade, leaving you with only the truth—you're falling for a jackass."

"Shut up," she groans as she pushes my hand off her thigh and lets out a huff before focusing on her phone a little too hard.

Georgie's monitor starts beeping, notifying me of a change in her condition, and the grin fades from my face. We both jump up and stride across the room, glancing over the monitor to figure out what's going on. Her heart rate has increased, and after double-checking all her other vitals, I'm able to put it down to a bad dream.

I give her little hand a gentle squeeze before taking my seat with a heavy heart. I hate the idea that she could be having a bad dream, but I hate it more that the dream is most likely a replay of the horrendous night she had. I wouldn't be surprised if she was traumatized by it for months to come.

Mel reaches across the couch and gives my leg a squeeze. "She's going to be . . ."

A deafening alarm sounds over the ward, cutting our conversation short, and we look at each other for a panic-filled moment before bursting to our feet. "What the hell is that?" I ask as I look over Georgie, who's seconds from bursting into tears as the deafening alarm assaults her ears.

Both our pagers go off at the same time, and I look down at mine. "Code Silver?" I question as I look up at Mel in horror.

"That's not . . ."

"Yeah," I breathe, the panic eating at me. "A shooter in the hospital."

"FUCK!"

Mel quickly assesses the situation before nodding to Georgia, clearly aware that I'm an extra set of hands on the pediatric ward. "Stay with her. Protect her with your fucking life." And with that, she's darting out the door, her mind already consumed with protecting the other children in her care.

I hurry to the door and lock it while staying right where Georgie can see me. Peering through the small window into the hallway, I watch Mel hurry to the nurses' station to speak with her supervisor. The pediatric ward is a flurry of panicked activity as they quickly go into their lockdown procedure, and as Mel turns back to me with horror on her face, my stomach drops.

She starts hurrying back to me to let me know what's going on when we hear the first terror-filled scream coming from the end of our hallway, realization dawning on both of our faces.

The gunman is on this ward.

Fuck.

A booming demand sounds from down the hall, sending my blood cold. "Where's my daughter?" he roars over the noise of the alarms and screams, the tone of his voice crystal clear, even behind the locked door of Georgie's room.

Fuck. Fuck. Fuck.

What the hell are we going to do? I try to go over the hospital's policies and procedures, but apart from locking the doors and covering the children, there's nothing else that could possibly help us now. The hospital would have gone into lockdown the second the alarm went off, meaning the big double doors leading in and out of the pediatric ward have been locked.

No escape.

No way for me to get Georgie out of here.

No way for the rest of the children to get to safety.

We're stuck here with a madman until someone comes to help.

"I'm scared," Georgie cries.

"Me too, sweet girl," I murmur, unable to take my gaze off Mel out in the hall. "Me too."

Terror fills my veins, and I watch as Mel's eyes widen, and she darts back behind the wall of the nurses' station, and I realize he must be coming this way. I glance back at Georgie, absolutely terrified when I hear the sound of a door being kicked in down the hall.

Ahh, fuck.

I shuffle back away from the door while keeping right where I can see Mel, the fear in her eyes crippling me. But I recognize the determination coming over her, and I have no doubt she's thinking about all the children on her ward, the little people she's come to care for.

My hands shake, and needing to get a better indication of where the gunman is, I creep toward the door and try to peer through the window, down the hall. I find him immediately, hovering in the doorway to one of the children's rooms, too fucking close to me and Mel. "Where is she?" he booms before raising his gun, pointing it inside the room, and pulling the trigger.

BANG!

I freeze, the sound reverberating through my chest and shaking the fucking walls.

Screams echo throughout the ward as I stare wide-eyed down the hallway at the people fleeing to find safety. I need to get down there. I need to check if somebody was hurt, but there's no way in hell I'm about to leave Georgie.

The man instantly ducks back out of the room and takes two big steps before kicking in the next door. His arm rises, followed by the screams, and then . . . *BANG!*

Fuck.

I look back at Mel who has tears streaming down her face. *Hide,* she mouths before slipping under the nurses' desk and squishing herself behind the metal filing cabinet.

With the sound of another door being kicked in and the realization that he won't stop until he's been through every room on this ward, I hurry away from the window and deeper into the room, frantically searching for something heavy enough to jam behind the door.

BANG!

My body jumps, mentally mapping the ward and trying to figure out how many more doors he's going to kick in before it's our turn.

Three.

Only three

Realizing my time is quickly dwindling, I hurry over to Georgie, my hands shaking, desperate to get her to safety. Moving right around to her side, Georgie screams as I recklessly start ripping the cords away from her.

Another door is kicked in.

Scream.

BANG!

I go as fast as I can, ripping the blankets off her and scooping her out of the bed. The bathroom is too far away, I'll never make it there.

Kick. *BANG! BANG!*

Fuck.

I find the supply closet and wipe my arm across the shelf, letting all the contents fall to the ground before jamming Georgie inside. "You need to stay really quiet, okay?" I beg as she screams for her daddy. "Please, Georgie. Please calm down. It's really important that you stay quiet, okay? Just like hide and seek. We need to be quiet. Don't let anyone find us. Do you understand me?"

With tears streaming down her face, she nods her head and sucks in a heavy breath, forcing herself to calm down.

"WHERE IS SHE?" the voice roars from the hallway.

Kick.

Scream.

BANG!

I hear a little boy scream and my heart breaks, tears staining my cheeks realizing it's the little boy with appendicitis, but I don't have time to get torn up over it, realizing we're next.

I slam the cupboard door shut on Georgie, hoping she has the strength to remain quiet, and I fly across the room, hearing his footsteps getting closer and closer to Georgie's door.

With no other options, I throw myself across the bed and grab the sheet, yanking it over my body, terrified that some part of me might be exposed. With terror in my veins, I try to calm my breathing when the door is kicked in, the sound of the wood splintering as it cracks and breaks right through the lock.

The door slams against the wall of Georgie's room and crashes with the force of his kick, yet despite the blaring alarms and the screaming from deeper within the ward, I've never heard such deathly silence.

Fear rattles my body, and I hold my breath as I hear him take a step inside the room, hoping like fuck Georgie can keep still and silent for just a moment longer. Tears stream down my face, and I bite down on my lip, forcing myself to keep still, my heart pounding, but if Georgie can be this brave, then so can I.

She needs me more than ever.

His footsteps creep through the room and my stomach drops, hearing as he gets closer. I see his shadow through the sheet, watch as he reaches toward it, then with a flick of his wrist, he grabs the sheet and tears it back off my body.

His manic stare locks onto mine, and I've never been so fucking terrified in my life. "Where's my fucking daughter?"

I clench my eyes as my body shakes with fear, refusing to look death in the eyes. I know it's coming. It's inevitable and I try to prepare, try to breathe through it, but nothing could ever prepare a person for this.

BANG!

FUCK.

Shooting pain tears through my shoulder, and I bite down on my lip, trying not to scream in agony, terrified for Georgie. My teeth rip through my lip with the force of my bite, and as I hold back my screams, I taste the blood in my mouth.

There's no doubt in my mind that I'm going to need stitches in that, maybe even surgery. The question is, can I make it to the point of receiving those stitches, or will I lose too much blood while I wait for help?

My shoulder aches, but I don't dare move until I'm certain he's gone, feeling the blood begin to soak through the bed. I need to check it out. I have to know what kind of damage has been done, but I'm terrified of looking, because the second I do, it becomes too fucking real.

The blood pools under me and runs off the bed, sounding like a fucking tap, I realize just how bad it is. I'm losing too much blood. If I don't get help soon, I'm not going to make it. I need to apply pressure before I pass out.

Hearing the gunman's footsteps leave the room, I let out a silent breath, jumping again when I hear the next door being kicked in.

Where the fuck is the hospital security? Where the hell are the police? The fucking SWAT team? Sean?

Sean? Oh, please let Sean be okay. I can only imagine the fear he's in for his little girl right now. And Mel, she would have had a front-row view of the man coming in here.

Those manic eyes haunt me as I shuffle off the edge of the bed, certain it's safe for me to move. Looking around the room, I see a splintered mess from the door and do what I can to avoid looking at the pool of blood on the floor.

Not knowing if he's going to come back, I'm all too aware of just how fast I have to be.

I dart across the room, hating how exposed and vulnerable I am without the door. Ripping open the supply cupboard, pain shoots through my arm, but I don't look, not yet. My arm dangles down by my side as I use my other to reach up and drag Georgie off the shelf.

She gasps as she looks at me, and I can only imagine what she's seeing, but I don't have time to dwell on it. I let her fall from the shelf and catch her over my good shoulder before bolting to the bathroom. I put her down in the shower and pull the curtain around to hide her just that bit more.

Then going back to the door, I look out at the room and run back to the supply cupboard. I grab anything and everything I can possibly find to help stop the bleeding and jam it down into the pockets of my scrubs. Then before racing back to the bathroom, I grab Georgie's asthma inhaler, all while my heart pounds out of my chest.

Racing back into the bathroom, I lock the door behind me and fall against it with a pained groan, the tears brimming in my eyes. We're not at the finish line yet, hell we're not even halfway. There's still a madman loose in the ward, and until I'm absolutely certain he is dealt with, I won't be leaving Georgie's side, or this bathroom for that matter.

Finding the strength to look at my wound, I move in front of the mirror and finally see what Georgie was seeing. Blood soaks my scrubs and trickles from my bitten lip, trailing down my arm and pooling on the floor beneath me.

Shit. This isn't going to be good.

I empty the pockets of my scrubs into the bathroom sink and reach for the bottom of my top. I try to remove it, but it's too hard. If I had scissors, I'd be able to cut it off, but I'm going to have to do it the hard way.

I walk back to the shower and gently pull the curtain back to see a sobbing Georgie. "Georgie, honey. Are you okay?" I ask, my voice breaking as it gets caught on the lump in my throat.

She looks up at me with terrified eyes, her tears streaming just as fast as mine. "I want my daddy."

"I know, sweet girl. He'll be here so soon, but until then, I need you to be brave and help me out. Do you think you could do that for me?" She nods her little head and I take a step back to sit on the toilet. "Can you see that I have a sore arm?" She nods again. "Okay, good. Well I need to take my shirt off so I can fix it. Can you help me do that?"

She gets up and walks toward me, rubbing the tears from her eyes in the process. She places a hand on my sore arm. "Sore?" she questions.

I try not to cringe at her touch as I feel myself starting to get weak. "Yes, honey. Very sore."

I talk her through the process of helping me to get my other arm out of my top before pulling it over my head and sliding the shirt down my bad side. I hold in my screams so as to not freak her out, but I nearly pass out from the pain. Somehow, I force myself to keep it together.

Georgie needs me to be alert. I cannot die in here with her. I cannot leave her with that trauma.

Once my shirt is gone, I grip the safety handle beside the toilet and pull myself to my feet before letting out a shaky breath and moving back in front of the mirror. Finally taking a good look at the damage, it actually hits me that this is so much more than a normal wound. It's a fucking bullet hole.

I got shot.

Turning around, I find the exit wound and let out a sigh of relief, realizing I won't have to fish for the bullet, but that doesn't do anything to take away from the magnitude of what's happened here today.

I try to rip open the packaging for the bandages, but with one hand, it's too hard, and Georgie tries to help but her little fingers just aren't strong enough. Taking them back, I brace the packaging between my teeth and rip, groaning in pain when the packaging scrapes along my cut lip.

"Come on. Come on," I mutter as I desperately try to break into it, aware of just how much blood I'm losing. I need to get this under control before I become a burden to Georgie. I'm supposed to be protecting her, but right now, I can't even protect myself.

I finally get the packaging open and instantly press it into the wound, hissing with pain before reeling it in, not wanting to scare Georgie any more than she already is.

Banging sounds on the bathroom door and has me dropping the bandages to the blood-stained floor and racing to Georgie, throwing my body in front of her, fear ripping through me.

"Gigi," I hear Mel's voice from the other side. "Are you in here? It's me. Open the fucking door."

"Fuck," I grunt, a fierce relief crashing through my veins. It's just Mel. Rushing to the door, I hastily unlock it, the blood on my hands making it slippery but I push through it and pull the door open just enough for Mel to slip in and lock it behind her.

She whips around with a wide, frantic stare. "Are you o—Fuck," she shrieks as she takes in the wound on my shoulder and lip. She instantly jumps into action, and I've never been so fucking grateful in my life.

"Georgie okay?" she asks, pressing the bandages hard into my shoulder and trying to control the bleeding before scrambling through the mess of supplies in the sink and starting to bandage me up.

"Fine," I tell her. "Just scared."

"Okay," she nods before moving onto my lip.

I pull her hand away from me, meeting her terrified stare. "What's going on out there?"

"Fucking everything," she says.

"Is he still on a rampage?"

"Yeah," she says as she lets out a shaky breath. "I've counted ten shots so far." She brings her hands back up to attend to my lip, and I push her away again. "Stop it," she demands, tears falling down her cheeks. "I need to fix this."

"No, you don't. It's fine. We can fix it later. We need to get out there and help."

"No. *I* need to get out there. You're injured, and you're just going to slow me down. You need to stay here and make sure Georgie is safe. Besides, if you don't get pain relief soon, you're gonna . . ."

She doesn't finish her sentence, and I know exactly what is rushing through her mind. "Fine," I tell her, knowing just how right she is, but

I try not to think about it.

"Okay. I'm out of here," she says, her hands shaking. "I just needed to make sure you were alright."

I nod my head, terrified for my best friend, but she's doing the right thing. The children on this ward need her now more than ever. "If you can, get any kids who don't have anyone in here. I'll do what I can."

She darts out of the room and returns only seconds later before tossing some pain relief through the door. It's not the strong stuff, but it should help.

With that, Mel disappears, and I send a silent plea that she'll be okay.

Chapter Sixteen

SEAN

The last fifteen hours have been horrific. I swear, every new day is another day where my world is challenged in some way. Today and last night just happen to be one of the worst challenges yet.

With a sigh, I reach across the counter and hand the woman at the hospital cafeteria a twenty-dollar bill before heading toward the tables and feeling so unbelievably grateful for Gigi. She's amazing, giving up her lunch break to sit with Georgie so I can have this small chance to eat and refuel. I'll never be able to thank her enough. I swear, I'll spend the rest of forever trying to make up for all the wonderful things she's done for me and Georgie. That's assuming she wants to give me forever. It's still new, only two weeks in, but I feel it in my gut, just like I did with Sara.

Like I said, she's fucking amazing. Undeniably incredible.

I'm just about finished my lunch when a deafening alarm screeches through the hospital, bringing the cafeteria to a standstill. Everybody glances around, panic in their eyes, then like a fucking movie, chaos erupts through the big room.

I stand, looking around, trying to figure out what the fuck is going on, searching for some kind of clue as to what caused the alarm. My only guess is a lost child or some sort of overwhelming emergency in the operating room. Hell, all I know is that an alarm like this can only cause this kind of havoc if it was life threatening.

The alarm is eerie, and as a million different scenarios rush through my mind, the pagers of every single hospital staff member in the cafeteria begin beeping. My heart races, not liking this one fucking bit, and as I start to make my way out of the cafeteria, wanting to get back to Georgie, I watch as every last hospital employee around me stops and looks down.

The strangest feeling settles over the cafeteria, and despite the blaring alarm, I could hear a fucking pin drop. Tension radiates through the room, and not a second later, their eyes fill with terror and they run full speed for the doors.

My stomach sinks, and I pick up my pace, following the crowd to the cafeteria exit. "What's going on?" I yell to a nurse as she runs past, but she ignores me in her hurry to get out. Within seconds, I find myself in the lobby with the rest of the crowd.

They push toward the main exit like a herd of animals, and I try to pull away from the crowd, desperate to get back up to the pediatric ward to find my little girl. Assuming this alarm is hospital-wide, she's bound to be freaking out. My only saving grace is that she has Gigi with her. But depending on what this alarm means, she might have to run.

The herd continues toward the parking lot exit, but panic ensues when they find the main doors locked, and I watch in horror as people try to break them down.

What the fuck is going on?

A man in a suit stands up on the reception desk. "Attention," he hollers across the lobby, having to say it three times before having to give an ear-shattering whistle to gain their attention.

Finally, some fucking answers.

It takes a moment, but eventually, everyone in the lobby turns to face the man, and he straightens his tie before clearing his throat. "Calm down," he instructs the crowd. "This is not a drill. I repeat. This is not a drill. As of three minutes ago, the hospital was put on lockdown. I need you all to keep calm and take a seat. The doors have been locked. Please keep your children with you at all times," he explains. "I'm sure the situation will be handled shortly. Your patience is appreciated."

"What situation?" I call out.

"That information is strictly off-limits," he replies, gaining outbursts from the massive crowd.

"Bullshit. We have the right to know if we're in danger," I tell him, begging him to challenge me on the law. "My daughter is upstairs."

He presses his lips together before turning to another man, who very wisely gives a nod. The suited guy turns back to the crowd, and the fear in his eyes instantly puts me on edge. "Please do not be alarmed, however, we currently have an active shooter on the third floor of the hospital," he explains. "Due to the lockdown, we are safe here, and I implore you all to remain calm. The situation is being handled, and I am sure you will all be allowed to go home to your families shortly."

Fuck, no. Third floor?

Pediatrics is on the third floor.

I make a fucking run for it.

The lawyer in me screams to tell the man to unlock the front doors to let the crowd out to safety, but they're not my priority, nor do I know anything about this hospital's lockdown policies and procedures. Either way, I couldn't give a single fuck right now.

Georgie and Gigi are on the third floor. They're right there, fending off a fucking armed shooter.

A million thoughts fly through my mind, but I don't give myself a chance to process them. All I know is that I need to get to them. I need to make sure they're alright.

I reach the elevator and hit the button three times, only it doesn't light up, and realizing this is due to the lockdown, I slam my fists against the door for the stairwell and race up the stairs, taking them two at a time.

I burst through the door on the third floor, letting it rebound off the wall behind. It slams with a bang, and I push myself forward before coming to a screeching stop at the doors of the Pediatric ward. I try to push through, but the big double doors don't budge.

BANG!

I freeze, my heart pounding.

Terrified screams echo through the hallway on the other side of the door, and the panic reaches an all-time high. It's one thing having someone tell you there's a fucking shooter, but hearing the sickening sound of the gunshot and knowing your sweet baby is stuck on the other side of those doors is the single most terrifying thing I have ever experienced.

Looking through the windows of the locked doors, I see right up the hallway, but nothing explains what the hell is going on. People are running around in terror, but I can't see who the fuck they're running from.

Mel stands in the nurses' station, desperately hiding behind a wall looking into Georgie's room, and I pray Gigi is still with her. She says something before ducking down and disappearing under the table, and not a second later, the hallway is dead silent, not a damn person to be seen.

My stare remains locked on Georgie's room when a man steps out of a room further up the hall. He takes two steps forward and positions himself in front of the next child's room. A sinking feeling settles in the pit of my stomach, and I watch in horror as his foot comes up and kicks in the door. He yells into the room, but when he raises his hand and I see a gun, my whole fucking world crumbles.

I shake my head, not believing this is really happening. "NO," I scream. "NO—"

BANG!

FUCK!

No. No, no, no, no.

My fists slam against the double doors, desperately trying to break them down, but they must be reinforced metal, purposely built for this very fucking reason, only I bet they never imagined the threat would be on the other side of the fucking doors.

I need to get in there.

"Fuck," I roar, frantically looking around.

I see a fire extinguisher on the wall halfway up the hall, and I sprint to get to it, before tearing it off the wall and doubling back. I run full speed ahead and hold up the extinguisher, using the momentum to try and break the window, but it's no fucking use.

BANG!

My head whips up, and I find myself pausing, desperate to find out where the hell he is, and not a moment later, the asshole appears in the hall once again. He yells something that's muffled by the doors before taking two long strides and placing himself right in front of Georgie's room.

"NO," I scream as he brings his booted foot up and kicks it in. "NO, you fucking bastard."

He strides into my baby's room, and I bring the fire extinguisher up and slam it against the window over and over again, the crippling fear blasting right through my chest. A crack appears in the window, and I give it everything I've got, my arms aching with the force.

BANG!

No. No. This isn't fucking happening. My sweet baby.

The gunman appears and rage pulses through my body as I vow with everything I am that I will fucking kill him.

The thought of my little girl bleeding out has me slamming into the window, way past the point of exhaustion, sweat dripping down my face as my muscles ache and burn. The desperation is like nothing I've ever known and it pushes me harder.

BANG!

Each gunshot is another life on my shoulders, and it has me ready to crumble, to fucking give up and accept that I'm not strong enough. I'm not the hero my little girl needs me to be, but fuck. I'll never give up on her. I'll never stop trying.

Slamming the extinguisher into the hard glass one more time, the window finally gives out under the pressure, and I don't hesitate to hoist myself up and through the narrow space, cutting my arms in the process. But nothing fucking matters to me right now, nothing apart from killing this motherfucker and hoping like fuck my sweet baby girl is alright.

Please, Gigi. Please be with her. Please make sure my little girl is okay.

My feet hit the ground, and as the bastard appears in the hallway, I take my fucking chance. Breaking out in a sprint, I soar up the long hallway, only just missing Mel as she darts out in front of me, racing into Georgie's room, and while I'd fucking kill to race in there with her, I have to take out the threat, I have to save these kids and the nurses, no matter the cost to my own fucking life.

The gunman goes to kick through another door when he realizes his fucking game is over. His eyes widen, seeing me charging toward him like a fucking bull, and his hand raises, the gun aimed right for my fucking head. But the bastard isn't going to get away with it that easily.

He pulls the fucking trigger, but I dart to the left, and before he even realizes he missed, I duck low and ram my shoulder straight into his stomach. The force catapults us back into the drywall, and it caves under our weight. I come down on him and get the sweetest satisfaction from the hollow thud of his head hitting the ground.

The gunman tries to fight me off, but I've got the upper hand. His arm flies back, still firmly clutching the gun, and I grab his wrist, easily overpowering him.

Tearing the gun out of his hand, I toss it down the hall, far out of his reach, and realize he's fucking nothing now he doesn't hold the power. He's weak. Pathetic.

Dead.

My fist slams into his jaw, and blood shoots from his mouth. Without missing a beat, I wrap my hands around his neck and squeeze, watching him gasp for air as he stares up at me in horror. My hands get tighter and tighter as I think about my little girl and all the other children he's hurt or traumatized today. He claws frantically at my hands, desperate for oxygen, but his fear only spurs me on.

"Sean," I hear my name screeched across the ward.

Reluctantly looking up, I find Mel racing toward me with a needle in her hand. She crashes to her knees, catching herself against the gunman's chest and slamming the needle straight into his neck, narrowly avoiding my hand. "It's a sedative. It will put him out long enough for the police to get here," she explains, hastily getting to her feet. "Now, I know you want to kill him, but let go. Gigi needs you."

My head whips up.

Gigi.

At that, all thoughts of the gunman are gone, and I get up off the fucker and race down to Georgie's room, my heart beating right out of my fucking chest.

Panic tears at me as I charge through the busted opening of the room. The door is in pieces on the ground. My gaze immediately whips to the bed, finding it drenched in blood, right in the spot I left my little girl.

Fear cripples me as the image of Sara's blood pooling over the bed haunts me, but I push it away, needing to find my daughter. I frantically look around the room. Supplies from a cupboard are thrown all over the floor, and I follow the blood to the bathroom.

Darting across the room, I reach for the bathroom door and give it a hard pull, but it's locked, not fucking budging. "Georgie, are you in there, baby girl?" I yell, desperate to find her. "It's Daddy."

The click of the door unlocking is like music to my ears, and as the door opens, my stomach sinks finding my little girl standing in the doorway drenched in blood. Horror tears through me, and I drop to my knees, looking her over.

"She's alright," I hear a deflated voice deeper in the bathroom.

Looking past Georgie, I gasp as I see Gigi slumped on the cold tiles in her bra. Blood covers her body and face, and she looks as though she's about to pass out. "Fuck," I grunt, rushing into the bathroom and dropping down beside her, not knowing the first fucking thing about how to help her.

Her eyes flutter as I touch her, and she tries to give me an encouraging smile, but I'm not fucking buying it. Trying to assess her injuries, I get a good look at her, and from the soaking bandages on her front and back, it's clear she's been shot right through her shoulder.

"What do I do?" I ask frantically, the desperation having a fucking choke hold on me.

"I . . . I need to help," she says with a tear in her eye.

"Gigi," I demand. "What do I do?"

She opens her mouth to say something, but nothing comes out, and I resist the urge to fucking shake her. She lets out a soft sigh as her eyes close again, and I see my whole fucking world crumbling all over again. "Daddy, hewlp her," Georgie begs with big tears in her eyes.

Having no other option, I scoop Gigi up in my arms and run out to the hallway to find the police piling in through the doors with a bunch of doctors and nurses flooding in behind them. They instantly scatter through the ward to offer their help wherever they can.

"HELP," I roar, desperate for anyone who'll listen.

A doctor runs straight up to me and takes a look at Gigi. His eyes widen as he recognizes her and orders me to place her down on the bed inside Georgie's room. "I need an available team in here, now," he calls out over the noise of the ward.

A nurse rushes in before me and strips the bloodied sheets off the bed, but she doesn't get a chance to put new ones down as I lay Gigi on the mattress. Georgie's vital signs monitor is now attached to Gigi as other nurses flurry around, preparing her for surgery.

"You're going to be okay," I tell her, hoping she can hear me. "You better fucking come back to me, Gigi, you hear me? I can't do this again."

Before I know what's happening, the bed is being wheeled out of the room with a nurse running up ahead, demanding that everyone clear the way.

I'm left in the room with a crying Georgie, and I hastily grab her a change of clothes and scoop her into my arms, not knowing what else I can do. "Are you alright, Georgie?" I ask, knowing she's going to have a lot of confusing emotions rushing through her right now, emotions that she wouldn't be able to understand.

She's never witnessed such awful things before, and I need to get her out of here. I need her to be safe with someone I trust so I can be here for Gigi.

Quickly getting Georgie changed into the clean clothes, I leave the bloodied ones behind, which is when I notice something discarded on the ground, and as I take a closer look, my eyes widen.

Holy fucking shit.

It's the bullet from Gigi's shoulder.

Pinching it between my fingers, I quickly slip it into my pocket, hoping like fuck Georgie doesn't ask me what it is. I know the police are probably going to want it, but they already have so much evidence to nail the fucker. They can do without this.

This bullet is going straight to Gigi. She deserves it as a trophy, something she can look at afterward to remind her just how strong she is. It might take her a little while to come around to the idea of it, but eventually, she might appreciate it.

Stepping out of the room with Georgie in my arms, I find most of the drama has died down. Police are still flooding the hallways and cries are heard throughout the ward. It looks as though most patients have either been seen or are in the middle of being looked after. Everyone else who's not needed is either in the waiting room or has disappeared to get out of the way.

"Hey," a familiar voice asks from beside me, and I turn to find Tom looking at me, relief flashing in his eyes. "You okay?" he questions as his gaze roams over Georgie, making sure she's alright.

"Only just," I tell him honestly.

"Have, umm . . . have you seen Mel? Is she alright?"

"Yeah, man. She's okay," I tell him.

He nods before looking back up at me with a cringe, knowing I'm not going to like whatever he has to say. "I know now isn't the best time, but I need to take your statement."

"Yeah sure," I say as he points to a chair, while mentally going over exactly what I need to say to ensure this guy rots in a jail cell.

I take a seat and he pulls out a recorder. "Just tell me exactly what happened through your eyes. Where you were when it started. What you saw. What you did."

Nodding, I do just that.

I tell him every last detail as it's fresh in my mind. I tell him how my heart stopped when I thought Georgie had been injured, how I nearly killed him myself, and how I found Gigi drenched in blood. The only part I skip past is the sedative Mel jammed into the bastard's neck. I can guarantee that wasn't part of hospital policy, and I'm not about to get her in trouble for her quick thinking. Though considering Tom's confusing feelings for her, he's probably happy I left that out.

I finish my statement and he looks at me with a cringe. "Do you mind if I ask Georgie her recap of what happened?"

I look at Georgie and know the story is going to be hard for her to tell, but ultimately, it's her decision if she's ready to tell it. "Do you want to tell Uncle Tom what happened today when the alarm went off?" I ask, knowing it's best to get this over and done with now while it's still fresh in her mind.

She looks up at me and her bottom lip pouts out. I feel as though she's about to say no when she surprises me with a nod and turns to Tom before she climbs across my lap and straight into his.

"Da loud nowse woked me up," she tells him.

"Oh no," he says. "That's not good. What happened when you woke up?"

"Gigi put me in da closet wike Daddy does when we pway hide and seek. She told me it was wreally important to be quiet."

Georgie's recap has my head falling into my hands, my elbows braced on my knees, every fucking detail like a knife to the chest. "What happened when you were in the closet?"

"I was wreally quiet and dere was a big bang," she says, clapping her hands together to emphasize how loud the bang was.

I cringe hearing it coming from her perspective, but at the same time, I'm relieved she didn't see Gigi getting shot. Hell, I don't know how I would have ever helped her through that.

"That's really good, Georgie. What came after the big bang?"

"Gigi took me to da bathwoom. She had lots of bwood and I had to take her shirt off."

"Why did you do that?" Tom prompts.

Georgie's brows furrow, clearly thinking this is a ridiculous question. "Cause she was bweeding, silly. She had big ouchy on her."

"Right, okay. Did anything else happen?"

"Da girl came in and Gigi squished me in da wall."

My heart aches as I realize what Gigi went through to protect my little girl. She jammed her in a closet, got shot in her place, and shielded her with her fucking body when she thought Georgie was at risk.

This woman is phenomenal.

Tom wraps up his interview with Georgie and looks up at me as she climbs back into my lap, regret heavy in his eyes. "Gigi is amazing," he tells me. "I owe her an apology."

"Yeah, man. You do."

His eyes find something behind me, and I turn to see Mel, which is when Tom flies out of his chair and bolts toward her. She falls into his arms and instantly bursts into tears, the emotions too hard to keep bottled inside. I'm not even going to pretend I know what's going on here, but at this moment, I'm happy she has him.

I get up and start to make my way out of the ward when a nurse stops me near the door. "Excuse me, Mr. Waters?" she says. I turn with a groan and give her a questioning look, hating that I'm appearing so rude right now. "I apologize, but Georgia is still an admitted patient here for observations. I completely understand if you'd like to discharge her. However, I cannot recommend it, especially with the stress today has brought. It would be easy for her to slip into another asthma attack."

"Shit," I groan under my breath. "Of course, but she needs to be on a different floor. I can't have her here."

"Indeed," she says with a compassionate nod. "I'll get her sorted out right away."

I thank her and she gets on her way, and with Georgie still in my arms, I head back over to Tom and grab his phone to call Logan. It's the second hardest phone call of my life—the first being the night I called Sara's parents to tell them their daughter was gone.

Logan agrees to come down and look after Georgie, making sure she gets settled in a new ward, leaving me to be there for Gigi when she finally wakes from surgery.

Chapter Seventeen

GIGI

Beep. Beep. Beep. Beep.

My head spins as I peel my eyes open to the bright hospital room, my day slowly coming back to me in bits and pieces, haunting my every thought. I mean, what a shitty day. Did I seriously get shot? As in a bullet pierced straight through my body and I'm still fucking alive? Holy shit. Who else goes to work and comes home at the end of the day with a gaping hole through their shoulder?

My body is groggy and heavy from being under, and I'm terrified to move in case I jostle myself and have to face the fact of how much trauma my body is currently suffering through.

My eyelids flutter open and closed as the memories continue to assault my mind like a horrendous nightmare.

The man. The gun. The terror. The pain.

It was awful. Today was easily the worst day of my life. I come to work to help people, to care for them, and watch as they heal. To me, the hospital has always been somewhere to call home, somewhere safe—a place of healing, not a place for mass shootings.

I mean, the look on little Geor—

Shit. Georgie.

My eyes fly back open. Where is she? Did Sean find her? Is she okay? So many questions fill my mind that I can barely register them all. She witnessed things that no three-year-old should ever have to see, and yet, if it weren't for her, I would have surely died today. She held me together; she was my motivation. Hell, what child would be brave enough to survive what she did today? She saw the blood pouring from my body, and instead of breaking down in fear, she rose to the occasion and helped where she could. Most adults would struggle with that, but not little Georgie Waters.

She's my hero.

I need to find her and make sure she's alright.

As I try to sit up in bed, the pain hits me, and before I can cry out in agony, an angelic voice fills the room. "Oh, hell no," Sean grunts as movement across the room steals my attention.

Sean flies up off the chair and then races to my side, gently pressing me back to the bed and refusing to let me move. His fingers linger on my skin as my face twists with pain, trying to get comfortable again.

"You're not going anywhere," he tells me.

Glancing up, I meet his exhausted stare, my hand finding his and clutching on with everything I have. "Georgie?" I question, fearing the worst.

A soft smile pulls across his lips as he reaches back and grips the dividing curtain, not daring to let go of my hand in the process. "She's fine," he tells me before pulling the curtain back to show me the bed beside me.

Warmth spreads through me, finding Georgie sitting happily in her bed, tucked under her uncle's arm as she plays a game on his phone. Though to be honest, with the cocktail of painkillers and surgery, I really couldn't tell which uncle it is. They all look the same.

Satisfied that he's answered my question, Sean gently slides the curtain back in place to give us a little privacy. "How are you feeling?" he questions, hooking his foot around the chair leg and dragging it closer as his thumb brushes across my knuckles.

"Like shit," I tell him honestly, not looking to sugarcoat it. I hate when my patients do that. It doesn't allow me to get a proper read on them.

"I bet," Sean smiles, reaching across my bed and pressing the call button for the nurse, probably wanting me to get checked over now that I'm awake.

"What happened? Did they get him?"

He cringes, and it's almost as if I can read his mind. He's hiding something. "You don't need to hear about this right now. Let's just focus on getting you better."

"Sean," I demand, not taking no for an answer, not today. "What happened? I need to know if he's behind bars or . . . dead. I'd feel a lot safer."

A sadness settles in his warm eyes, and he presses his lips into a hard line, considering his options, but he finally lets out a sigh before giving it to me straight. "The asshole is still in the hospital and will be for another few hours, but he has a police escort, and the second they can release him, he'll be behind bars."

An odd disappointment rumbles through my chest. As a nurse, my every instinct is to help people and make them better, but for the first time in my life, I find myself wishing this man was dead. "Huh?" I question. None of this makes sense to my groggy brain. "Why's he still here?"

He gives me a tight smile. "Because someone hit him with a sedative strong enough to take out a fucking elephant."

"Oh," I say, wishing I could feel happier about that, but I don't think happiness is something I'm going to be capable of for quite some time, especially considering how many innocent lives might have been lost here today.

Katrina, one of the night shift nurses, pops her head through the curtain and gives me a sad smile, and the heaviness in her eyes speaks volumes, but I can see how desperately she's trying to keep herself together in the wake of this tragedy. "Can I come in?" she asks, gingerly walking in, not bothering to wait for a response, the same way all of us nurses do.

I give her a small smile as she goes about checking my chart and vitals before adjusting the flow rate on my morphine to make me comfortable. She pours me a glass of water, and I hit the button on the side of my bed, raising me into a sitting position before greedily accepting the water and taking a drink, my throat so dry and sore after being out.

Satisfied I'm doing alright, Katrina gives me a smile before telling me she'll notify the doctor that I'm awake, and with that, she slips out before I get a chance to ask her about everyone else who was on the pediatric ward today.

"How's Mel?" I ask Sean. She had gone through so much today and risked her life by running around the rooms and helping everyone she could. I hope she's not alone tonight.

"She's doing okay," he tells me. "I think she's in shock. She was here waiting, but I sent her home. She didn't want to go, but she was exhausted. Tom had to drag her out of here."

"I bet," I say with a pained smile, one that doesn't reach my eyes.

We sit in silence for a little while, and I find the quieter the room is, the quicker I notice the pain fading away. "Gigi?" Sean questions, breaking the silence and pulling me out of my head. I turn toward him and wait for whatever it is he has to say. "Georgie told me everything you did for her."

My lips pull into a tight line. I see the big, whopping, thank you on his lips, but I don't want it. What happened today isn't something I want to be praised for. I did what I had to do, just like any other decent human being would have done in my position. I don't want to be recognized for that. I don't want a constant reminder of this day. I just want to move on and get back to life.

"Don't," I say, cutting him off. "I know what you're going to say, and I don't want you to. I just . . . I want to forget today happened."

"Gigi," he sighs, raw emotion in his eyes. "Trust me, ignoring it is not going to help you forget. It's going to eat you up inside until you can no longer breathe. One day, you'll think you're fine, and the next . . ."

He cuts himself off as a tear rolls down my face, and I watch as he leans forward and quickly wipes it away. "You protected my little girl by risking your own life, Gigi," he tells me. "You would have given yours for hers. I'm not about to pretend that didn't happen."

I close my eyes and let out a slow breath. "I did what I had to do," I tell him quietly, the whole thing playing like a horror movie in my mind.

Sean stands and leans in toward me so our faces are just inches apart, those dark eyes of his boring into mine. "You did so much more than that," he whispers before closing the gap and pressing a gentle kiss to my lips.

If I wasn't having such a shitty day, I probably would have eaten that up and given him everything I had, but not now, I need a few moments to find myself. "Thank you, Gigi," he murmurs as his forehead rests against mine.

"How are you feeling now?" he questions as he moves back and takes his seat again, his gaze shifting over me. "Is the morphine helping? Do you need more water?"

His thumb moves across my knuckles, and I concentrate on that, not wanting to feel any other part of my body right now. "I'm okay," I tell him and watch as relief comes to his dark eyes. "I'm starting to feel the morphine. It's helping."

"Good," he murmurs as he lets out a breath.

Dr. Monroe comes in through the curtain and relief fills my veins, knowing I had the best trauma surgeon working on me today. He demands I have six weeks off to heal, and I let out a groan. I absolutely love my job, and the thought of having any time off kills me. I can't even sneak back early since I work in the same damn place as the guy.

He checks my chart, and after moving across to check Georgie's and confirming she's looking great, he strides out of the room, leaving me feeling deflated. I let out a sigh and immediately start pouting, the heaviness on my heart too much to bear. I mean, what the hell am I going to do with six weeks off?

"You okay?" Sean asks.

"No."

His eyes go wide as he flies to his feet, his gaze sailing over my body, ready to jump into action and help me in any little way he can. "What's wrong?" he rushes out. "What's hurting?"

"No. No, it's not that," I tell him. "I'm just—"

"You're upset about having so much time off," he finishes for me, understanding dawning in his dark eyes, only his brows furrow, clearly confused.

"Yeah. Wouldn't you be?"

"No," he scoffs. "I'd give anything to have more time off to spend with Georgie."

I glance away, my gaze sailing out the window and taking in the wide world just outside this hospital. "Yeah, well, I don't have a kid."

"Fair enough," he says, trying to hide a smirk.

Letting out a sigh, I give him my truth. "My work is all I have. It's what I live for, and I love what I do. Having six weeks just sitting at home . . . All I'm going to do is replay it over and over again. Being here at work is what I need."

Sean gives me a tight smile, and I see the understanding in his eyes, but I can also see how much he wishes he could give me what I want. "I'm sorry, Gigi," he murmurs, squeezing my hand.

"You wouldn't happen to know where my phone is, do you?" I ask, wanting to move on. "I should probably call my parents and Mel."

"Yeah, right here," he says as he reaches across to the little table beside the bed and hands me my phone. He gets up and leans over, pressing another gentle kiss to my lips. "I'll give you some privacy."

"Thanks," I smile, watching as he walks away, probably to check on Georgie, but my hand feels oddly empty without him. He pulls the curtain closed behind him, and suddenly the idea of having to call my parents and tell them what happened is the most daunting thing in the world.

Pulling up my mother's number, I hit call, and it rings five times before going to her voicemail, so I give Dad a try. It starts ringing out, and I fear that's going to go to voicemail as well, but he picks up with just moments to spare. "Pumpkin, how are you?" he says, his usual chirpiness making me want to break down in tears.

"Hey Daddy," I say, my voice breaking as I struggle to get my words out. "Are you with Mom?"

"What's going on?" he questions, instantly worried.

"Dad," I repeat, quickly getting frustrated. "Are you with Mom? Can you put me on speaker?"

He mutters something under his breath, and I hear him walking around the house before talking to Mom in the background. He presses a few wrong buttons before finally putting me on speaker. "Honey, is that you? Are you alright?" my mother asks, concern thick in her voice.

"Hi Mom, are you sitting down?" I ask.

"I knew we were going to get this call sooner or later," Dad grumbles to himself.

"Dad," I snap, knowing exactly what's going through his head. "I'm not pregnant. There's been an incident at the hospital."

Mom gasps as Dad finally zips his lips. "What kind of incident?" she questions.

I take a deep breath, unsure if I can get the sentence out without breaking down. "There was a gunman on my floor today," I start.

"Stop that," Mom cuts in, undeniable fear in her tone. "You stop that right now."

"I wish I could, Mom," I sigh.

"How bad is it?" Dad asks, needing the cold, hard facts.

Shit. This is harder than I thought. I take a breath and rip it off like a Band-Aid. "Okay, first, you need to know that I'm alright. I was locked down in the same ward as the gunman and was shot. The bullet went straight through my shoulder, nothing too serious. I've spent the afternoon in surgery, and now I'm doing okay."

"Oh, honey," Mom sobs.

I try my hardest to soothe her, but it's not going to happen until she can lay her eyes on me and see for herself. "Alright, Pumpkin," Dad says, his usual strong tone wavering. "We're coming now."

"Thanks, Dad. See you soon."

Ending the call, I let out a breath. That couldn't have been easy for them. Getting the phone call to say your child has been injured must be awful, and I don't doubt they'll be here in record time, probably breaking a shitload of traffic laws in the process.

With my phone still in my hand, I hash out a quick text to Mel, tears now freely trailing down my face.

Gigi – I'm okay.

She texts back almost immediately.

Mel – Thank fuck, you're awake. I'm on my way.

I can just imagine her running around our apartment in a flurry, grabbing her stuff along the way while trying to remember a few things to grab for me, though I have no doubt there will be a second or third trip home to get the things she's forgotten. The thought brings a smile to my face and is enough to keep the tears at bay.

With the most important people in my life on their way, I take a moment to catch up. I close my eyes and take a few slow, deep breaths. With each one, I find a small piece of myself, and eventually I'm able to pull myself together.

It doesn't take long before my parents show up and instantly check me over. Mom fusses about with tears in her eyes as she orders the nurses to grab more blankets and pillows, all of which I don't need, but if it's going to help ease her mind, I'll deal with it. Hell, I've been the nurse on the other end of this a million times before, and there's nothing I wouldn't do to help put those scared parents at ease.

Sean comes back in, and I do the quick introductions, barely getting a chance to tell them anything about him before Mel bursts through the door with Tom hot on her heels. I have to resist scowling at him, still not forgiving him for the speeding ticket laying in the backseat of my car.

Mel throws herself at me, making both my mother and Sean gasp, but I trust her completely, and she holds me tighter than any of them have. She cries, which only brings on a round of my own tears, and then being the Mel I know and love, the second her tears are dry, she dives for my chart. She quickly scans over it and within seconds is going off on a rant about Katrina, the night nurse, for not giving me the absolute strongest pain meds available.

Yawns start ripping through me, and with my parents satisfied that I'm still alive, they get on their way, promising to be back first thing in the morning. They walk out the door accompanied by Logan, which is when Tom clears his throat to gain my attention. I turn to him with a raised brow, wondering where the hell this is going to go.

"I, umm . . . owe you an apology," he says, looking as though just saying the words alone could have him spontaneously combusting and burning in a blazing inferno right here in my hospital room.

"No shit," I grunt.

"Would you shut up and listen?" he demands.

I gape at him. "I just got shot and you want to yell at me?" I say, glancing at Mel. "Really, girl? Are you really sure this is your best option? Out of all the guys who'd kill to have you, you want this one?"

Mel rolls her eyes as Tom lets out a frustrated groan, making Sean turn on him, anger blasting through his stare. "Dude, seriously?"

Tom's groan turns into a sigh, and he swivels his gaze back to me, clearly wishing he were anywhere but here, but what can I say? He brought this on himself. He didn't need to come here, but he did, and now I'm going to milk it for all it's worth. "How can I make it up to you?"

I try not to smirk, knowing this particular asshole is putty in my hands right now. "You can start by dealing with that phony speeding ticket for starters," I tell him.

"Done," he says, holding my stare and making me wonder if he truly is a genuine person, maybe just someone who's a little rough around the edges, or maybe a lot rough. Either way, I need to come to terms with the fact that he's an asshole who means well. After all, if he truly was an asshole, Mel wouldn't be entertaining this little flirtation between them.

I hold his stare for a while, dragging this out and making him sweat, and after a moment, I finally let out a breath and nod, accepting what will be and putting our drama behind us.

Tom eventually manages to pull Mel out of the room, leaving just me and Sean with Georgie fast asleep on the opposite side of the open curtain.

Georgie's doctor comes in and clears her to go home, and after being discharged, Sean wraps her in his arms and brings her over to my side before taking a seat with his little girl safely in his lap.

I watch him for a moment, wondering why the hell he isn't scrambling to get her out of here. "What are you doing?" I question.

"We're keeping you company," he explains as Georgie gets comfortable on his lap and tries to sleep against his chest, somewhere I wouldn't mind sleeping right about now.

"Uhh, no you're not."

He gives me a blank stare, clearly not seeing what the problem is. "Why the hell not?" he argues.

"Where should I start?" I say. "Firstly, Georgie has been stuck in a hospital for the past twenty-four hours and has gone through things no child should ever have to go through, not to mention, I don't think you've actually slept in well over twenty-four hours. So, you both need to get home to your own beds."

"And secondly?" he grunts, knowing damn well I'm right.

"And secondly," I say, putting the cherry on the top of the cake. "I want to go to sleep."

Sean groans, and just like that, I know I've won this round, but there's still hesitation in his eyes, something that pulls me right in. "I don't want to leave you," he admits.

My heart flutters as a brilliant warmth begins spreading through me, but I push it aside, all too aware of the exhausted child in his arms.

"If I could have my way, I'd never let you leave," I tell him. "But you need to get her home. You're no good to her if you're too tired to catch another attack."

With a sigh, Sean places Georgie down on the end of my bed and starts making his way over to me. He leans down and presses his lips to mine in the sweetest kiss, lingering a little too long considering his little girl can't take her eyes off us.

Butterflies swarm in the pit of my stomach, and as he pulls back, he meets my stare, a soft smile settling on his face. "Do you mind if I come by tomorrow?"

"I'd like that," I say, a blush spreading over my cheeks.

His eyes soften, taking me in. "Do you need me to bring anything?"

"Just yourself," I smile.

"Okay," he whispers as he takes a step back and collects Georgie off the bed. He heads toward the door before turning back. "You know you can call me, right? Even if you're just lonely. I'll come."

My heart warms, but after the hell he's been through, there's no way I'd even consider asking him to come back so soon. Though, that doesn't mean I can't send a slew of flirty texts. "Thank you," I whisper before he flashes me the kindest smile and, just like that, disappears out the door.

Finally alone, I try my best to get comfortable in my bed and close my eyes. Today has been awful, but there have certainly been some bittersweet moments, moments that I will desperately cling to in order to fade out the bad.

Another yawn rips through me and pulls on the stitches holding my lip together, and I come to terms with the fact that this is going to be something I'll be dealing with a lot over the next few days. But all that matters is when Sean kisses me, all I feel is the sweetest sin, not an ounce of pain.

Unable to find comfort, I call the nurse and get the stronger pain meds that Mel insisted I should be taking, and the second they're blissfully floating through my system, I close my eyes and dream about what could have happened if I weren't in Georgie's room today.

Chapter Eighteen

SEAN

It's been four weeks since the shooting, making it six weeks since Gigi and I started doing this little dance, and I'm not going to lie, today I'm nervous. So far, it's been great, apart from the obvious, but I can't help but feel as though things are starting to get a little more serious.

Since Gigi was hurt, I've been doing everything I can to try and be there for her, but she's over it. She clearly doesn't enjoy people fussing over her, which she has coming at her in full force.

The second she was starting to feel better, she made that fact well known with one of the best tantrums I think I've ever seen—Georgie's included. She told her parents to back off, she told Mel to take her pain meds and shove them up her ass, and of course, she couldn't resist dragging Tom into the action. I'm just grateful that he stood and took it like a man.

On the other hand, I was the lucky bastard who came out as the knight in shining armor, and I have to admit, it felt pretty fucking good.

I know this frustration mainly comes from being holed up in her little apartment when she wants to get back to work so badly. Being a midwife makes her feel whole, and the fact that she's unable to do that right now is killing her.

The second she said she was feeling better and the pain had mostly eased, I offered to take her out. She deserves it, even if it's only for a little while to get her out of the apartment to feel like a normal human being again. And honestly, I can't wait to be the one who offers her that freedom.

So, here I am, standing in front of her door, ready to be her hero. Lifting my hand, I gently knock, and after a minute with no response, my brows start to furrow. Knowing Gigi, she would have been waiting by the door, her coat in hand. I wouldn't have even gotten a hello before she was flying down the hall. "Gigi?" I call through the door.

Still, there's no answer.

I'm sure she's here. Her car was parked right out front. "Gigi?" I call again.

Still nothing.

Maybe she's showering or has forgotten. Though, had she

forgotten, she still would have answered the door. Despite everything I hear in my line of work about bastards who barge into women's apartments, I try the handle and hate that I find it unlocked. "Gigi, I'm coming in," I warn her before pushing the door open.

I step into the little apartment and look around, and I have to check that I've stepped into the right one. The place is a mess, which is not who Gigi is. I haven't known her for long, but one of the many things I've learned is that she's a clean freak. She hates the thought of people seeing her home messy. Hell, she told me she used to power-clean right before Mel would invite a Tinder date over, despite never having to see the guy again.

Dishes lay discarded on the counter, blankets and pillows are all over the living room, and Gigi is nowhere to be seen. Not hearing the shower, I figure she must be in her room, so I walk down the hallway, poking my head into the open bathroom as I go.

Reaching her room, I gently knock on the open bedroom door, and the sight before me breaks my heart.

Gigi lays wrapped up in hundreds of blankets, shivering. Her eyes are closed, but from the pained look on her face, she's not sleeping. Making my way over to her, I sit on the edge of the bed and can't help dropping my hand to her thigh. "Are you okay?" I ask.

"Sick," she mutters, her voice hoarse and clearly sore.

Bringing my hand up, I press it against her forehead and feel she has a fever. "Shit, Gigi. You're hot."

"No," she says, squeezing her eyes closed and I realize she most likely has a migraine to go with it. "Cold."

"Have you had anything for it?" I ask her.

"Can't get out of bed."

Of course not.

I gently squeeze her leg before getting up and heading out to the kitchen. I rifle through her cupboards and drawers until I find a glass and some painkillers. After filling the glass with water, I head back down to her room and help her sit up. She's so stubborn that I practically force the painkillers down her throat.

From the look of her and her apartment, it looks as though she's been sick for a little while. "Where's Mel?" I ask, a little annoyed with her friend for not looking after her better.

"She's working a double. She doesn't know I'm sick."

"Why didn't you call me?" I ask.

"Because," she groans, her bottom lip pouting out. "I didn't want you to see me like this."

I shake my head and roll my eyes. "Fuck, you're stubborn," I tell her, realizing just how much I like that about her. "Lay down and try to get some sleep."

"Where are you going?" she questions, reaching for me but not having enough energy to sit up and take my hand before her arm flops back to the bed.

"None of your damn business," I tell her as I head back out to the living room.

Making quick work of her home, I put the place back together. The blankets are folded and shoved back in the linen closet, and after twenty minutes, the dishes are done and Gigi's home is sparkling, just the way she likes it.

Once I'm done, I make my way back down to her room to check on her and find her arms crossed over her perfect chest, the most stunning scowl stretched across her face. "Did you just do my dishes?"

"So, what if I did?" I tell her.

"You shouldn't have."

"Tough shit," I tell her, glad to see the painkillers have started to kick in. "Let's go."

"What?" she sputters, her brows furrowing. "I appreciate you coming over here and helping me out, but I'm really not up for doing anything right now."

I arch a brow, not taking no for an answer. "I told you that I was going to get you out of this apartment today, and that's exactly what I intend to do."

She raises a brow at me, the challenge clear in her eyes, but clearly she hasn't worked out who she's talking to. "And where do you think you're taking me? I can barely sit up, let alone go for an outing."

"My place."

"Your place?" she asks slowly, the interest in her tone making it sound as though my place is a mystical land filled with treasure and secrets.

"My place," I confirm. "Besides, I got Georgie this little doctor kit after she said she wants to be just like you. So, it will give her a chance to use it."

Gigi's whole face lights up at hearing about Georgie, and honestly, mine does too. Georgie is crazy about Gigi. Ever since the shooting,

Georgie has formed an attachment to her, and I can't blame the kid. So have I. "Fine," Gigi grumbles as she throws the blankets back. "Can I at least shower first?"

"Nope, I just saw your shower," I tell her. "It's fucking tiny. I don't know how you even fit in there. You can use mine."

She rolls her eyes and tries to stand out of bed, only the movement makes her wobble and she has to reach out to the wall to balance herself. But I'm not having it. Stepping into her, I scoop her up into my arms, and as she folds in against my chest, I can't deny how fucking right this is.

Gigi curls her arms around my neck to hold on, and as I start making my way out of her room, she lifts her head and gasps. "Oh shit. My phone."

Turning back, I make my way to her bedside table, and she scoops up the phone before ordering me to her kitchen counter where she grabs her keys. Satisfied that she's got what she needs, I lock up her apartment and quickly deposit her into my truck.

Climbing in beside her, I start the engine, watching as her head lolls against the window and her eyes close. All the movement probably isn't great for her. She reaches forward and turns the hot air on full blast. "Are you doing alright?" I ask nervously. "You're not going to hurl in my truck, are you?"

"Mmmm," she replies.

"Is that a yes or a no?" I ask, pulling out into traffic.

Gigi shrugs her shoulders, those gorgeous eyes still closed. "I really couldn't be sure to tell the truth."

Ahhh, fuck. I step on the gas to avoid chunks being blown in my car, and fifteen minutes later, I pull up in my driveway, smirking at the way Gigi stares up at my house in wonder. "What the fuck is this?" she grunts.

"What's that supposed to mean?" I question as I hop out and head around to her side.

I open her door and take her hand to help her down. "Your house. It's like . . . I don't know. A grown-up house."

I burst out laughing, and she cringes at the noise. "Sorry," I say as I lead her up the stairs with my hand clutching her hip, making sure she doesn't fall. "What were you expecting?"

"I don't know, not this. Everything about you has been perfect so far. Statistically, it's going to go downhill at some point, right? I mean, surely my luck is bound to run out sooner or later."

I grin at her, watching the way she rolls her eyes, knowing damn well where this is going. "You think I'm perfect, huh?"

"Shut up," she groans, a beautiful flush spreading over her cheeks.

"I'm far from perfect, Gigi. But I do have my shit together," I tell her as I pull her into my arms. "Besides, I think I'm the lucky bastard when it comes to you and me."

She presses her lips together and gently shakes her head.

"Come on," I say, unlocking my front door. "Let me get you inside before you pass out on my doorstep."

With a grateful nod, she allows me to pull her into my home, and I watch as she looks around with interest but doesn't have the energy to comment. Though, I'm sure the second she's feeling better, she's going to go on a rampage.

Leading her to my living room, she looks at my massive couch with longing before instantly falling into it and snuggling into the cushions. After making sure she's alright, I run upstairs to one of the many spare bedrooms and strip the bed of its pillows and blankets before hurrying back down to Gigi.

She greedily accepts them, and I help spread them out on the couch and make her comfortable before grabbing the TV remote and showing her how to use the complex thing. She finds Netflix and puts on a ridiculous show that I wouldn't watch in a million years, but instead of watching it, she turns the volume down and watches me.

Sitting at her feet, I pull them into my lap and get comfortable, ready to be at her beck and call. "What?" I ask when she doesn't look away.

"Why are you doing this?"

I squeeze her foot as her eyes bore into mine. "Do I need a reason?"

She shrugs her shoulders. "I don't know. Apart from my parents and Mel, no one has ever gone out of their way for me before."

Grabbing hold of her feet, I drag her down the couch before pulling her up into my lap. "I don't see it as going out of my way," I tell her, making sure I have her undivided attention. "I see it as taking care of what's *mine.*"

Her eyes sparkle, and I watch as a small smile spreads over her face. "Yours, huh?" she murmurs.

I press a kiss to her forehead and pull her into my arms, holding her close as her head falls against my shoulder and she snuggles into me. "Definitely mine."

Running my hands up and down her back, it doesn't take long before she falls asleep, and once she's fully out, I pick her up and lay her back down on the couch, pulling the blankets right up to her chin. She slips her hands under the pillow and lets out a gentle sigh, more than content, and with that, I hit mute on the TV and give her peace to sleep.

Heading into the kitchen, I look up a recipe for chicken soup and study it for a minute before deciding this kitchen shit is too hard for me. Sara always did that, and after three long years, I still haven't been able to figure it out. I'll pick some up from the store when I get Georgie from preschool.

Wanting Gigi to have everything she needs, I duck back into the living room and place some more painkillers and water on the table before scrawling out a note to let her know I'm heading out to pick up Georgie and that we'll be home in thirty minutes.

With that, I head out the door and get on my way, quickly collecting Georgie and finding out she was a cheeky girl again today. I give her another award-winning lecture and duck into the store. Georgie sits up in the cart and grabs things off the shelves, and because the thought of having Gigi in my home brings me the sweetest peace I've had in years, I let the little munchkin get away with it.

On the drive home, I let Georgie know we have a special guest at home and that she needs to be on her best behavior because Gigi isn't feeling very well. And the moment the words are out of my mouth,

Georgie's little face lights up, realizing she can finally use her doctor kit on a real patient.

When we get home, Georgie runs up the stairs as fast as her little legs will take her, then because she can't reach the handle yet, she stomps her feet when it takes me too long to get to the door.

As soon as I open the door, she bolts inside with an excited squeal, and I cringe, hoping like fuck Georgie doesn't wake Gigi. I'll have to talk to her again about following instructions.

Heading into the kitchen, I dump the shopping bags on the counter when I hear a shuffling coming from the couch and groan, having no doubt Georgie is in there bugging Gigi. Making my way into the living room, I prepare to tell Georgie to scram when I find her sitting up in Gigi's lap, begging her to put her shows on.

Gigi glances up at me, and I let out a relieved sigh seeing the color has returned to her cheeks and the painkillers have been taken. A soft smile spreads across her face, and I perch myself on the armrest of the couch, unable to take my gaze off her. "How are you feeling?" I ask.

"Better," she tells me, her voice not so hoarse anymore. "My head still hurts, but the painkillers helped a lot."

"Good," I smile. "Are you hungry?"

She nods her head and is about to say something when Georgie demands her undivided attention, and with my girls settled, I go back to the kitchen and try to figure out this damn soup.

As I cook, I listen in amusement as Georgie runs out of the living room, disappears, and returns a moment later with her doctor kit in her hand. "Oh, Georgie," I hear dramatically from Gigi as my little girl laughs. "I'm so sick. If only there was a doctor around."

Georgie squeals in delight and I cringe, betting that the noise is killing Gigi's head. "Lay down," Georgie demands. "Sick people have to lie down. That's what my daddy says."

After twenty minutes and two glorious tantrums from Georgie, we sit at the table to eat, and I can't tear my eyes away from Gigi as she curiously looks around. "You're dying to go exploring, aren't you?" I say, a grin creeping across my face, loving that she's nosey.

A guilty expression cuts across her beautiful face, her eyes shining with laughter as she returns her gaze to me. "I might be," she admits. "But you can't blame me. A girl has to go snooping to make sure there are no glaring red flags hidden away."

I laugh, more than happy to show her it all. "I'll give you the grand tour as soon as you're done."

"Thank you," she mouths across the table. I give her a wink and watch in delight as her cheeks flush the most stunning shade of red.

As soon as we've finished, I clear the table and take her hand. I lead her around the house, showing off the home Sara and I built together.

Starting from the bottom, I lead her down into the basement that's been transformed into a home gym and bachelor pad, somewhere Tom and I usually take advantage of on game nights. Next up, I take her around the ground level, which she's pretty much already seen, but when we start climbing the stairs, a strange nervousness creeps into my chest, knowing exactly what she'll see when she reaches the top.

Gigi pauses at the very top of the stairs, taking in the huge canvas print of Sara and me on our wedding day, and I stand in silence, unsure of what to say as I watch her. She studies it, taking in every inch of the canvas, and I try to work out what the hell is going through her head, but she's giving nothing away.

It's a strange feeling, standing here with my girlfriend while looking at my wife, but just like any time I'm in front of a picture of Sara, that familiar pain plagues my heart, and I can't help but stare into those blazing blue eyes I miss so much.

I get distracted looking at the old picture when Gigi squeezes my hand and gives me a warm smile. "She was beautiful, Sean," she tells me. "Georgie is . . . they could have been twins."

"That, they could," I tell her, and with that, I lead her down the hall and show her the rest of my home—the home I've always been so proud of.

Chapter Nineteen

GIGI

This place is amazing. I've been in Sean's home all day, and even now, at the end of the night tucking Georgie in bed, I still can't come to terms with how magnificent it is. Every corner I turn, every new room, just blows me away.

Sean's home is fit for a queen. Every inch of the place is designed with absolute love. Sean explained that his brother, Carter, was the one who built it, but Sara was the one behind the design, and it shows.

The only space where I could actually see Sean's true input was the bachelor pad in the basement downstairs. It was like walking into the most extravagant man cave I've ever seen. He was so proud of it. The whole room was packed with gym equipment, all the gaming consoles in the world, the biggest flat screen I've ever seen, and of course, a pool table and a ping pong table with a game of beer pong set up on it. Though, I can't actually picture someone like Sean playing a game like that.

Don't get me wrong, the rest of the house has his touch as well, but it's more of *their* touch rather than just his. It was like having a bucket of iced water tipped over my head. Hearing about his wife and seeing it are two very different things.

Ever since the shooting, I've seen Sean nearly every day, which I'm loving, but I feel like we're not progressing. When it comes to hand-holding, stolen glances, and soft kisses, we're good, but I need more. I'm ready to take the next step with him, and while I know we agreed to take things slow, I'm left wondering just how slow he meant. I have to keep reminding myself just how hard this is for him. Moving on from the love of your life couldn't be easy. Though there's no denying the intrusive thoughts that make me feel like second best, like I'm a replacement for the real thing.

Seeing the pictures of how happy they were on their wedding day reminds me that he will never truly be all mine. He will forever share a piece of his soul with the woman he lost, and that's just something I'm going to have to get used to. Honestly, I don't think I'll have any problems with it, I just hope Sean can find room in his heart to share it with me.

In no way do I want to take any of the essence of Sara away. It's so important to Georgie that she knows her mother. Even though she only met her on the day she was born, I'd like to think she will know her through Sean's memories and her presence within their home. I guess it's actually kind of beautiful.

Dinner came and went, and before I knew it, Georgie was begging me to do her nighttime routine, so here I am, tucking her into her bed, which apparently is a big girl bed made only for big girls. Definitely not a regular bed that should be confused for regular sleeping.

I somehow get roped into singing *Twinkle, Twinkle, Little Star,* which instantly has her snoring on my shoulder. I squirm out from under her and pack the six books she demanded I read back onto her bookshelf before turning on the baby monitor and slipping out the door.

Heading back toward the stairs, I see a black and white photo of Sara hanging on the wall, and I can't help but stop and stare. She is nothing short of radiant. It's no wonder Sean was so drawn to her when they first met. The woman is unbelievably stunning, and with both her and Sean's genes, there's no doubt in my mind that Georgie is going to have lines of boys pining for her attention.

I find myself studying her eyes, her cheekbones, the soft flow of her hair, and pretty much every inch of the photograph, desperate to know the woman who stole Sean's heart. I'm not going to lie; I find myself a little jealous of the love they had for each other.

Leaning back on the opposite wall, I look at her, and with tears in my eyes, I tell her every damn thing that's within my heart. "Hi Sara, I know I never knew you when you were here, but from what I've heard and seen of you, you were an incredible woman and would have made one hell of a mother."

"Woman to woman, I have to tell you that I'm falling madly in love with your husband. He is . . . wow, he's everything. He's the kindest man I have ever met. He's been through hell and back, and despite everything, he is still the strongest man I have ever met.

"I honestly don't know what to believe about the afterlife, so I don't know if you're looking down on him and Georgie, but in case you're not, you should know that he's an amazing father. Georgie is his whole world, and he's doing an incredible job of raising her. Though, I'm sure you already know that. It's no secret what kind of man he is.

"Surely you must also know that when you passed, his heart shattered. Sara . . . I want to put it back together for him. I want to bring joy and happiness back to his life. When I look at the photographs of the two of you together, I see that happiness in his eyes. I need to bring that back to him."

Taking a shaky breath, I wipe the tears off my face. "It's important to me that you know I would never try to replace you. You were a massive part of his life, and you were the woman who taught him how to love. In fact, you're still a massive part of his life and forever will be. What you were to him made him the incredible man he is today.

"I know I can't really ask for your blessing, so I'm going to have faith that you would want him to be happy. I will never be able to amount to the woman you were, but I swear to you, Sara, I'm going to try every single day. If this thing between us is as real for him as it is for me, then I will spend the rest of my life bringing him and your little girl joy, and I promise you that I will never allow them to forget you.

"I guess . . . There's really no great way of saying this, but your passing has led me to the greatest happiness known to humankind, and I want to say thank you. My heart truly aches for you, that you left this world so young and had to leave Sean and Georgie behind. Though I know you'll be waiting for them on the other side. I just hope when that time comes, you'll have room for me too."

With tears streaming down my face, I spare one last glance at Sara's photo and step into the bathroom, needing a second to compose myself. I take a few slow breaths, finally feeling at peace with the fact that Sean will forever have another woman in his life.

Being in this home makes me feel as though I've met her now. There was something peaceful about pouring my heart out to her, and I find myself wondering if she's who I'll come to when I'm feeling conflicted or need help figuring out how to be in Georgie's life. Assuming Sean wants me there.

It's been a shitty day, but Sean came in and swept me off my feet like a knight in shining armor, but I'm not gonna lie, I hate that I haven't showered, and now, standing in the bathroom, I can't help but look longingly toward the big shower. Though I should probably ask him before stripping off my clothes in his house and jumping in.

Heading back down the stairs, I pass the canvas print of Sean and Sara's wedding day and find myself smiling at Sara as I pass her, feeling as though we share a secret connection, and I hope to God that she approves of me being the woman in her husband's life and the woman who will no doubt spend the rest of her life helping to raise her daughter.

Finding Sean on the couch exactly where I left him, I give him a warm smile when he glances up at me. "I thought I was going to have to go find you soon," he murmurs as he pats the space beside him.

I inch closer to him while keeping on my feet. "Georgie insisted on six books and a song," I explain.

"Oh, God, I'm sorry," he laughs. "She sure is going to love having you around."

Fuck, that feels good to hear.

"I bet," I say, unable to keep my smile from turning into a wide grin. "Would it be weird if I showered? I miss feeling human."

The second the words are out of my mouth, I instantly start freaking out. I mean, I just went straight ahead and assumed I was staying here tonight. What if he was about to ask me to leave for the night? But then, it's a Friday night, and Georgie is already in bed. He's a sensible guy. If he had intended on taking me home, he would have done that before doing Georgie's bedtime routine.

Oh shit, this could be really embarrassing if I'm wrong.

"Oh, sure," he says, getting to his feet. He places his hand on my lower back, and I've come to realize this is where he always places his hand whenever we're walking, like a true gentleman, and I absolutely love it. Hell, I crave it.

He leads me up the stairs and stops at a cupboard where he pulls out a towel and hands it to me before leading me back to the bathroom and placing a gentle kiss on my lips. With that, he smiles and backs out, closing the door as he leaves.

My heart races, and butterflies swarm through my stomach.

Whatever this is between us feels so special, and I hope to God that he feels it too. Quickly undressing, I step into the shower and turn on the taps.

Warm water cascades over me like a tropical waterfall, and after feeling like shit for most of the day, it's everything I've been needing. I let the water wash over my hair before deciding to quickly wash it, only this bathroom is solely used for Georgie, so I have to make do with children's shampoo.

Ten minutes later, I step out of the shower and towel off my body before getting as much water out of my hair as possible. Wrapping my towel around myself, I start searching through the cupboard and let out a sigh of relief as I find Georgie's hairbrush and get to work braiding my hair.

Turning to my pile of clothes that lay discarded on the floor—the very clothes I've been wearing for nearly two days—I realize just how underprepared I am for this. When we left my apartment, I wasn't thinking clearly. New clothes? Clean underwear? My phone charger? Shit. If I knew today would have ended in a possible sleepover, I would have come more prepared.

With a cringe and dread resting in the pit of my stomach, I double-check that my towel is on securely before doing the only thing I can do and stepping out of the bathroom. Trudging up the hall toward Sean's bedroom, I gently knock before poking my head through the door.

Sean stands across the room with his back to me, wearing nothing but a pair of track pants and my gaze eats him up like a Thanksgiving turkey.

He's absolutely gorgeous.

My jaw drops taking him in, my gaze greedily roaming over the strong muscles of his back, and as he turns to face me, I just about collapse from starvation at his bedroom door. My knees go weak, and I try to be respectful, try to remember that this was their room. But damn it, I'm about to come just thinking about another woman's husband.

Wow.

His skin is perfectly sun-kissed, his shoulders wide and strong, and his chest has me desperate to dig my fingers into him and take a bite. He slowly strides toward me, and I can't help but settle my gaze on his defined abs. Every passing second has me clenching my thighs and planting my feet on the ground so I don't jump him.

But what really gets me is the deep V that's practically a big fucking arrow to what I'm sure is going to be all my Christmases coming at once. "Um . . ." I find myself saying like a complete loser as he grins at me with a knowing smirk. "I, um . . ."

Fuck me, he winked.

I'm a goner.

How the hell did I get this lucky? My perfect match is Shrek, not this glorious man who looks like the best sex I'll ever have. Any woman looking at his body would risk a spontaneous orgasm. In fact, it's very possible I'm having one right now.

God, he knows what he's doing to me.

Reaching me, he pulls the door wider and I suck in a breath just as his hand twines around the back of my neck and pulls me closer, his intense stare holding me captive. My hands brace against Sean's strong chest, and he doesn't say a damn word before closing the gap and dropping his warm lips to mine.

He kisses me so deeply that the hunger is almost too much to bear, and as the nagging thought of Sara remains in the back of my head, I pull him out into the hallway, and he instantly presses me up against the wall. I moan into him wanting so much more, but I don't want to rush what I know he isn't ready to give.

Sean's strong hand grips my thigh and pulls it up around his hip as he grinds against me, and a soft moan slips from between my lips, my eyes fluttering with intense need as his rock-hard erection presses against my bare pussy.

His lips drop to my neck, and my nails dig into his back when he pulls back, his breath hard and fast. "Fuck," he mutters, needing to close his eyes to find control.

"Yeah," I breathe, my hand moving back to his chest and splaying across his skin.

My heart starts to return to normal, and despite the need pulsing through my veins, I unhook my knee from around his hip, desperately wishing for so much more as I glance up and meet his heavy stare. "You seem to have forgotten your clothes," I tell him, a poor excuse for not being able to resist him.

"Look who's talking," he says, that glorious smirk returning to his lips as his fingers trail across the top of my towel, brushing along the curve of my breast and leaving nothing but burning desire behind. "I was in the middle of getting dressed. You knowingly walked out here in just a towel."

I catch his hand in mine, stopping the movement before the desire completely overwhelms me. "I came to ask for some clothes."

"Really now?" he teases as if I had an ulterior motive.

I grin up at him. "Don't be a jerk. How was I to know you were putting on a show?"

He laughs as he laces his fingers through mine and pulls me across the hallway to his room, only I stop in the doorway, refusing to take another step. Sean turns back and his brows furrow before giving me a questioning look. "Something wrong?" he asks as he steps into the walk-in closet and starts rifling through his things.

My face scrunches, not sure just how honest I should be about this, or if I should even bring it up at all, but I don't want to start this relationship with mistruths. "Yeah, sorry. I just . . . I don't want to impose in here," I say, giving him a sad smile. "This room was your personal space with Sara. I don't want to tarnish the memory she left here. That's yours and yours alone."

A faraway look flickers through his eyes, and I watch as he truly considers my words before finally nodding, appreciation in his dark gaze. "Thank you," he finally says, making his way back to me with a white shirt and sweatpants in his hands.

I offer him a smile as he hands me the clothes, and yet I find myself still stuck in his doorway, not ready to walk away. His hand comes up and he runs his fingers down the side of my face, making me tilt into him, those soft eyes locked on mine. "What's on your mind?" he asks.

Glancing past him, I take in the picture of Sara on his bedside table and press my lips into a hard line. "Do you think she would approve of me?" I ask, nervousness plaguing me as I look back up at him.

A softness creeps into his eyes. "Yeah," he says, his smile widening. "She sure as hell would."

I let out a heavy breath, and I let go of the anxiousness that's been buried deep inside me since the moment I first saw the canvas at the top of the stairs. "You have no idea how happy that makes me."

With that, Sean leans down and presses his lips to mine again, only this time, we manage to control ourselves. "I might be being a little bold here," he says, his lips moving against mine, "but I think you've worked out that I'm not taking you home tonight."

"Yeah," I laugh. "I worked that one out."

"Good," he smiles before taking my hand and leading me back to the bathroom. "Get yourself dressed and then we're gonna go downstairs and pretend to watch a movie while I kiss you like a fucking horny teenager."

Sounds fucking perfect to me.

After getting dressed, Sean leads me back down to the living room and all but deposits me on the couch, and I watch him as he walks over to the massive fireplace and expertly lights it up, filling the room with the sweetest warmth. "Do you need any more painkillers?" he asks as he drops onto the couch beside me and pulls me into his arms.

"No," I tell him as he reaches for the discarded blanket on the floor and pulls it over us. "I'm perfectly fine."

"Good," he says before handing me the complex remote and

demanding I choose only my favorite movie in the world, and honestly, making that decision is more pressure than he will ever understand. I mean, how do I choose between *The Notebook* and *A Walk to Remember?* Though, considering their ending, perhaps neither is appropriate.

We lay together on the couch, his warm arms wrapped around me as his fingers roam up and down my arm, and within fifteen minutes of watching the movie, I find myself getting sleepy. Glancing up at Sean, I notice his furrowed brows, and I roll in his arm to meet his stare. "What's wrong?" I ask, hoping that he isn't having second thoughts.

He takes the remote and lowers the volume before bringing his gaze back to mine, a seriousness in his eyes. "I was just wondering if it bothers you that I've been married and have a child?"

"No," I tell him honestly. "I'm thankful for it."

His brows furrow further, and I can tell he wasn't expecting my answer, Hell, he wasn't just not expecting it, it downright confuses him. "How so?" he questions.

"Your marriage is what made you the man you are today," I tell him, reaching up and placing my hand on the side of his face. "Without that, you could be anyone or anywhere, and that may not have led you to me."

His eyes shine as he takes in my answer. "And Georgie?"

"She may be the cheekiest little girl I've ever come across," I tell him. "But she is quickly becoming the light of my life."

His face fills with adoration as he locks his arm around me tighter, our bodies melting together as he brings his lips down on mine once again. "You're incredible, Gi."

My face flames, and I gently press my hand to his chest. "Sean," I start, feeling a little nervous but needing to get this out. "I don't think you're ready to hear this, and I don't want you to feel pressured to say anything back. I know we agreed to take things slow, but the last few weeks with you have been amazing. You know, despite the whole being shot thing."

I pause, hoping I'm doing the right thing, and when he encourages me to continue by squeezing my hand, I let out a shaky breath and give it to him straight. "I'm falling in love with you, Sean."

His eyes fill with love, and he drops his forehead to mine, a smile pulling across his lips. "About fucking time, baby," he murmurs, dropping his lips to mine and kissing me with everything he's got.

Undeniable happiness soars through my chest, and I kiss him back, not even caring that he hasn't said it back. I knew he wasn't ready, but I know his heart is in the right place, and I see him starting to heal. He's working on it, and if he wasn't feeling it, I wouldn't be here in his home, sharing the space he shared with Sara and having this amazing moment with him.

And true to his word, we pretend to watch the movie while spending the next hour making out like horny teenagers, my self-control nowhere to be seen.

Chapter Twenty

SEAN

The early morning sun shines through my bedroom window on Thursday morning, and the first thing I want to do is reach for a bottle of whiskey. Hell, it doesn't even have to be whiskey, it can be any form of alcohol that's going to take the pain away.

I've purposely left Georgie with Cassie and Jax and made sure I have no court appearances or appointments. Because today fucking sucks. Just like it did last year and the year before that.

Because five years ago, I stood in front of my family and friends and vowed to Sara that I would love her until the end of time. Yet here

I am, falling in love with another woman. What kind of monster am I?

Reaching over to my bedside table, my gaze settles over the picture of Sara as I grab my phone and silence it for the tenth time this morning. My family should know better by now.

Adjusting myself in bed, I glance at my phone. Fuck. It's only 9:10 a.m. It's going to be a long-ass day. Scanning through my notifications, I make sure there's nothing important before swiping away all the missed calls and text messages from my family and promptly turning it off.

I'm not going to be good company today. All they want is to show they care and be there for me on a hard day, but fuck them. If I want to drown in a sea of self-pity then that's exactly what I'm going to do.

Rolling over in bed, my hand stretches out to the empty, cold space beside me, and a pain like no other blasts through my chest.

Why the fuck did you have to go, Sara? You ruined all our plans. We were supposed to grow old together, have a tribe of kids to screw up, and live the happiest lives together. But not anymore. You left. You left me and Georgie to work it out on our own. How could you do that to us?

Climbing out of bed, I force myself through a shower. I don't bother turning on the hot water, hoping that the chill manages to wake me up from this depression, but it's no use. Only a new day is going to help me now.

The thought of texting Gigi shoots through me, and I instantly want to punish myself. How could I even think of her today? My wife is rotting in the ground, and I'm thinking about texting my girlfriend so she doesn't worry about me today. Fuck, I'm a disgrace.

The day drags on, just as I knew it would, and by lunchtime, I'm pushing my way through the door of the worst fucking dive bar in town and handing the bartender my keys, knowing when I leave this place, I'm not going to be in any state to drive. Hell, at this point, I don't even care if the fucker steals my truck. As long as I get to drown my sorrows, I'm good.

I sit at the bar with my elbows braced on the counter—one drink after another, desperately trying to dull the ache, but I should have known better. Nothing will ever ease this kind of pain.

Hours pass, and I'm shocked when the bar starts getting busy. That's when I realize it's well past dark, and not wanting to be this pathetic fuck up, I hightail it out of there, finishing off what's left in my glass.

I stumble down the sidewalk, only stopping when I pass the liquor store. Disgust fills me, remembering my first date with Gigi, how I walked around with a hand on her lower back, practically claiming her. Was I thinking about Sara then? Was I thinking about her when I took Gigi back to my home? The home I built with Sara. No. I fucking wasn't. Where were my fucking vows then? Where was my loyalty?

What the hell is wrong with Gigi to even bother with someone like me?

I'm broken. I put on a good show for Georgie, but soon enough she'll grow up and realize that her father is nothing. *Has nothing.*

Fuck.

After purchasing a bottle of rum, I stumble out of the store and start walking the long trek to the cemetery. I weave my way through the angel statues and headstones before walking the familiar steps toward Sara.

I bring Georgie here all the time so she can talk to her mommy, but being here alone on the day that's supposed to be filled with love is fucking awful.

I stand before her as a shallow, empty man and drop to my knees, just staring at her grave. "Happy anniversary, baby," I whisper, lifting the rum to my lips and willing it to dull the ache.

How did it ever come to this?

A lump forms in my throat as I lift my gaze and read her name across the headstone. *In loving memory, Sara Jane Waters. Wife. Daughter. Mother.*

Tears sting my eyes, and as I sit here in front of my wife, I feel nothing but hollow. I thought I was starting to heal with Gigi, and maybe I am, but right now, it's just . . . nothing. I'm empty, desperately clinging onto the ghosts of my past.

I fall from my knees into a distraught pile in the cool grass, willing myself to hold the sobs at bay. I need Georgie. I need to seek out the comfort I find within her, but I refuse to allow her to see me this way.

The flowers Georgie and I left here last week look atrocious, and I curse myself for not bringing her new ones. She deserves the best flowers money can buy, especially on our fucking wedding anniversary. I was too caught up in my grief and selfish need to dull the pain that I forgot to bring her flowers.

FUCK.

Anger shoots through me, and I launch the bottle of rum across the cemetery. The bottle shatters against a tree into thousands of pieces. "I'm so sorry," I tell her, feeling like a pathetic piece of shit. "You deserved so much better than me."

I sit in silence, lost in my memories. I owe it to Sara to tell her what's going on with me. She deserves a conversation, and even though I'm more than aware she isn't here anymore, I know she's here in spirit, always looking down on me and Georgie.

"It hurts, baby," I breathe, the words getting stuck on the lump in my throat. "Why'd you have to go? I feel like I'm starting to find myself again until days like this come around, then I'm nothing. Sara, I'm nothing without you."

My head hangs as the grief overwhelms me.

"I just . . . please. I need you in my arms again. Come back, baby. I promise, I will never let you go again. Please, I'll be better. I'll put the trash out. I'll clean more. Anything, I'll do anything, baby. Just come home to me. I need you. Don't you see how badly I need you?"

I sit, wallowing in my grief until the lump in my throat disappears, and I prepare to be upfront. "I've met someone," I tell her. "I'm sorry. I love you so much, Sara, but I think I love her too. She's helping the pain go away, and she adores Georgie. I think you'll like her. I was scared at first. I didn't know how to be with anyone else, but she slotted straight into my life. And what's more, she respects us and she respects you. But, I just . . ." I let out a shaky breath. "I just need you to let me know I'm doing the right thing."

The chill has well and truly seeped into the air, but the liquor in my body is keeping me warm, so I sit here for hours until I can no longer bear it. The overwhelming need to curl up next to her headstone hits me, but I know I can't do that, and I push myself to my feet and stand before her for just a moment.

"Sara," I whisper. "I know you love Georgie, but please don't take her from me. I know it's you who keeps calling out to her. She's desperate to meet her mommy, but let me hold on to her. She's all I have left of you. We'll all be together again one day, and when we are, we'll have until the end of time, but please, baby. Please bless her with a long life. Let her find a love like ours. Let her experience life and all its beauties. Let her have children and raise them the way we didn't get to do together. Give her a chance to have the world."

With a heavy, pained sigh, I look up at the sky and blow her a kiss before finally backing away from her headstone, each step sending a searing pain right through my chest.

Finding myself wandering the streets, I pass the same liquor store from earlier and head in to grab another bottle for the night, cracking it open before the payment has even gone through. The cool liquid burns on its way down my throat, and I welcome it like I welcome Gigi's touch.

Ahhhh, Gigi. She's a gem. She's like the devil who's come to torture me, especially today. I wish it could be easy between us, that I could simply invite her into my life and promise her the world. Only Sara keeps holding me back.

What the fuck is wrong with me? Sara's dead. *Gone.* It should be simple with Gigi. I should be able to wake up every day with her by my side. Instead, I hold her at arm's length.

She told me she was falling in love with me and she was fucking right, I wasn't ready to hear it. Hell, the way fear blasted through my chest and crippled me was torture. Luckily for me, she said I didn't have to say anything. Otherwise, I'm sure I would have fucked it up right then and there.

But on the other hand . . . hearing those words from her was incredible, and I don't know how she's doing it, but bit by bit, she's thawing me from the inside out, and every day, I find it just that bit easier to breathe.

Gigi is amazing, and I'm a fucking bastard. She deserves more, just like Sara did.

Before I know it, my hand is raised into a fist and banging on the familiar door. I wobble on my feet as I wait for it to open, and I shove a hand out to steady myself, gripping the door frame above.

The door is ripped open, and I instantly fall into the room, stumbling forward.

Oops. Maybe that wasn't the doorframe I was holding.

Oh well.

I crash into someone who manages to somehow dodge me before I go hurtling down to the ground. My eyes focus as someone hovers over me, looking down at me in concern, and as I see Gigi's gorgeous face, a wide smile stretches over my lips. "Well, hey, sweet cheeks," I slur, trying to reach up and pull her into my chest, all the way down here on the floor.

Gigi bats me away as I try to pull myself up, the world spinning from all the way down here. "Are you drunk?" she questions with distaste.

"Ummmmmm, maybe," I grin, my hand braced against the wall to keep me upright as my other reaches out for her. If I could just lose myself in her body, maybe I'd forget about everything else. Get her naked and feel her burning skin under my fingers.

"Don't even think about it," she mutters, batting me away again.

"Come on, babe. You can't resist me," I grin, remembering just how delicious she looked wrapped in that towel and how desperately I wished I could give her what she wanted. "You love me, remember?"

"Sean," she snaps, stepping into me and shoving me hard against her closed door, though how it got closed is a mystery to me. "First off, you're drunk. You smell like rum, you can hardly stand straight, and it's all over you. Secondly, you're being an arrogant asshole. I've been messaging you all day. Your sister called because she was worried about you and no one could find you. And thirdly, if you think you're about to get something from me, you're dead wrong."

Ha. *Dead.* You know who's dead? My wife.

"Babe," I say, letting out a heavy breath and moving into her, my hands at her waist. "I'm gonna take a wild guess that you're not feeling it tonight?"

"Damn right I'm not feeling it," she argues, disgust and anger in her eyes, making me realize I am being an arrogant asshole. "You're a mess."

Damn straight I'm a fucking mess. "I'm drunk."

"I see that," she says.

"What the hell is going on out here?" Mel asks as she comes out of the hallway. She takes one look at me and scrunches up her face, probably assuming I'm here to screw Gigi well into the morning. She grabs her bag off the kitchen counter and walks toward us before giving Gigi a quick hug. "I'll leave you guys to it," she says before reaching for the door handle behind me.

"You going to tell Tom how much you hate him while you screw his brains out?" Gigi asks as I move out of Mel's way, hoping like fuck I can keep on my feet.

Mel can't help but grin at Gigi before she silently slips out the door, leaving us alone.

"Come on," Gigi says, taking my hand and leading me down the hallway. She pulls me into the bathroom and immediately grabs the hem of my shirt before pulling it up over my head. I help her to fully remove it, which is when her hands come down on my chest and the electricity instantly pulses between us.

My skin burns from her touch, and I absolutely love it, I fucking crave it. Her eyes fill with desire, and I slide my arms around her waist, pulling her in before dropping my lips to hers, and fuck, the sound of her soft moan breathes life into me.

Fuck, she's everything.

My hands travel down to her perfect ass, giving it a firm squeeze before taking hold and lifting her onto the vanity. Her legs wrap around my waist, and for a moment, I wonder if she's changed her mind before she gently pushes me back.

My brows furrow, and I look down at her with confusion. "We're not doing this," she says.

I lean in, pressing my lips to the base of her neck, unable to get enough. "Why the hell not?" I ask, my lips moving over her skin as she tilts her head, opening up for more.

Gigi's fingers trail up to the back of my head, holding me to her. "Because you're drunk, Sean. And not the good kind of drunk. Something's going on with you right now, and I have absolutely no idea what it is, but I don't like it. So, you need to shower and preferably brush your teeth, then I'll put you to bed."

With a sigh, I lift my gaze back to hers. "That's not how I was hoping tonight was going to go."

"You've made that perfectly clear, but unfortunately for you, I'm not some whorebag who you get to take advantage of to dull the ache," she says, clearly realizing that whatever this is about has something to do with Sara. "Now hurry up and get your ass in the shower."

I step back from her and reach for the button of my jeans, watching as her gaze follows the movement, and I take my sweet time, popping the button, loving the way desire flashes in her eyes. "You staying or leaving?" I ask, making it perfectly clear that the invitation is still there.

"Leaving," she finally says, her chest rising and falling with rapid pants as her gaze lifts back to mine. "Definitely leaving. Our first time is not going to be while you're drunk and dangerously close to hurling all through my bathroom."

Okay. She has a good fucking point.

With that, she jumps down from the vanity and all but runs out of the bathroom, leaving me to get cleaned up in her tiny shower. I take my time, stealing someone's toothbrush, and after the hot water assaults my skin, I somehow start to sober up despite the disgusting amount of alcohol working its way through my body.

Striding out of her bathroom ten minutes later in nothing but a pair of jeans, I find Gigi curled up on her couch with a cushion squished under her face. She looks up at my movement and climbs off the couch, silently taking my hand and leading me into the kitchen. She hands me a glass of water before dragging me down the hallway into her room. "Get in," she says, grabbing the blankets on her bed and pulling them back.

I raise a brow at her. "Are you seriously putting me to bed?"

"Yep," she says. "Now, get in."

I do as she says before patting the space beside me. "You getting in, too?"

She bites her bottom lip and is silently thinking about it. "Are you going to maul me?" she questions.

"Depends," I grin.

"On?"

"If you want me to."

"You know, I do," she tells me before kneeling on the edge of the bed and slowly creeping toward me with both desire and reluctance in her blazing eyes. She drops down into my arms, curling her body beside me. She goes quiet for a moment, deep in thought before finally glancing up and meeting my eyes. "We will," she murmurs. "But only when it's me you're thinking about."

Her comment hits me like a freight train. She's right. I'm not being fair to her right now. "I'm sorry," I whisper into her hair.

"It's okay," she whispers, a sadness filling her tone. "Do you want to talk about it? I mean, you don't have to, but I just thought it might help."

I let out a sigh as I realize that she deserves to know. I fully intend for this woman to be part of my life, which means I need to open up and completely let her into my life.

Giving myself a moment to breathe, I give it to her straight. "It was supposed to be mine and Sara's fifth wedding anniversary today."

Gigi gasps and her eyes fill with pain before she closes them and holds me a little tighter, her hand so soothing against my chest. "I'm so sorry," she whispers.

"I know," I tell her, and with that, I pull her tighter against me, desperately clinging to the comfort she can offer, and as her fingers draw little circles against my chest, I close my eyes and finally allow this hellish day to come to an end.

Chapter Twenty-One

GIGI

Lounging on my couch with my feet carelessly hanging over the side, I cradle my coffee mug in my cold hands when the front door flies open and Mel barges in. I peer at her over the back of the couch, taking in the startled look on her face. "Just getting in?" I grin.

She lets out a sigh before dumping her handbag and the mail on the entryway table. "Yes," she groans.

She flops down onto the couch beside me before taking in the heavenly aroma of my coffee and changing her mind. She gets back up again and heads into the kitchen to start fussing with the old coffee machine, hoping it's down to play ball twice in one morning. "How was your night?" she questions, her tone low as she watches me from the kitchen, her brows bouncing. "Is he still here?"

A smile tears across my face at the chance of talking about Sean. "Yeah, he's still in bed," I tell her. "He's going to have a wicked hangover though."

"I bet," she murmurs, tapping on the side of the coffee machine when it doesn't start up straight away. "Did you guys happen to talk?"

"Not really," I tell her with a heavy sigh, feeling a little lost after everything that happened last night. I was only just starting to feel content in this relationship. Hell, I'd even told him I was falling for him, and then he had to go and hit me with that. But I get it. He has every right to crumble on days like that, but it was an eye-opener to just how much he's still hurting.

"Oh," she murmurs, her brows furrowed as she comes over and leans across the back of the couch as the coffee machine finally kicks into gear. "So, you don't really know what last night was about then?"

"Yeah, actually," I say. "It would have been his fifth wedding anniversary with Sara, but apart from that, he didn't give me anything more."

"Oh shit, that must have been hard," she sighs, pressing her lips into a tight line and catching my eye. "But what about you? It's hard enough trying to navigate a new relationship, but you've got that to think about as well. Are you . . . okay with it all?"

"Yeah," I tell her, truly meaning it. "I've come to terms with the fact that there's another woman in his life, but I'm not going to lie.

Nights like last night . . . It can make me feel second best, but we have a unique situation, and I want to be there for him."

"You sure?"

I reach over the back of the couch and give her hand a squeeze. "Yes, I'm perfectly fine with it. Sara made him the incredible man he is today, and I honestly wouldn't have it any other way. You know, apart from the crippling hurt. If I could take that away, I would."

"Good," she smiles. "I'm happy for you. You've been so desperate to find Prince Charming and you finally have."

"Hey," I scold. "I wasn't desperate."

"You were, babe," she laughs, prancing back into the kitchen to collect her coffee from the machine and double-checking that it's not going to give her third-degree burns. She makes her way back to the couch and drops in beside me, pulling her legs up under her. "So, tell me all about it. Did you finally get him in the sack?"

The second her question is out, coffee comes sputtering out of my mouth, and I have to wipe my sleeve across my face to mop it all up.

"I'll take that as a no," she grumbles, clearly disappointed in me.

"Shhhhhhhh," I demand as my eyes flick back to the hallway to check he's still safely in my room and out of earshot. "We're taking it slow, remember? Besides, it's not like it's been easy for us. He has his demons to deal with, and I got shot."

"Excuses," she grunts. "If you guys take it any slower, you'll be going backward. I mean, you've been dating for nearly two months, you should be screwing like rabbits instead of acting like an old married couple."

She's completely right, but then, she doesn't understand our reasoning. Sex to her is for fun, it's not romantic, it's not about love, it's about who's the first to reach the finish line with a screaming orgasm.

Not wanting to have to defend this to her, I let out a sigh and focus on her. "How was Tom?"

She rolls her eyes, clearly seeing my question for what it is; a horrible way of changing the topic. I don't want to explain how when I'm finally physical with him, I don't want him mentally having a threesome with his dead wife and me. "He's fine," she grunts.

"That's all you have to say about it? I thought you had a strict *no-sleepover* rule."

"We do," she grumbles under her breath before lifting her mug to her lips and taking a long, drawn-out sip, averting her stare.

"What's going on, Mel?" I say, fixing her with a hard stare. After all, if she can demand answers out of me, then I'll damn well do the same to her.

"Nothing. It's just casual sex," she says.

I let out a huff as I lean forward and place my coffee mug on the table so I can make a show of crossing my arms. "Casual sex is not supposed to be every damn night. That's why it's called *casual.* Besides, Sean and I have been doing whatever this is for two months now, which means you've been dancing around Tom for two months as well."

Mel lets out a sigh before glancing up at me, and when her bottom lip starts to wobble and she starts blinking back tears, horror bursts through my chest. Mel is the strongest woman I know. Nothing breaks her.

"What the hell?" I panic, wide-eyed. "What happened?"

"I . . . I think I like him," she blurts out.

Sweet baby Jesus. What has Tom done to my best friend?

I fall into a fit of uncontrollable laughter, gripping my stomach when it starts to hurt. "Holy shit, Mel," I say, gasping for breath. "That's fucking hilarious."

"Shut up," she whines. "I don't know what to do."

Somehow managing to pull myself together, I give her a pointed stare, hoping like fuck she decides to take me seriously. "You stop being such a little bitch about it and man up. Tell him how you feel and see how it goes. What do you have to lose?"

"My dignity," she scoffs. "Tom isn't like Sean. He's not going to swoon and give me everything I've ever wanted in life. He's the more dickish version of me. He's gonna freak out and run for the hills. I can't tell him this."

"I think you're not giving him enough credit," I tell her. "If Tom is so much like you, then why is he having sleepovers with you? It's a two-way street, and he's giving just as much as he's taking. He likes you, Mel. And like you, he's probably too scared to come out and say it."

She silently leans back into the couch and puts her feet up on the coffee table as she continues to pout, and realizing she's putting an end to the conversation, I turn on the TV and finish off my coffee while Mel eventually gets up and takes a shower.

Twenty minutes later, she returns, dressed and ready for work, making me more jealous than I've ever been in my life. I look over at her and can't help but sigh as I take her in. "You're so weird," she grunts before quickly pouring a bowl of cereal and annihilating it.

"Huh? Why?"

"Because you must be the only person I know who doesn't enjoy having paid time off work," she explains.

"I can't help it," I tell her, feeling like I'm going to burst if I get holed up in this apartment for much longer. "I love my job. I mean, who else can say they shove their hands up pussies all day long and pull out slimy little humans?"

"Good point," she grunts, absolutely disgusted. "How much longer now?"

"I'm good to go back on Monday," I tell her. "I saw Dr. Monroe yesterday, and he signed off on everything as long as I promised to see a therapist every now and then to check in with my mental health."

Mel nods and blows out her cheeks. "It's really been six weeks already?" she asks.

"Already? It feels like I've been cooped up in this little apartment for months."

"Hey," she scolds. "Don't knock the apartment."

"Who cares about the apartment? I get to go back to work," I grin.

Mel rolls her eyes and gets up to wash her bowl, grabbing my empty coffee mug in the process. She grabs her bag off the entryway table before picking up the mail and skimming through it. "Hey," she says with a frown as she walks toward me and hands me an envelope. "There's a letter for each of us from the hospital."

My brows furrow as I take mine from her and glance over the

envelope, and the longer the paper rests in my hands, the heavier the dread becomes in my stomach. "It'll be about the shooting," I tell her as we start ripping into them.

"No doubt," she grunts.

Opening the letter, I start scanning over it, and the further I get, the wider my eyes become.

Holy shit.

"Fuck yeah," Mel cheers, pumping her fists into the sky as I read through the letter thoroughly, my heart pounding right out of my chest. "I knew today was going to be a good day."

"You getting a payout too?" I question.

"Sure am," she beams, blinking rapidly as though unable to believe what's right in front of her face. "It's not enough to buy my island, but certainly enough for a new set of tits."

As if on cue, we switch our letters and get busy reading again. "Wow, thirty-five thousand dollars? Not bad," I tell her as I look back up at her to see her eyes practically bugging out of her head, realizing just how much my payout is.

"Holy shit, dude," she grunts in disbelief. "You're getting one hundred and seventy-three thousand big ones."

"Apparently," I murmur, unable to wrap my head around it.

She stares at me, confusion flashing in her eyes. "What's wrong? You're not happy about this?" she questions. "I'm fucking thrilled."

"I bet you are," I laugh before shrugging my shoulders, unease pulsing through my veins. "I just don't think you can put a price on getting shot. Like, who's out there determining a figure on what my trauma is worth?"

She lets out a sigh and gives my good shoulder a squeeze. "I'm sorry," she says quietly. "That was insensitive of me. I'm just . . . I'm excited."

"It's okay," I say before taking the letter back from her and glancing over it again. "Is this even legal? I mean, what are they trying to achieve? Is it hush money?"

"When I hear *is it legal* and *hush money* in the same sentence, it's usually right before I put some bastard behind bars," comes a groggy, sleepy voice from behind us.

I turn around to find Sean heading up the hallway, his hand resting against his chest while showing off those show-stopping, orgasm-inducing abs. An almighty yawn rips out of him as I get up off the couch and grab him some painkillers and a glass of water.

He greedily accepts them from me, swallowing the pills and following them down with the water before pulling me into his arms and pressing a kiss to my lips. "Morning," he murmurs, his lips moving against mine.

"Good morning to you, too," I say, pleased he managed to make it through the night without redecorating my home with vomit.

"Ugh, you two are going to make me taste my breakfast again," Mel grunts before pulling her bag higher on her shoulder and blowing me a kiss. "I have to go. Will I see you for dinner?"

My mouth opens to answer but Sean gets in first. "Nope."

Glancing up at him with furrowed brows, I go to ask why the hell not, but he's clearly not giving anything away.

Mel slips out the door, and as Sean tightens his hold around me and kisses me again, I melt into him. I've been kissed by a few guys in my twenty-six years, but nothing will ever compare to this. Overwhelming passion and emotion pour through him when he touches me, and I simply can't get enough.

Leading Sean over to the couch, I grab my discarded letter before handing it to him. "What do you make of this?" I ask as he takes it from me. "I don't quite understand it."

He reads through it, and from the look on his face, the painkillers haven't quite kicked in yet, but he forces his way through the entire thing. "Looks as though the hospital is giving the staff and families involved in the shooting a payout in hopes they don't get sued for negligence."

"What?" I grunt, my eyes widening. "Why would anyone do that? The hospital isn't to blame. The shooter is."

"I agree, but people are greedy. All they see are dollar signs, and if there's a chance to make a quick buck, they'll take it. Besides, they know they'll never get anything out of the shooter, so they'll go after the hospital instead."

"What do you mean?" I question as Sean falls onto the couch and pulls me down with him.

"The hospital will be sued for negligence and probably a shitload of other things which could ruin them. The last thing the hospital needs is a highly publicized court case. Its reputation will be dragged through the mud and they'll be up for millions of dollars."

"Shit," I mutter, looking at him. "What do I do?"

"I can't answer that for you, babe."

Damn him and his moral high ground. "Well . . . what are my options?"

"The way I see it, you have three," he starts. "You could ignore the letter and forget anything ever happened. You could sue the hospital and come out a very wealthy woman, though probably never work there again, or you could accept the money in this letter and put it behind you."

I consider my options for a while, but there's one very clear winner. There's no way I could ever sue the hospital. That place is my home, and I could never place blame for being shot on them. But do I deserve some sort of compensation for the shit I've been through? Hell yes. It just feels wrong taking it from the hospital instead of the asshole who barged through the doors of a children's wing with a gun in his hand.

"And if I accept the money?" I ask.

"Then you'll most likely have a meeting with the bigwigs at the hospital, sign some papers declaring that you won't pursue any legal action against the hospital, and go home with a check."

"That easy, huh?"

"That easy," he confirms. "You can put it all in the past and move forward."

"That sounds pretty good to me."

"I bet it does," he says, before brushing his fingers over my shoulder and slipping the fabric of my shirt down, revealing the skin beneath. His gaze settles over the healing wound, checking how it's healing, just as he has done every time I've seen him since the shooting.

His fingers lightly brush over the angry red scar before he presses the softest kiss to my skin and sends goosebumps soaring across my body. Adjusting myself on his lap, I straddle him and feel his strong hands slide around my waist, not daring to let go, and as I meet those deep eyes that I love so much, he blows me away.

"I love you, Gigi," he murmurs, his gaze boring into mine as his thumbs brush over my skin. I suck in a breath, not having expected that, especially so soon after last night. "I'm sorry it's taken me until now to tell you, but I think I knew the second you answered the door the day we went riding. You looked radiant, and I felt my heart kickstart again. Only it terrified me because it meant I was starting to move on."

My heart swells, but I sit quietly, sensing he has more to say. "I talked to Sara last night, and believe me, I know how crazy that sounds. But I was at the cemetery, and I feel like if there was any time that she was there listening, last night would have been it."

His lips press into a hard line, and it's clear his memories of being at the cemetery are hard to swallow. "I told her all about you and realized she would be okay with it. The second I figured that out, everything just kind of settled within me. I'm still pissed that she's gone, and I miss her every fucking second, but I no longer feel as though falling for another woman is betraying her memory."

Tears well in my eyes as I snuggle into him, slipping my arms under his so I can hold him tight. "She already knew," I whisper, my head resting against his wide chest.

"What do you mean?"

"That day you kidnapped me," I start, a fond smile settling across my face. "I saw that picture of her in the hallway upstairs, you know the black and white one outside Georgie's room?" He nods and I lift my head to smile up at him. "After tucking her in, I stopped to talk to her."

"And what did you tell her?" he questions, his gaze narrowing as a soft smile pulls at the corner of his lips.

My cheeks flush, feeling shy, and I squish my face into his neck, a wide smile stretching across my face. "That you're the kindest, sexiest, most incredible man I've ever met and it's all thanks to her that you're here in my life. Then I told her how you're an amazing father and that you're doing an amazing job of raising Georgie."

"And?" he prompts, knowing there's more, his eyes sparkling.

I pull my cheek from the nook of his neck so I can see his perfect face, my gaze settling on his. "I told her that you were hurting and that I want to bring you happiness."

Emotion shines bright in his eyes, and he squeezes my waist as if trying to comfort me, but I don't need it, not now, not when I'm already in his warm arms. "You've already brought me so much happiness," he tells me. "I adore you and so does Georgie. I couldn't have asked for anything better."

Sean's hand comes up and gently pushes a stray lock of hair behind my ear before curling around the back of my neck to pull me in, only I hold back. "Sean?" I murmur, my heart racing. "I love you, too."

His chin tilts up to mine, and he gives me everything he's got, kissing me deeply as I curl my arms around his neck, never more content in my whole life than what I am right now. When we pull back to catch our breath, I drop my forehead to his, reveling in the feel of his hands gently moving over my back. "I'm sorry you had to see me like that last night."

"It's okay," I sigh. "I understand it, and honestly, it was actually a little entertaining."

"You're kidding, right?" he scoffs. "I barged in here like a dirty drunk hoping to get between your legs."

"Yeah," I grin, the memory of his raging cock pressed against my clit still so fresh in my mind. "I kinda liked it."

Sean gives me a wicked smile, shaking his head before letting out a breath, and just when I think he's about to make some kind of dirty joke, a strange hesitance flickers in his gaze. His hand digs into his pocket, and he visibly swallows as his eyes meet mine. "I've got something for you," he tells me. "I honestly don't know how you're going to take it, though."

My face falls, panic soaring through my chest. "Tell me that's not a fucking ring, because like . . . I know we did the whole *I love you* thing, but this is way too soon, and no offense, but you are not even a little bit ready. I mean, don't get me wrong, I know you'd be an incredible husband to me, but hold the fuck up."

Sean laughs, not saying a damn word as he stares back at me, silently watching me freak out before putting me out of my misery. "You done?" he questions.

I swallow hard and nod, hoping like fuck I've misunderstood. "Depends."

He takes my hand and flips it so he can see my open palm, and as my brows furrow, he places a mangled piece of metal right in the center before sitting back and watching me with deep curiosity.

I study the metal in my hand, having absolutely no idea what it is, when it hits me. It's a bullet.

Confusion rocks through me, and my gaze shifts from Sean's to the bullet and back again. I don't know how to take this or even what to think. Is this *my* bullet?

"This isn't . . ." I question, meeting his intense stare.

He nods ever so slightly, and I watch the hesitation creep back into his eyes as he second-guesses if this was a good idea. "Yeah, it is," he tells me with a slight cringe. "I found it after you were taken into surgery and thought you'd want it one day. But if it's too much, I can get rid of it. I didn't mean to freak you out or anything."

Lifting my hand, I take a deeper look at the bullet, taking in the squished metal and remembering the fierce, burning agony this little fucker caused.

Sean closes my hand around the metal and forces my eyes back to his. "I know you don't like talking about it, but I wanted you to have it as a reminder of what you've achieved. You went through this awful thing and have come out the end. So many others would have crumbled going through that, but you soared. You showed unbelievable amounts of strength, and I'm so fucking proud of you. So, don't think of this as a reminder of the fear and pain from that day, but use it as your motivation to always keep going."

I open my palm and look down at the bullet in a new light.

He's right. I shouldn't fear this scrappy piece of metal. After all, I conquered it and survived. It can't hurt me anymore. Hell, I made this bullet my bitch. It should go up on a pedestal so each time I look at it, I'll remember that I kicked ass.

Seeing the change on my face, Sean lights up. "Do you have plans for today?" he questions.

"Nope," I smile as his hands run up and down my back.

"Good," he smiles. "Then I'm kidnapping you again."

"Careful now," I tell him, a wicked grin stretching across my lips. "I know this kickass lawyer who'd bust your ass wide open for even suggesting such horrendous things."

Sean laughs. "Let me at him," he tells me, his lips crushing to mine.

With that, he lifts me off the couch and places me safely on my feet before ordering me to grab some clothes. I do as I'm told, and before I know it, Sean is stealing my car keys out of my hand and pulling out of my parking spot.

Chapter Twenty-Two

SEAN

With Gigi's hand in mine, I drive her car down my driveway and find a police cruiser parked next to my truck. Tom is halfway up the stairs with my keys in his hand when he hears the sound of Gigi's tires on the driveway and turns around, the relief in his eyes almost comical.

Gigi and I get out of her car and meet him halfway. "Hey," he says as he tosses my keys. "Just started my shift when I found your truck parked outside some rundown bar."

"Yeah, thanks," I say as he looks me over, making sure I'm doing alright after yesterday.

Gigi gives Tom a tight smile, and I hand her my keys so she can head on inside. Tom offers her a polite nod, and it's clear these two are going to have to work on their relationship. Though, I'm sure her fear of Tom breaking Mel's heart doesn't help the situation.

"How are you feeling?" Tom questions once Gigi is inside and closes the door behind her.

"Good, actually," I tell him. "Really good."

"Good, then learn to answer your fucking phone," he grunts. "We've all been trying to get a hold of you. Your sister was worried you were laying in a gutter somewhere, Logan and Carter were searching local bars, and I was checking hospitals."

"Shit," I grunt, starting to regret my decision to turn my phone off. "Sorry. I went to the cemetery to check in with Sara, then ended up at Gigi's place."

"Yeah, I see that now," he says. "We checked the cemetery but must have just missed you. We all ruled out Gigi's place thinking that was the last place you'd want to be yesterday."

"I mean, if you bothered to check in with Mel, you would have known I was there," I tell him, specifically remembering Mel leaving to go to Tom's place, though something tells me not a lot of talking was happening.

Tom rolls his eyes before letting out a breath and nodding up the stairs to where Gigi disappeared. "So, it's serious, huh?" he questions.

"Yeah, man," I say, a little unsure how he's going to react.

It's clear he's deep in thought before he slowly begins to nod and press his lips together. He claps me on the shoulder. "I'm happy for you," he finally says.

"Really?" I question.

"Really," he confirms. "Don't get me wrong, I miss Sara. I fucking loved her like a sister, but at some point, I have to accept that she's really gone and that you need to start living again. I think Gigi will be good for you."

"She is," I agree.

"Alright, man. I have to run, but do me a favor," he says, a guilty expression flickering in his eyes. "When you turn on your phone, just go ahead and delete your voice messages. There's no need to listen to that shit."

I laugh as he walks away and drops down into his cruiser with his partner patiently waiting in the car. After a quick wave to them, I turn on my heel and head inside, finding Gigi sitting up on the kitchen counter, waiting patiently and looking fucking radiant. "Hi," I murmur as I walk toward her.

Her face flushes as I reach her, and I can't resist sliding my hands up her thighs as she slowly opens her legs, allowing me to get even closer. "What are the plans today?" she questions as her hands come to a stop on my chest, her legs locking around my hips.

"I don't need to pick up Georgie till three," I tell her, a wicked grin stretching across my lips. "So until then, consider yourself my hostage."

"Hostage, huh?" she asks, her fingers roaming over my chest. "Should I be screaming?"

I lean into her and run my nose along her neck, inhaling that addictive scent before kissing her soft, sensitive skin, loving the way she tilts her head, silently begging for more. "Oh, you'll definitely be screaming," I rumble against her skin.

"Really now?" she questions, excitement drumming in her eyes as she pulls back and meets my stare, her bright eyes boring into mine.

I give a slow definite nod, letting her know just how serious I am. I've been resisting her too fucking long, keeping her at arm's length because I've been scared, but not anymore. She deserves to be loved in the way she craves, and damn it, I wanna give it to her. I want to give her everything I've got.

Reaching out to her, I run my fingers down the side of her face, and she leans into my touch as my hunger for her intensifies. My hand slides around the back of her neck, and before I know it, I'm pulling her into me, our bodies crashing together with urgency.

Gigi wraps her arms around my neck as I catch her lips in mine, kissing her deeply and letting her feel just how fucking desperately I need her.

She moans into me before releasing her hold around my neck and dropping her hands to the hem of my shirt, grabbing the material, and yanking it up between our bodies. She tosses the shirt aside and the second her hands come down on my body, electricity fills my veins.

"Oh, God," she groans against my lips as I grind against her.

Needing so much more, I grip her shirt and pull it over her head, my hands immediately coming down on her body as my lips roam over the base of her neck. Feeling my way over her back, I unclasp her black bra and she quickly pulls the straps down her arms before tossing it away.

The hunger burning through me intensifies, and my hands roam over her sweet tits, my thumb rolling over her pebbled nipple as she arches her back, pushing them firmly into my hands, her soft groans like music to my ears. "Fuck, you're beautiful," I murmur, my lips returning to hers.

Gigi reaches down between us and starts working my belt buckle, and a deep rumble vibrates through my chest, the anticipation of feeling her hands on my body almost too much to bear. She gets the buckle and the button undone before it becomes too much, and I scoop her off the kitchen counter, lifting her into my arms.

She clings onto me, her lips on mine as I walk through to the living room and drop down onto the couch as she straddles me. This new position has her full tits right in front of my face, and I don't hesitate to close my mouth over her nipple and flick my tongue, watching the way her body jolts on top of me.

Gigi grips onto me, groaning with undeniable pleasure, and I can't wait to see just how fucking beautiful she is when she comes. "Fuck, Sean," she breathes, grinding that sweet pussy down against my cock.

My eyes roll.

I need to fucking taste her.

Bracing my arm around her waist, I lift her just enough to tear her pants down her legs, taking her thong right along with it before throwing her down on the couch, watching the way her eyes heat with intense desire and her chest heaves with needy pants.

I come down over her, grinning wide as I kiss her deeply, and then just when she goes to lock her arms around me, I make my way down her body, listening to her sweet inhale of breath.

"Oh shit," she groans, the anticipation making her eyes flutter.

My lips roam over her body, tasting every fucking inch of her and stopping to tease those pretty nipples, loving the way her back arches off the couch, so fucking sensitive to my touch.

Keeping my hand cupped around her firm breast, I make my way down, skimming over her waist and hips as she shifts under me, opening her legs to allow me in, and goddamn it, I can't wait. Meeting her heavy gaze, I watch as she braces herself on her elbows, wanting to see every last second, and fuck, if that's what she likes then I'll put on the best show she's ever seen.

Dropping my face, I close my mouth over her clit and her whole body jolts under me as her head falls back in undeniable pleasure. "Oh, God, Sean," she groans, spurring me on.

My tongue works over her clit, and I give her everything she needs, licking, sucking, rolling, and then because my fucking queen deserves it all, I reach up beneath my chin and slowly slide two fingers deep inside her.

"Oh, God, yes," she cries.

I'm rock fucking hard at just the thought of having my fingers buried inside of her, and God damn, she's delicious. I could take this sweet cunt every day of forever and never grow bored.

I work her, quickly learning what she likes, splitting my fingers and massaging her walls as she grips the couch cushions, her hands balling into fists. "Shit, Sean," she pants. "Don't stop. I'm gonna come."

Fuck, yeah she is.

Giving her everything I've got, I suck her clit while flicking my tongue and rolling my fingers inside her. Pushing even deeper, I feel her walls clench down around me, and she comes hard, throwing her head back as the orgasm tears through her body.

She's fucking radiant, and I don't dare stop, wanting to drag it out, tasting her arousal on my tongue.

Gigi's eyes clench, a heavy breath escaping through her lips as her hand knots into my hair and her legs tighten around my shoulders. "Oh, God, yes," she cries, heavily panting as she reaches her high, her body jolting and quivering under my touch.

I don't dare stop until she comes down from her high and her body finally starts to relax, then lifting my head, I meet her eyes as I roll my tongue over my lips, savoring every last drop of her arousal, watching as her eyes flame with hunger.

"Holy shit," she says, still panting, her heated gaze locked on mine.

Her tongue rolls over her lips, and I know she's only moments from scrambling over to me and repaying the favor, but I'm not nearly done with her yet, and something tells me the second she wraps her warm lips around me, I'll be a fucking goner, and I'm not about to let that happen. No, I'm going to drag out every last second of this.

Climbing back up her body, Gigi reaches between us and finishes undoing my pants before diving inside and curling her tight fist around me, and fuck, it's everything. I haven't felt a woman's touch in over three years, and the way she works up and down my cock has me ready to fucking lose it.

My lips crash down on hers, letting her taste herself on my lips, and she groans into my mouth before using her other hand to finally push my pants down, freeing me completely. I adjust myself over her, settling between her legs, so fucking ready to take her, but I won't dare until I have her begging for it.

Reaching down between us, I find her center and roll my fingers over her clit, grinning against her lips as her body jolts beneath me, still so sensitive from her first orgasm. But I hope she's ready because I won't be stopping until she can't fucking walk.

Gigi hooks her leg over my hip, opening herself to me, and I meet her eye, watching as that beautiful flush spreads over her cheeks.

"Sean," she groans. "Don't make me wait."

"I don't want to rush this, babe," I murmur against her lips, but my own patience is wearing thin. I need her just as bad.

"Please," she begs, hooking her arm around my neck and pulling my lips down to hers. "This is torture. I need to feel you inside me. I wanna feel how you stretch my walls and fill me. God, Sean. Please."

Fuck. That does it.

Adjusting myself between her legs, I slip my arm beneath her knee and pull it up just as I guide my cock to her entrance and then finally push inside. Gigi sucks in a deep gasp, her fingers digging into my back, and I don't dare stop until I'm fully seated inside her warm cunt, her walls stretching around me.

"Fuck, babe," I groan as my fingers squeeze her waist, her sweet pussy clenching around me and making my eyes roll. A weaker man would come from just being seated inside this woman, but me, I'm going to hold on until it kills me.

I take my time, slowly pulling back as I catch her lips in mine, both of us lost in the undeniable pleasure. Then reaching down between us, I work her clit and really start to move.

Gigi gasps into my mouth and I swallow it with pride, in a world of fucking ecstasy.

"Sean," she mutters as I pull all the way back only to slam all the way back inside her.

I take her right to the edge until I feel her walls starting to clench around me, but I'm not nearly done. Not yet.

Scooping my arm around her waist, I pull us both up on the couch until I'm settled in the seat on the cushion and she's straddling me, my cock buried even deeper as I hold onto her waist. "Oh, God," she groans, plastering her body to mine as she hooks her arms around my neck and starts riding me like a fucking cowgirl.

My eyes flutter, my fingers digging into her waist as she bounces up and down on my cock and grinds her clit against my pelvis. And when I adjust my hips to add more pressure on her clit, she gasps before completely detonating.

Her pussy clenches down around me and she groans low, barely able to move as she comes undone, her walls convulsing around me. Bracing my arm around her waist, I keep her moving and watch as her eyes roll and she tips her head back, giving me the perfect opportunity to close my lips over her sensitive skin.

As her sweet cunt drops down over me again, I reach my fucking limit and come hard, allowing myself the release my body has been desperate for since the second she walked into my life. I shoot hot spurts of cum deep inside her as her high continues tearing through her body, squeezing my cock so tight I fear I might actually lose it.

Holding her tight to my body, I breathe her in as we each start coming down, and when she's finally able to breathe again, she melts into me, completely spent. "That was incredible," she murmurs as she draws little circles on my skin with her finger, something I've realized she can't help but do.

"You're fucking incredible," I tell her, my hand moving around her body and grabbing a firm hold of her ass. She kisses me eagerly, and as the hunger slams back into me, I pick her up off the couch and make my way into the bathroom.

Neither of us had a chance to shower this morning, and the thought of getting all wet and soapy with her has me almost ready to fucking explode.

Setting Gigi down on the vanity, I reach in to turn on the taps. Then turning back around to get my girl, I find her hungry stare firmly plastered to my ass. "Would you like to take a photo?" I question, a wicked smirk stretching across my lips.

"Mmmm," she groans. "Only if I can frame it and put it up on my bedside table."

"You're fucking trouble, Gigi," I tell her, stepping right into her and scooping her off the vanity, only to pin her up against the cold tiles of the shower, laughing as she screeches and tries to get away from them.

"Hold still, baby," I grumble, leaning into her and pressing my lips against her neck. "I'm not finished with you yet."

Reaching for the body wash, I flick it open with my thumb before up-ending it and letting the cool liquid slowly run out, dropping against the curve of her breasts.

She sucks in a breath, and I give the bottle a little squeeze, watching as cold soap lands against her and runs down her body, leaving a cool trail behind. Her eyes flame as she silently watches me place the bottle back on the shelf.

Then just when she thinks she's got a handle on this, the cool liquid reaches that heavenly place between her legs and she lets out a low groan.

Glancing down her body, I take my time, appreciating every inch of it. I bring my hand up and touch the soap on her breasts and slowly begin spreading it over her delicious curves. She closes her eyes in satisfaction, but they pop open the second my fingers follow the trail of soap that leads down her stomach.

Cupping her pussy, I give a gentle squeeze, grinning as she grinds down against me, but I don't give her what she needs, not yet. Instead, I spread the soap over her body and she moves with me, taking in every sensual touch.

My hands roam over her body, exploring every inch of her, and as she pulls me in, our bodies rub together, the soap lathering between us and driving me wild with need. She kisses me and squeezes her hand between us before taking my very hard dick in her hand. She pumps it a few times before grinning and dropping to her knees.

The water rinses off the soap, and before I know it, she's taking me in her mouth, and I lean against the tiles while she takes me deep. She works me up and down and my eyes roll in my head, feeling my balls tighten. Her tongue is like fucking magic, and she quickly brings me to the edge, but I need to be inside her again, need to feel the way her tight cunt squeezes around my cock.

Grabbing her arms, I pull her to her feet and she pouts for just a moment, and I realize she couldn't wait to make me come, but I'll make it up to her tenfold.

Spinning her around, I take her hips as she thrusts her ass back toward me, bracing her hands against the cold tiles. I line myself up with her entrance, and as my fingers bite into her hips, I slam into her. Gigi screams out and pushes back against the wall, taking me deeper, and I pound into her until we're both coming undone in a blazing release of ecstasy.

As soon as we're done, Gigi collapses against my chest, more than exhausted on her shaky legs. Not wanting her to hurt herself in the shower, I reach around and shut off the water before grabbing a towel and wrapping it around her.

The need to take her to my bed burns within me, but I know she isn't comfortable in there, so I take us downstairs to the living room and fall onto the massive couch before pulling her into my arms. She snuggles into me as though this is the only place she would ever want to be, and with a few hours to spare before I have to get Georgie, I put on a movie. It only takes a minute for Gigi to fall into a peaceful sleep in my arms.

I lay awake beside her feeling completely at ease for the first time in three years. This woman has somehow managed to put the broken pieces of my heart back together. When I told her I was in love with her, I meant every last word, and I can't wait to see how our relationship develops from here. All I know is that I won't ever let her go.

When this whole *start dating again* bullshit was thrown my way, I was convinced it would feel as though I was attempting to replace Sara, but now with Gigi in my arms, I see just how wrong I was. Sara is still right there, always in my heart and mind, right alongside Gigi. Sara is the mother of my child and the woman I married. She always will be, and nothing can take that away. But Gigi is my future, and she accepts that Sara will forever be a part of my life. Not only that, but she respects and encourages it, which is so much more than I could ever ask for. Gigi is everything I needed to bring me back to life.

I wake Gigi with a kiss an hour before I need to leave, and she smiles up at me, warming my thawing heart. "Hi," she murmurs.

"Are you hungry?" I question.

"I could eat," she says with a smile, her voice thick with sleep.

"Good," I tell her as my finger runs down her cheek, past her neck, and between those perfect breasts. "As much as I hate to say this," I tell her with a heavy sigh, "you need to get dressed."

"Really?" she frowns.

A laugh rumbles through my chest. "Yeah, babe."

She sits up on the couch and rubs at her tired eyes. "Do you know where you tossed my clothes?"

"Unfortunately," I mutter under my breath, hating that she needs to cover up that beautiful body.

Gigi gives me a cheeky as fuck grin as she puts on an award-winning show while getting dressed into her underwear. I get up off the couch and head over to the kitchen counter where her top lays carelessly on the floor. Scooping it up, I make my way back into the living room and reluctantly hand it over, watching with disappointment as she pulls it over her head. "I should have burned it," I tell her.

With that, I get myself dressed, grab my shit off the table, and take her hand in mine to lead her out the door.

Chapter Twenty-Three

GIGI

Sitting in the cutest little princess bed with Georgie curled up beside me, I close her bedtime story and get ready to tuck her in, wondering how the hell she so easily twists my arm. "Can you wread it again?" she asks, looking up at me with those big blue eyes, ones I've come to realize look exactly like her mom's.

"No," I laugh as I bop her nose with my finger. "I've already read it three times."

She lets out a little huff before a cheeky sparkle lights up her eyes. "You could wread a different one," she suggests. "You haven't wread a different one free times."

"Georgie," I warn, trying to keep the smile from tearing across my face, knowing damn well if she were to try just one more time, I would cave.

"Fine," she pouts, and I can just imagine that if we were anywhere else and she wasn't curled up in her bed, she'd be stomping her little foot right about now. "Do you have to go?"

"No, not yet," I smile as I reach over and grab her inhaler. "But you do need to take your medicine first."

She instantly sits up and does an excellent job of taking slow deep breaths as I administer her Ventolin. Then as soon as she's done, I replace the inhaler with a glass of water and she does a damn good job on that too, making me nervous about her bed sheets for the middle of the night.

She snuggles back into my side, and I curl my arm around her little body as Sean appears in her doorway, probably wondering why the hell this tuck-in is taking so long. "Do you want to know a secret?" I whisper.

"Uh-huh," she says excitedly, her little head vigorously nodding up and down.

A wide grin cuts across my face and I try my best to smother it before giving her a serious stare. "My name isn't Gigi," I tell her.

Her mouth drops as she looks up at me in horror, her little mind blown. "Yes, it is," she demands, her brows furrowed. "My daddy said it is."

I shake my head and she looks at me as if I'm the biggest liar on the planet, and I don't doubt she's already planning on telling her daddy all about my wicked ways. "Gigi is my nickname, just like Georgie is your nickname."

"Really?" she asks, with wide eyes.

"Uh-huh. My actual name is Georgia, just like yours."

She sucks in the biggest breath I've ever seen, and I'm thankful she's just had her inhaler. Excitement booms over her face. "Wow," she laughs as she looks to her daddy for confirmation, clearly not believing it until her daddy says it's so. He gives her a nod and she turns back to me before holding me tighter, her face squished into my shoulder. And call me crazy, but it's almost as if she's connecting herself to me with an invisible tether.

Placing her book on the floor, I scooch down in her bed, and she does the same before curling into my side again. I run my fingers through her hair and watch as the world's biggest yawn rips through her chest. "Can I tell you something?" I say, quietly.

I feel her head nodding against my arm, as a strange nervousness settles into my heart. "I'm in love with your daddy, and if it's alright with you, I'd like to spend some more time with the two of you."

She's silent for a moment, and as I look down at her, I find her brows furrowed, and it's clear she's deep in thought. Curiosity filters through my veins, and I glance at Sean, finding the same look in his eyes.

I give her the moment she needs to work out the thoughts floating around in her head, and when she finally looks back up at me with hope in her eyes, she tears me apart. "Are you going to be my mommy?"

Oh shit.

How the hell am I going to answer this without tearing her heart open? Sean walks into the room and sits at the edge of the bed, his hand resting on her little foot. He glances at me, and I can tell he's about to answer, but I shake my head, hoping he's okay with me taking the lead on this one.

Reaching across to Georgie's bedside table, I take the photo of Sara and hold it above us so she can see it perfectly. "I wish I was lucky enough to be your mommy because you're the most beautiful little girl I've ever met. But you already have a mommy and even though she doesn't get to be here, I bet she wouldn't be too happy with me if I stole you away."

Georgie shakes her head and her bottom lip pouts out. "Is this your mommy in the picture?" I ask.

"Uh-huh," she says, reaching up and taking the picture out of my hands. "Daddy says she's my mommy, but I don't know her."

"I know, sweetie, but I bet she knows you," I tell her. "I think she looks down on you every single day to make sure you're safe and happy."

"Wreally?"

"Yeah, Georgie."

She lets out a broken sigh, and I look up at Sean, a little unsure of what to do, and I watch as he squeezes her foot, bringing her attention to him. "What's wrong, baby?" he asks.

She looks up at him with her heart on her sleeve and the pain in her eyes nearly kills me. "All da kids at preschool get picked up by dere mommies."

My heart shatters, and I pull her in closer, tucking her into my chest and holding her tight as little tears appear in her eyes. The pain is clear across Sean's face, and I desperately want to pull him in too, but I don't dare let go of Georgie. "Would it be alright if I picked you up from preschool sometimes?" I ask.

"But you're not my mommy," she says.

"I know," I tell her, my hand brushing over her hair. "But I'm going to love you like one."

Her little face instantly brightens and a cheeky sparkle returns to her eyes. "So, I can hab anoder book?"

Sean lets out an amused sigh and rolls his eyes, realizing we just got played by a three-year-old. "What am I going to do with you, Georgie Girl?" he murmurs, grabbing another book off of her bookshelf and ordering us to scooch over. He climbs in and Georgie instantly starts giggling like she's just gotten away with murder. She has her father wrapped around her little finger. Hell, she's got me there too.

Sean reads her the story before she finally accepts it's time for bed and pulls her blankets right up to her chin. He kisses her on the forehead, and after switching on the baby monitor, we make our way out of her room.

Sean takes my hand as we walk down the hallway. Right before we hit the stairs, he tugs my hand, bringing me to a stop and crowding me against the wall. He presses a soft, lingering kiss to my lips, and when he pulls back, I stare up into his eyes, completely breathless. "You're amazing with her," he tells me.

I smile up at him. "I can't help it. She's beautiful."

"She is," he agrees, undeniable love shining in his eyes. "Will you stay here tonight?"

"Are you sure?" I question. I mean, I've been here all day, the last thing I want to do is push my luck. He said he loved me this morning, but now we're in his home with the memory of his wife. I don't want to rush it and force him to take a step back.

His eyes soften. "I'm positive," he tells me, sincerity in his deep tone.

"Then I'd like nothing more."

A big cheesy smile cuts across his face, and he scoops me up into his arms and starts walking back down the hallway. And as he approaches his bedroom, a slight panic pulses through me when he walks straight past it and into one of his many spare rooms.

He lays me down on the bed and comes down on top of me, propping himself up on his elbows and caging me between them. "I'm meeting my family for lunch tomorrow. Did you want to come?"

Wow. This is a big step.

I know I've already met the family, but this will be meeting the family as the woman he loves, not the woman who he was roped into taking out. "I'd love to," I murmur. "Your family is hilarious."

"Yeah," he grunts sarcastically. "They think so."

I grin up at him and hook my legs around his waist. "You're such a dork," I giggle.

He grabs my arms and pins them to the bed before slipping his hand up my shirt and trailing it higher toward my tits. "Oh yeah?" he questions, his lips on my neck. "Tell me, can a dork fuck you like I can?"

Oh, God.

The hunger bursts through his eyes, and the way he looks down at me has me weak, and I realize just how much I love this side of him.

"I'm waiting," he challenges, demanding me to answer.

Pressing my lips together in a firm line I shake my head, refusing to give in to him, despite knowing damn well that nobody could ever fuck me the way he does. He releases my arms and pushes back to his knees, and as his hands run down my body, goosebumps spread across my skin.

His eyes flame, loving my body's reaction to his touch, which lights a fire within me. "You're trouble, Gigi," he murmurs as his fingers gently brush across my stomach.

"You've got no idea," I tell him, and as he leans back down, he presses a kiss to my stomach before another on my hip. He raises back up and hooks his fingers into the waistband of my thong before sliding it down my legs, and I eagerly welcome his every touch.

Sean climbs back up my body and presses his lips to mine as he shimmies my shirt up between us, and the second my clothes are gone, I wrap my arms around him and latch onto the material of his shirt. I pull it up over his head and throw it aside before digging my nails into his back, desperate for anything he's willing to give me.

He wedges his body between my legs and slowly makes his way down as anticipation builds in my stomach, knowing whatever he has in store for me is going to be amazing. With his face between my legs, I've never felt so exposed, yet with Sean, all it does is turn me on that much more.

Just like on the couch this morning, I find myself pushing up onto my elbows as his face ducks down, his eyes shining with the darkest desire. His arms scoop under my thighs and wrap around my body, cupping my tits, and with that, he closes the gap, his warm lips closing over my clit and driving me wild.

His tongue grazes past my clit, and the tiny touch has my eyes closing in pure delight, my head falling back as I try to tighten my legs around him. And then he goes to fucking town.

My hands fist into the sheets as he adds his fingers into the mix, working my body in a way that only Sean Waters could possibly do, and it doesn't take long until my world is exploding.

I come around his fingers, but he continues his sensual assault on my body as I ride out one hell of an orgasm. My breath comes hard and fast and he climbs back up my body with a proud grin before kissing me deeply, letting me taste myself as his thick cock settles between my legs.

Reaching down, I curl my hand around his base and work my way up, loving the feel of those angry veins beneath my fingers. I pump a few times before adjusting myself and guiding him into me. He pushes up, and I swear, every time this man is inside me, he somehow manages to fill me more than before.

Sean holds me tight, and I let out a needy groan as he sets his pace, working my body just right. His lips never leave mine, and as I tighten my legs around him, he makes the sweetest love to me. "I love you, Gigi," he tells me as he looks down into my eyes, pushing my body closer to the edge.

Wow. Nothing is better than this.

His hands slide up my body and find mine before lacing our fingers together. "I love you, too," I murmur as his lips come back to mine, my heart swelling with undeniable happiness.

My grip on his hand tightens as we both get closer to what is going to be an amazing finale, and as we continue moving as one, our bodies are pushed to their limits, growing sweaty and hot in the best ways. Hell, I've never felt so alive.

Sean thrusts up into me one more time, and I groan out as my orgasm rips through me, my walls clenching down around his glorious cock just as he comes with me, both of us in a world of utter bliss.

As we come down from the high, Sean drops his forehead to mine as I desperately try to catch my breath, my chest heaving with heavy pants. "Wow," I murmur, my hand still clutched so tightly in his. "I've never felt a connection like this before."

His eyes shine with adoration, and I see my whole future playing out before me. "You're incredible, Gigi," he tells me. "It's only going to get better from here on out."

"I can't wait," I smile.

He reaches down and pulls the blanket right up over our heads, grabbing me by the waist and rolling us until I'm on top, and after blowing my mind three more times, I finally curl into his side as he presses a kiss to my temple. "Sweet dreams, beautiful girl."

"Sweet dreams, Sean."

Chapter Twenty-Four

SEAN

After pulling up outside Gigi's apartment complex, I head around to Georgie's door to unbuckle her from her car seat, only she puts up a fight, demanding that Gigi be the one to unbuckle her. And at this point, I'm positive my daughter loves Gigi more than she loves me.

Naturally, Gigi is more than happy to jump in and struts around the side of my truck, looking smug as fuck with that wide grin stretching across her face.

Gigi unbuckles her and pulls Georgie out of the truck, and as she goes to settle her on her feet, Georgie screams and demands to be held. I'm about to object and step in when Gigi's face beams with delight, and she effortlessly perches my daughter on her hip.

I shake my head, realizing just how much trouble these two together are going to be. It's all good and sweet now, but what about when they figure out how easy it'll be to gang up on me?

Shit.

After holding the door open for my girls, we walk up the hallway to Gigi's apartment, my hand on Gigi's lower back as she holds onto my daughter. Reaching Gigi's door, I quickly open it for her and usher my girls inside, and the second Gigi puts Georgie down, she takes off like a fucking rocket, running around the apartment like a dog that just got hit with the zoomies.

Glancing up from Georgie, I find Mel walking around the kitchen, her legs so far apart that I fear she may end up in the splits. I go to say something when Gigi beats me to it, grunting at her best friend. "Why the hell are you walking like that?"

Mel turns a ferocious glare on Gigi and it quickly turns into a pout. "I got a hot wax this morning and the bitch burned my pussy. I have blisters, Gigi," she cries. "Fucking blisters on my vag."

Fuck. Don't laugh. Don't fucking laugh. It won't be worth it. Hold it together, man. Come on, you can do this.

Gigi hurries over to Mel as I force myself to look away and find my composure, pressing my lips into a hard line, desperately trying to muffle my laugh. "Are you sure Tom didn't give you an STD?" Gigi questions, making it that much harder.

"I don't have a fucking STD, Gi," Mel snaps before pulling herself out of Gigi's arms and grabbing the hem of her skirt. She rips it right up her body to show Gigi her burns just as Georgie appears from around the corner.

Georgie's eyes go wide before she slaps a hand over her eyes and I quickly grab her, pulling her away and shoving her face into my thigh to block her view as Gigi gets busy inspecting her best friend's pussy. "Shit, Mel. This is bad. Have you put anything on it?"

"Not yet," she whines as she finally drops her skirt back into place. "It hurts too bad."

"Go sit down," Gigi orders. "I have a good burn cream in the medicine cabinet."

Gigi disappears down the hallway and Georgie and I stand awkwardly by the front door, watching as Mel waddles over to the couch and falls straight onto her back. She throws one leg up over the backrest while leaving the other on the ground, I guess to air out her pussy. I don't fucking know, but seeing your best friend's girl spread eagle on her couch is more than a little uncomfortable.

Mel's head pops up from the couch and she looks at me through her open legs. "Hey, Sean," she says with a tight smile.

"Mel," I nod, trying to keep it short and simple.

"Sorry, I, uhh . . . didn't realize Georgie had come back into the room," she says about the display she put my impressionable daughter through. I mean, I wouldn't be surprised if Georgie starts flashing herself to the kids at preschool on Monday.

"It's fine," I say, wanting to move right along.

Gigi appears moments later and bursts into laughter as she takes

Mel in on the couch. "Here," she finally says as she hands her the cream. "I'd offer to do it for you but I'm not putting my hands all over your STD-ridden cooch."

"It's not an STD," Mel throws back at her, catching Gigi's grin and realizing she's just teasing. "Besides, anyone would be lucky to get to spread cream all over my coochy, I know Tom enjoys it."

"Uggghhhhh," Gigi says, pretending to gag.

"You know you love it," Mel laughs as I follow Gigi back down the hallway to her bedroom. I put Georgie down and she goes nuts with a new room to explore, diving through all of Gigi's things.

I drop down on the edge of Gigi's bed as she rifles through her closet and pulls out a pair of dark jeans and a black top before quickly pulling them on. She grabs her boots and a jacket then fluffs up her hair in her tiny mirror, and all I can do is stare. She looks stunning, and I can't wait to show her off to my family again.

We leave Mel behind to tend to her scorched pussy, and before I know it, we're pulling up at the restaurant. Georgie does a repeat performance and demands Gigi get her out of her car seat, and to be honest, I'm fucking jealous.

I love doing things for Georgie, even the small things like getting her out of my truck, but I guess I'm going to have to get used to sharing. I love that Georgie loves Gigi, but it would be nice if Georgie could pretend that she still remembers who I am every now and then. Though as she gets used to Gigi being around, she'll settle back into her old self. For now, she's just excited.

As we walk into the restaurant, all hell breaks loose. Brianna and

Carter's twins notice us first and squeal at the same time, making all heads turn our way, and with that everyone is on their feet. They crowd up, saying hello and checking on Georgie while putting in the extra effort to welcome Gigi.

After the long, drawn-out hellos, we get comfortable at the table while Georgie crawls around under it, giggling like a hyena as she unties everyone's shoelaces. The waiter comes and takes our orders and returns moments later with a few bottles of champagne before getting busy filling a glass for everyone.

Everyone is having a great time when Cassie speaks up, her narrowed gaze locked on her best friend. "What's the matter with you?" she asks, staring at Brianna. "You're not drinking."

My gaze flicks down to Brianna's champagne and realize it's been left untouched, which isn't a cause for alarm, apart from the fact it's Brianna. She never skips out on a good drink. Then before she has a chance to say anything, I realize my thoughts have been right. Carter and Bri are expecting another baby.

A grin rips across my face as Brianna looks at Carter, letting him take the lead on this one. He laces his fingers through hers on the table before glancing back at everyone, pride flashing in his eyes. Carter's chest inflates as if he's about to say something when Logan flies to his feet with his drink in his hand. "Fuck yeah," he cheers, raising his glass to Brianna and Carter.

Cheers boom through the restaurant while Cassie stares at her best friend in confusion, her brows furrowed. "What the fuck am I missing here?" she questions.

"Babe," Jax chuckles. "Your brother knocked up your best friend again."

"What?" she screeches as she flies to her feet and practically crawls across the table to get to her best friend, having to stop halfway as she starts sobbing with uncontrollable happiness.

Logan clears his throat and gains the table's attention. "While we're at it," he says, looking down at his wife with love. "Elle's pregnant, too."

What. The. Fuck?

A grin rips across my face, and I hardly know where to look. Do I smile at Bri? Do I smile at Elle? Do I look at Georgie to see if she understands what's going on? Do I collapse to the ground out of pure happiness?

Holy shit.

I came here today expecting one pregnancy announcement, but two? Wow. Our family is growing, and I can't wait to meet these little guys.

Fuck, I wish Mom and Dad were here to see this. I could just imagine Mom's face.

Gigi squeezes my hand under the table and gives me a beaming smile, and I can't help but feel just how right it is to have her here with my family, my two worlds colliding. And damn it, I can't resist leaning over and pressing a kiss to her warm lips.

I order another bottle of champagne for the table, and just as the party really gets started, a short Italian man frantically rushes into the restaurant, screaming for help. "Please, someone," he yells in a thick

Italian accent. "I need a doctor. My wife is having a baby."

Without even a moment of hesitation, Gigi flies to her feet and shoots toward the man, and I follow behind in case she needs anything. "My name is Gigi. I'm a trained midwife," she says to the man, her hand on his shoulder in a calming gesture. "Where's your wife?"

"She's in the car," he rushes out before flying back out of the restaurant door. "We were on the way to the hospital, but she's not going to make it. I can see the baby's head."

"Shit," she grunts under her breath as we hurry out behind them. "Sir, have you called an ambulance?"

He looks startled at the question, and I pull my phone out to begin dialing.

Reaching the car, we find the public starting to crowd around, and Gigi simply barges past them before leaning down in the open car door and taking the woman's hand, so fucking calm as she looks at the woman screaming out in pain. "Hi ma'am, I'm Gigi. I'm going to help you," she says, squeezing her hand. "Are you able to get out of the car?"

The woman tries to move but she's too far along, and she hastily shakes her head, panic flashing in her eyes. "I need to push," she screams at Gigi.

"Alright," she says as calmly as ever before turning to me. "Can you help her out of the car?"

I nod and throw my phone to Logan who catches it and instantly continues the conversation with the emergency operator. Then diving into the open doorway with the woman's husband, we help get her out as Gigi demands someone grab a shit load of towels and blankets. Though I don't know where the fuck we'll find them out in the street.

The waiter from the restaurant brings out bottled water with a pile of clean tablecloths and we finally get the woman down on the ground. Her husband climbs in behind her to help support her back, and I stand patiently beside Gigi, waiting for any instructions if she needs help. Then all too aware of the onlookers, Gigi spares me a quick glance. "Can you get someone to hold up a blanket? She needs privacy."

I get straight to it and within seconds Jax is right there, quickly unfolding one of the many tablecloths and handing one end to a guy in the street, making a partition between the onlookers and the woman.

"Alright, ma'am, I'm going to remove your underwear," she tells the woman as she reaches forward. "What's your name?"

"I'm Lucia," she practically screams at Gigi.

"Okay, Lucia. I can see your baby's head, so you're going to have to prepare to push on your next contraction," she says, blowing me the fuck away with how calm and professional she is, but then she goes and glances up at me. "Grab someone who's not squeamish and get down here. One at each leg."

Ahh, fuck.

I do as she instructs, and before I know it, both Logan and I are in the firing zone, glancing up at each other over the woman's legs, horror in both our eyes.

"How far out is the ambulance?" Gigi questions.

"Still a few minutes. There's an accident backing up traffic," Logan explains.

"Shit, alright," Gigi says, pressing her lips into a hard line. "Looks like we're delivering this baby."

Fear flashes in Lucia's eyes as she looks at Gigi. "The contraction is coming."

Gigi explains to Lucia how she wants her to push as Logan's eyes widen, and judging by the look in his eyes, I'd bet he's wondering how the fuck our nice lunch turned into this.

Gigi gets me and Logan to hold the woman's legs up, and I've never felt so uncomfortable in my life, but there's not a damn thing we can do about it before the woman starts screaming. Her husband does his best to calm her, but she's squeezing the life out of his hand, making him scream right along with her. "Okay, Lucia," Gigi says over the noise. "You're going to give a great big push while Sean counts back from ten."

Shit. I momentarily forget what the fuck numbers are before jumping into action and trying to remember what the fuck comes after seven. "Slower," Gigi murmurs, her voice low.

We get all the way down to one when her contraction stops, and I feel like both me and Logan are breathing just as hard as the woman. "Another push on the next contraction and we'll have the head out. You're doing great Lucia."

Just as I knew she would, Gigi coaches her through the next one, and I find myself staring down at the baby's head sticking out of its mother's vagina—not exactly the sight I thought I'd be looking at after eating my lunch.

Gigi checks the positioning of the umbilical cord and explains what's going to happen next as I hear my daughter in the background asking what's going on and wondering where her daddy has gone. Hoping like fuck one of her aunties has got her rather than leaving her to run around the street by herself.

The next contraction has the baby coming the rest of the way out, and it's so fucking gross, but it's also incredibly beautiful. If I was a weaker man, I'd be tearing up right now, the same way the woman's husband is sobbing behind her.

Witnessing a child being brought into the world is a miracle. I didn't get to see Georgie's birth like that, but nonetheless, it was still extraordinary.

Gigi reaches through the woman's legs and places the baby boy on his mother's chest as Lucia tears up, looking down at her little man. Cheers and applause are heard all around, and I feel the greatest sense of pride in Gigi. What she has done today for this family was incredible. I can't imagine what would have happened if she wasn't here.

"Thank you," the new mother says as she looks up at us all. She gives a grateful smile to Gigi who looks as though she's on cloud fucking nine.

Tablecloths and towels are tossed around, and the new parents go about cleaning him off when the ambulance finally arrives. Gigi jumps up off the ground and talks to the paramedic, who by the looks of it, is a friend of hers.

The woman is checked over by the paramedics before she's moved into the ambulance with her new baby and husband, leaving us all behind. Gigi smiles, but the rest of us just gape in shock. The second the ambulance disappears around the corner, I take Gigi by the hand and pull her into my arms, not giving a shit about the state of her clothes. "You were amazing," I say as I press my lips against hers.

She looks up at me, quickly searching my eyes to make sure I'm okay before finally deciding she's happy with what she sees. "That was incredible," she tells me. "I absolutely love it, bringing life into the world. It's the best feeling you'll ever know."

"I'll place it right behind loving you and Georgie," I murmur.

She grins up at me before rolling her eyes, but nonetheless, she melts into my chest. "You're so cheesy."

"You love it."

"I do," she tells me. "I can't wait to get back to work on Monday."

"I know," I laugh, my hand dangerously low on her back. "You tell me three times every day."

With that, I lead her back into the restaurant where my family instantly commends her for everything she's done, but Logan is as white as a fucking ghost as he sits beside his wife silently, looking as though he's about to pass out.

Sitting back with Georgie in my lap, I watch proudly as Gigi and the girls talk all about it, going over everything and telling them how incredible it was when she turns back to me, her eyes sparkling with undeniable joy.

Reaching out, I take her hand, seeing my whole future right there by my side. "I love you," I tell her, bringing her hand to my lips and pressing a gentle kiss just above her knuckles, hoping like fuck the paramedics gave her the good shit to clean her hands with.

Gigi's face flames as she notices the eyes of my whole family on us, but despite the attention, she can't help but say it back.

Chapter Twenty-Five

GIGI

Walking around the maternity ward, I quickly check on my patients one last time before heading over to Sue to let her know I'm done for the day. She lets out a relieved sigh as I hand her my paperwork and gives me a fond smile. "It's so good to have you back, Gigi," she says, taking the papers from me.

"Thanks, I've missed it so much," I tell her. "It was only six weeks, but it felt like a lifetime."

"I know, honey," she says, giving me a sad smile and reaching out to squeeze my hand. "I'm just happy to have someone back on this floor who I don't need to constantly be chasing."

I give her a big smile before saying goodnight and heading out to grab my things, feeling a little off this afternoon after overhearing a few nurses gossiping about the shooting, talking about how the shooter was a father of a little girl who died during surgery the week before. He'd been struggling mentally with the loss and had gotten it in his head that the hospital was keeping her from him.

I shook it off, but the thoughts stuck with me right through my shift.

I've been back at work for just over a week, and for the most part, it's been amazing. I've always had a fire within me when I work, but since being back, that fire has only gotten stronger. I don't know if it's because I've missed it so much since being off or because I'm just a happier person since having Sean in my life and finding this intense, beautiful love.

Fuck, I'm so head over heels in love with him.

Letting out a lovesick sigh, I collapse onto the couch in the nurses' lounge, my phone in hand. My feet are aching, but I swear, I'd happily stick around and do the night shift if I was asked.

Unlocking my phone, I go to text Mel and see how she's doing when I find a text already waiting from her.

Mel – Still going to be another hour. Tom is going to pick me up. Go home and spend the night with your man. Love you xxx

Getting back to my feet, a wide smile stretches over my face, and I quickly reply as I make my way to the door, more than happy to get out of here if it means spending the night with Sean.

Gigi – No problem. I'll see you tomorrow. Love you, too. Xx

Making my way out to my car, I bring up Sean's number and shove the phone between my ear and shoulder as I search through my bag for my keys. He answers almost immediately and a soft smile begins spreading over my lips when I hear his deep voice. "Well . . . look who's dying for my attention again?" he jokes.

"Shut up," I laugh, finally finding the keys and unlocking the car. "What are you doing?"

"Just getting home," he tells me. "I had a massive day in court."

"Oh, that's right. How'd your case go?" I ask.

"Do you even need to ask?" he scoffs. "You should know by now that I never lose."

"Ooooh," I tease, dropping down into my car and pulling the door closed behind me. "You know, I think I remember seeing somewhere that you only had a 98% conviction rate, not 100, and honestly . . . aren't you embarrassed?"

"Not at all," he laughs. "I did that on purpose. It's important that those other lawyers think they might stand a chance against me. 100% just seems too unachievable for them. You know, I'm all about the little people."

"Ha," I laugh. "That seems about right."

He lets out a laugh that wraps right around me. "Are you heading home?" he asks.

"I was going to, but Mel's working late and seeing Tom tonight."

"Oh, I see how it is," he teases. "Your original plan bailed and now you want me."

I scoff, unable to wipe the wide grin off my face as I jam the key into the ignition and start my car. "Ugh. Presumptuous much? I never said I wanted to go to your place."

"Like you could fucking resist," he tells me, and damn it, he's never been so right.

"I know," I laugh. "You're always my first choice. You know that, right?"

"I do," he murmurs. "Now hurry up and get that sweet ass over here. Georgie's cooking."

Oh no.

A laugh rumbles through my chest, a wide grin stretched across my face as I picture our impending doom so perfectly. "I can't wait," I tell him. He says a quick goodbye, and I end the call, throwing my phone down on the passenger side before putting my car in reverse and backing out of my spot.

Fifteen minutes later, I pull into Sean's ridiculously long driveway before coming to a stop right at the top. Reaching into the back, I grab my overnight bag that I've learned to always keep packed and ready to go. As I get out of the car, I find myself staring up at the big house, still amazed by its sheer size.

Not bothering to knock, I push my way through the door and the smell of burned Bolognese sauce instantly assaults my senses. A grin pulls at my lips, and I kick my shoes off before walking deeper into

Sean's house. From the kitchen doorway, I find Georgie standing on a chair and stirring her pot of sauce while Sean stands protectively behind her.

"Hi," I smile, taking it all in.

Georgie squeals and pushes her dad out of the way so she can launch herself off the chair and bolt toward me. I catch her in my arms and pull her in tight as Sean turns off the stove and walks over to us, wrapping his arms around both of us and pressing his lips to mine in the sweetest kiss.

"Eeeewwwwwwwww," Georgie whines, dragging it out until she physically can't hold the word a second longer. "No kissing."

Sean kisses me again, and I feel the smile on his lips as he teases his little girl. "But I like kissing her," he tells her.

"No," she demands, shoving her little fist into his chest and pushing him away. "She's mine."

"Nu-uh," he fights back. "She's mine."

Georgie scrunches her face up and sticks her tongue out at her daddy, so I put her down before this shit gets out of hand. Then hearing her shows in the living room, she forgets all about me and takes off like a rocket, singing her songs at the top of her lungs.

With Georgie out of my arms, Sean lunges for me, and I fall right into him where I belong. His hands find my ass, and he lifts me right up onto the counter, stepping between my legs and bringing his lips down on mine in a deep kiss.

"How was your day?" he asks, giving me a moment to catch my breath.

"Amazing. I could pull babies out of vaginas all day," I tell him, watching as he shudders, the memory of helping Lucia deliver her baby on the street still too fresh in his mind. "I wish there were more hours in the day."

"Me too," he agrees, leaning in and letting his lips brush over mine as he talks. "But not so I can work more."

I reach forward and hook my fingers into the waistband of his pants and pull him right into me. "Pray, tell. What would you do with your extra hours?" I whisper as I look up at him through my lashes.

His hands wrap around my body, and he scoots me to the very edge of the counter so that I feel his very hard cock grinding against my core. "You," he tells me. "Always you."

A fond smile stretches across my lips as I look up at him, meeting those intense, dark eyes. I couldn't agree more. If I could spend my life with him between the sheets, I would.

Sean's hand wraps around the back of my neck, and I tilt my chin up just as his warm lips come down on the sensitive skin below my ear, and I have to force myself not to moan, knowing Georgie is in the other room.

My hands slip up under his shirt and roam over his strong chest, never wanting to take my hands off him. "Dinner smells . . . interesting," I tell him.

"Yeah," he chuckles, a fondness flashing in his eyes. "I ordered pizza the second she said she wanted to cook."

"Oh, thank God," I breathe just as the doorbell sounds through the house.

"Good timing," he tells me, reluctantly pulling away to answer the door.

Jumping down from the counter, I pull some plates out of the cupboard before putting them out on the dining table then doubling back for some glasses. "Georgie, honey. Dinner is ready."

She comes bolting out of the living room and flies up into her chair at the table, excitement brimming in her bright eyes. Sean comes in with the pizza and Georgie's face falls. "Where's my sketti?" she asks, the disappointment in her tone breaking my heart.

Sean opens his mouth to answer, but I see him stumbling over how to explain her dinner wasn't edible, so I fix a pout on my face and reach across the table to take her little hand in mine. "Your daddy burned the sauce while you were playing," I tell her.

She sucks in a breath, completely horrified as she looks at her father. "Daddy," she whines.

"I'm sorry, baby," he says, taking the seat beside her and opening the pizza box.

"Maybe you should give him some cooking lessons," I suggest, ever so helpful.

Georgie's whole face brightens, and the way her eyes beam back at me has me feeling as though I could do or be anything I want in this big wide world. "Yeah, and den you could helwp when you live wid us."

"Oh no," Sean breathes, dropping his face into his hand.

My heart starts to race, and I look at Sean, taking in the dread etched into his handsome face. "I'm sorry?" I ask, willing my heart to calm for just a moment. I mean, I could have sworn she said that I was going to live with them.

Seeing Sean hasn't responded, Georgie takes it into her own hands again, digging Sean a deeper hole. "Daddy towld me you were going to live wid us."

I look over at Sean before turning back to Georgie with a comforting smile. "Did he just?"

She nods her head before scooping up a slice of pizza and shoving it into her mouth as Sean glances up and looks at his daughter. "Thanks, kid," he grunts.

"Dat's okay, Daddy," she says, oblivious to the tension now floating around the room.

Sean's gaze shifts to mine, and I see the question deep within them, and I watch as he gets up and walks around the table. He drops down to one knee beside me, and I gasp as I take him in, my stomach in knots.

He takes in the look on my face before glancing down at his position, his eyes widening in horror. "Oh shit, no," he rushes out. "This is really not going how I imagined it would."

Sean shakes his head, dragging a hand down his face before glancing back up at me. "Sorry, I just needed to be closer to you."

Letting out a relieved breath, I feel my heart finally begin to return to a normal rate. Marriage is not something I see for us. Don't get me wrong. I fully intend to spend the rest of my life with him, but he has a wife. She may not be here anymore, but it's not a territory I want to go stomping all over. At least, I don't think so. Maybe in a few years we can revisit the topic.

Sean's hand squeezes my thigh and pulls me out of my thoughts. "I wanted to do something special and blow you away with a grand gesture when I asked you to move in, but someone has a big mouth."

I can't help but flick my gaze back to Georgia, finding her completely engrossed in her pizza. A smile rips across my face, so damn in love with this little girl. Glancing back at Sean, I take his hands and clutch them as though they are my only lifeline. "Are you sure?" I question. "It's not too soon?"

"It's not soon enough," he tells me. "I want you here every day, Gigi. I want us to build a life together. I want to wake up every morning and see your beautiful face looking back at me. What we have is something I'll never find again. So yeah, I'm ready to take that leap with you and start the rest of our lives."

I blink back tears as I reach up and take his face in my hands, warmth spreading through my chest and making my heart swell with love. "You're not going to change your mind?" I ask.

He shakes his head, not taking his eyes off mine for even a second. "No, Gigi. Never," he tells me, pulling me into him and kissing me deeply. The second he releases my lips, he rests his forehead against mine and laces our fingers together. "What do you say, babe? Would you like to move in with us?"

A smile spreads over my face. "Yes," I whisper, the tears falling down my cheeks. "I'd love to."

Sean beams back at me before pulling me right into his arms, scooping me off the chair and getting to his feet, spinning us around as he kisses me with everything he's got.

"Eeewwwwwwwww," comes from that sweet little voice across the table.

I laugh, pulling back just enough to break our kiss, but when I meet his gaze, I find him deep in thought, a slight crease appearing between his eyes. "What's wrong?" I ask.

"I have one condition," he says, settling me back on my feet and keeping his hands on my waist. My mind rushes through all the possibilities, wondering what it could be, and I give a slow nod, desperate to hear this mystery condition. "I want you sleeping in my bedroom."

My eyes widen, and I suck in a breath. Could I do that? Can I sleep in the same bed where his wife once slept? Unease rattles my chest, and I bite down on my healed lip, knowing that for him, I'll try. "I'll make a deal with you," I say.

"Go ahead," he says, his gaze narrowing in suspicion, looking a little terrified.

"I'll sleep in your bedroom if you get a new bed . . . and mattress," I say. "Oh, and new sheets. I want to love you, Sean, but I don't want to replace her. We need our own bed, one that's just ours."

He nods, understanding in his eyes. "I can do that," he tells me.

"I wasn't quite finished," I tell him with a cringe, not sure how he's going to take this one.

"What else, your highness?"

I swallow hard as I prepare for the one thing he might have a problem with. "Can we limit the photos of Sara in the bedroom to just one small one?" His brows furrow as I continue, really hoping he understands where I'm coming from. Then sparing a glance at Georgie, I cringe and try to get this out without saying too much. "We can't be, umm . . . you know, going to town in there while she's staring at me uhhhh . . . playing hide and seek with her husband."

He lets out a breath and I know it's hard for him to let me in like this, but he's trying so hard to give me his whole world. "You have yourself a deal," he murmurs, as I make myself a promise to put those same photos in another area of the house, somewhere I know Sean will see them every day.

"Thank you," I whisper.

He takes my hand in his before letting out a breath. "Now that's out of the way," he grins before dropping down to one knee again.

"Don't push your luck," I laugh.

Sean smirks up at me before flying to his feet and lifting me back into his arms and crushing his lips down on mine. "It was worth a shot," he tells me before finally allowing us to finish our dinner, only the whole time he holds me in his lap.

It's well after Georgie's bedtime when I finally get a chance to check in with Mel, and I crash down on the oversized couch, my phone in hand.

Gigi – So, uhh . . . I sort of agreed to move in with Sean.

Mel – Thank fuck!!!! I started moving my shit into Tom's place two weeks ago.

Gigi – WHAT! How the hell could you not tell me?

Mel – I was too busy denying it. I'll tell you all about it in the morning. Right now, I have a man tied up with chocolate syrup dripping all over his body. Though, I forgot the whipped cream. Do you think he'll be pissed if I left him like this while I ducked down to the store to get some?

Gigi – You have some serious issues, girl!

I barely have a chance to hit send when a strong hand curls around my ankle and starts dragging me down the couch. I squeal, trying to roll over, and before I know it, Sean is hovering over me, his knee pressed up against my center. "I fucking love you so much, Gigi."

A soft smile pulls at my lips as I lock my arms around his neck, pulling him down to kiss him. "I love you, too," I tell him as I look deeply into his warm eyes. "Before you, I thought there was something wrong with me, like I was somehow not good enough or deserving of someone like you, and then you showed up on my Tinder and brought back the woman I used to be."

"You always were that woman, you just didn't know it," he tells me as he pushes my hair behind my ear then kisses me deeply. "Actually," he says, pulling back. "That reminds me. Can I have your phone for a minute?"

My brows furrow and I watch him with a deep suspicion. "Why?"

"I need to delete that damn app."

I let out a laugh and hand him my phone, watching as he goes about deleting my Tinder account and removing the app off the phone. Then after tossing my phone aside, his arms curl around my body, and he lifts me right off the couch and into his arms. "Come on," he says, his lips brushing over mine. "Let me take you to bed."

I smile as I melt into him, my eyes locked so heavily on his. "I'd like nothing more." And with that, he closes the gap and brings his lips down on mine, walking us up the stairs before making me the happiest woman in the world.

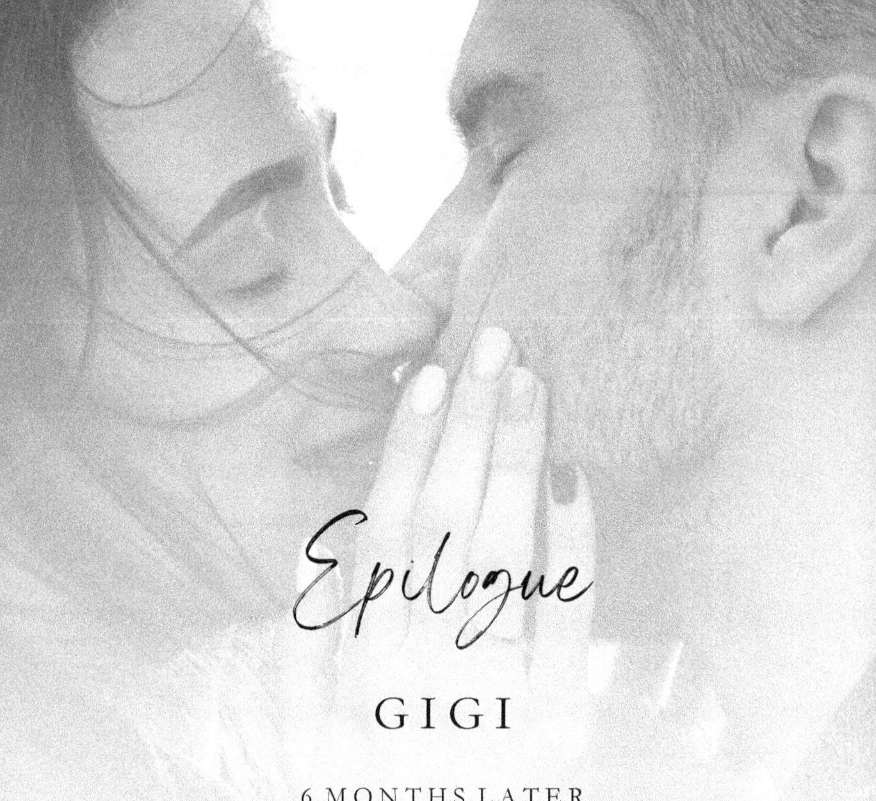

Epilogue

GIGI

6 MONTHS LATER

I sit with all of the girls, including Mel and Georgie, in my living room as we sip champagne. Well Cassie, Mel, and I sip champagne while Elle and Bri throw back as much juice as their little hearts desire since they are busily cooking my future nieces or nephews.

Sean has gone away for a boys' weekend, and knowing those guys, there's no telling what kind of shit they're getting up to, but it doesn't matter to me because I am having the time of my life with the girls.

The house is filled with kids, and it's amazing. It's all I've ever wanted out of life. Having a big family, having the career of my dreams, and having a man who I love and cherish.

I've got it all.

It's been an amazing day when Mel stands up and addresses all the girls. "I feel like dressing up," she says with a big girly grin on her face.

"What?" I mutter, gaping at my best friend. I know she gets a little over the top when she's drinking, but getting all dressed up is simply not her.

"I want to dress up," she repeats. "You know, put on a fancy dress, make my hair all pretty and do my makeup. I mean, what are girl weekends for if we can't dress up? We could go out afterwards, looking like the hottest bunch of bitches in Denver."

"Oooh, I wouldn't mind," Cassie speaks up. "I never get to get all sexy anymore. It's work clothes and then pajamas. I mean, have I told you guys how I tried pole dancing once? Now that was sexy."

"Oh please," Brianna scoffs, a smirk on her lips. "I get sexy every night."

"I bet you do," Cassie laughs as I try not to spit my champagne all over the room.

"So, that's settled then," Elle says. "We're getting beautified."

"Ooooh," Mel shouts. "I'm hiring a hairdresser, masseur, and makeup artist. If we're doing this, then we're doing it right." She pulls her phone out and starts a Google search on mobile makeup artists and hairdressers in the area.

A grin creeps across my face. This isn't how I expected my day to go, but being pampered and getting dressed up sounds absolutely perfect, and I find myself bursting with excitement. I top off the girls' champagne glasses, and before we know it, a hairdresser is knocking on the door while a masseur sets up a table in the living room.

Two hours later, I feel like a queen. I've had a massage, my hair is falling in soft ringlets, my nails are manicured, and my makeup looks absolutely stunning. Hell, all the girls look stunning, but nobody looks better than little Georgie.

Once our team of makeup artists and hairdressers finish packing up, I close the door behind them and send them on their way before turning to Mel. "Thanks," I smile. "This was a great idea."

"It's not over yet," she tells me, her eyes sparkling with excitement. "We still need to put on nice dresses and go out. I think we should go for dinner."

"Oh, hell yeah," Cassie says. "There's no way in hell I'm not going out and showing myself off. Only, I'm gonna need one of you hoes to take some photos of me for Jax. Gotta keep that man on his toes."

"Agreed," Elle says.

As I top up our champagne glasses, I can't tear the smile off my face. We all head upstairs, each with a child or two in our arms, and raid my jewelry and dresses. I don't have many to choose from, but what little I do have is perfect for the job.

I pick out a yellow sundress and Mel shakes her head. "Nope. Too casual," she says before pulling out a floor-length cream dress that I wore to a fundraiser the hospital had put on a few months ago, which is also when the victims of the shooting were formally awarded their payouts.

I still feel a little strange about the money in my bank account, but it's honestly been kind of amazing not having to worry about the financial aspect of life. Not to mention, Mel was so thrilled she scheduled her boob job right away, and I swear, they look amazing. Though, she's still a little sore.

With a smile, I take the dress from her and slip into it while the others get dressed. Even Georgie comes to me with a sequined dress from her closet, and I help pull it over her head before adding just a little lip gloss to finish off the look.

Over the past six months, Georgie and I have become best friends, and I can't get enough of it. Sean adores watching us together, and I adore watching him watching us together. He's always missed having a mother figure for Georgie, and I've easily slipped into that role. But I'm not going to lie, there have been times when I've found myself staring up at the picture of Sara at the top of the stairs and wondering if I'm doing it right.

The sun is just beginning to set when we finally step out of the house, each of us looking our absolute best. It's a beautiful night, but what surprises me more is the limo parked right at the bottom of the stairs, the driver standing by the back door in a suit.

"What the hell?" I gasp as the girls go nuts. "Who did this?"

"I don't know. It could have been Carter," Bri says, her eyes sparkling with the thought. "I told him we were dressing up and going out."

I smile at Bri, "Remind me to thank that husband of yours."

"Don't worry, I'll thank him enough for all of us," she says with a wink. "With these pregnancy hormones, I haven't been able to keep off of him. Good thing he's the devil in bed."

"Ewww," Cassie groans. "You have to stop talking about your sex life around me."

Georgie looks up at me, pulling on my dress to get my attention. "What's sex, Gigi?"

Ahhhh shit.

Every single eye goes wide.

Cassie slaps a hand over her mouth while the rest of us burst into uncontrollable laughter. "That's something you'll have to talk to your daddy about when you're a bit older," I tell her, watching as she pouts, wanting answers right here and now. Though I have to admit, when she does finally decide to talk to her daddy about it, I'd love to be a fly on the wall. Watching Sean sweat is one of my favorite things to do.

The driver opens the car door and all talk of sex fades away, Georgie's eyes lighting up like Christmas morning. The driver explains that he's had car seats put in for all the kids, and I smile at the tiny details Carter remembered. Bri really did get herself a good man, not better than mine though. Close maybe.

We all climb in, and the second the kids are buckled in and safe, the driver hits the gas, and it doesn't take long before I realize he's heading in the wrong direction. I go to say something when he rolls to a stop outside a very familiar park, and as I glance out the window, a wide smile stretches across my face, finding the park set up with the sweetest little wedding.

Little white chairs are set up with rose petals scattered down the aisle, but nothing beats the beautiful lanterns hanging from the trees, casting a light glow over the setting below.

"Wow," I whisper to Mel, taking it all in. "That's beautiful. Take a picture. If I ever get married, that's how I'd want it to be."

"Okay," she agrees as she goes about pulling her phone out and taking a quick photo.

Movement across the park catches my attention, and I shift my gaze, my brows furrowing as I find Sean striding toward the limo, a breathtaking smile pulling at his lips.

What in the sweet baby Jesus is going on here?

My gaze travels over him in a suit, and my mouth starts to water. I love him in his suits. Every morning he leaves to go to court, I have to physically restrain myself to keep from jumping him. But this suit? Mmmmm. This suit is special.

I distantly notice his brothers, Jax, and Tom behind him and my heart starts to race. I have no fucking idea what's going on. I mean, what the hell? He's supposed to be on a boys' weekend riding, not looking like sex on legs in a suit and making my ovaries scream.

Movement from the opposite side of the park catches my eyes, which is when I notice my parents and my closest friends and colleagues. "What the hell is going on?" I ask the girls, but not one of them says a word as they try to hide their secretive smiles and make their way out of the limo.

"Mel," I warn, needing answers, my hands starting to sweat. "What's going on?"

She turns back to me with a proud smile and pulls me into her arms, her eyes welling with tears. "You look beautiful," she says before scooting out of the car.

I follow behind, and by the time I'm safely on the pavement, Sean is right there taking both my hands in his. He looks at me with love in his eyes as the rest of our group heads toward the empty chairs under the lanterns.

"Fuck, you're breathtaking," he says as he pulls me in and presses a kiss to my forehead.

"Sean?" I ask, pulling back to peer up into his dark eyes. "What the hell is going on?"

"I'm about to make you my wife," he tells me with a fierce determination that has my heart lurching in my chest.

I shake my head, my mind thoroughly blown. "But," I start to protest.

"No buts, Gigi. We're doing this," he tells me, squeezing my hands and letting me see the sincerity and raw honesty in his eyes. "I know this is what you want. You want it so bad but you're scared to talk to me about it because you think it's too soon or that I don't want it, too, but I do. I want it all with you."

"What about Sara?" I murmur as I look up at him through my lashes.

"Sara would be rolling over in her grave if I didn't take this step with you. She's always wanted what's best for me, and that's you. I love you so much it hurts, and I couldn't imagine living my life without you. I already know what it feels like to lose someone, and I'll be damned if I ever let you get away."

Sean pauses, giving me just a second to wrap my head around this before going on. "I want to give you the world, just like you've done for me. So, what do you say, Gigi?" he asks as he gets down on one knee with my hand firmly in his. "Will you do me the greatest honor of becoming my wife?"

Holy shit.

I gape at the man who holds my whole heart as absolute joy pulses through my veins and fills me with elation, tears welling in my eyes and escaping down my cheeks.

I wait barely a second before it becomes too much, and I launch myself at him, my arms flying around him as he stumbles back onto the pavement, holding me tight. "Yes. Yes, of course, I will," I tell him, my lips crashing down over his as he laughs through our kiss, his grip so damn tight on my body.

Sean eventually gets us back to our feet when his hands fall to mine, squeezing them tight. "Come on," he tells me. "Let's go make an honest woman out of you."

With that, he turns toward our family and friends who all stand congregated around the white chairs with the lanterns sparkling so beautifully above them. "She said yes," he calls out for them.

Booming cheers and applause echo throughout the park, and I have no doubt that it's heard right up the street. Then with a beaming smile across my face, I walk with Sean down to our family, ready to start the beginning of the rest of our lives.

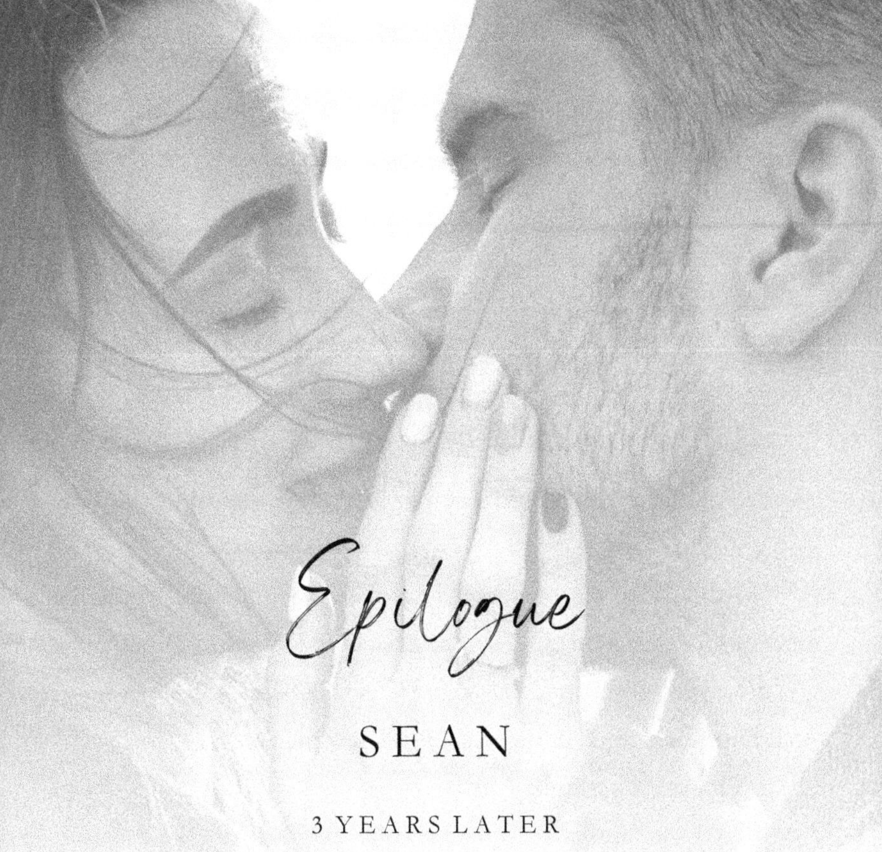

Epilogue

SEAN

3 YEARS LATER

My bedroom door is all but kicked down as Georgie comes barging in and throws herself into the center of our bed. "It's my birthday! It's my birthday!" she screeches, the excitement overwhelming her. "I'm six now. I'm a big girl."

"Yeah, you are," I say, sitting up in bed next to Gigi just in time for Georgie to come barreling into my arms and knock me right back down to my pillow, her squeals waking her baby sister.

Gigi reaches over and takes little Sara out of her bassinet and holds her close to her chest as she soothes the screaming baby. Georgie crawls in between me and Gigi, and I pull her in close before pressing a big kiss to her cheek, "Happy birthday, my big girl."

She beams up at me, but a baby is soon thrust into my arms as Georgie is stolen from beside me and pulled into Gigi's arms. "Happy Birthday," Gigi booms as she squishes Georgie into her so hard I fear her head might pop off.

Georgie giggles, but it's not over yet as Gigi pins her to the bed and starts smothering her with kisses. She squeals and laughs, trying to push Gigi off her, not getting away with it until little baby Sara starts crying for her breakfast.

We switch children and Gigi whips her tits out before getting the baby fed. I watch with pure joy. Sara is only two months old, and I still get the biggest thrill out of watching Gigi with her. Georgie never got to do this stuff with her mom, so it's all new for me.

It's fucking incredible.

"Do I get presents?" Georgie asks, standing on the bed and bouncing so hard the baby pops off Gigi's tit, sending milk squirting across the bed.

"You sure do," I laugh, climbing out of bed as Gigi hastily shoves her tit back in the baby's mouth and starts mopping up the spilled milk. "But you have to go put your slippers on."

With that, she bolts out the door, and Gigi and I meet her on the staircase, the baby still clutched in Gigi's arms. We make our way down the stairs as a family, and as we reach the bottom, I turn and glance down at Georgie. "You need to close your eyes," I tell her.

She grins up at me and puts her hand over her eyes, with her fingers slightly splayed so she can peek right through the cracks. Knowing my daughter too well, I pull a blindfold out of my pocket and wrap it around her head as she groans, then just for good measure, I spin her a few times.

She giggles as I guide her down the hallway with Gigi following behind to record the moment, and I open the door to the room we currently have all her toys stashed in. "Happy Birthday, beautiful girl," I tell her, removing the blindfold.

Her eyes bug out of her head as she takes in the room that my brothers and I spent all of yesterday redoing. Rather than a plain room with toys in it, it's now been transformed into a very pink princess castle filled with everything a princess could possibly need.

"Wow," she screams before diving straight in.

I turn back to Gigi and give her a massive grin that matches the one already plastered on her face. "That couldn't have gone any better," I tell her as I step back and wrap my arm around her waist, both of us looking in on our birthday girl.

Gigi finishes feeding Sara before handing her off to me and disappearing to the kitchen, and I get comfortable in Georgie's castle while she goes absolutely nuts, playing with everything.

Soon enough, Gigi returns with a massive stack of pancakes and sits down beside me as Georgie's nose acts as a food radar and comes crashing down between us, narrowly missing her sister.

Leaning back against the wall, I sit with my perfect family, watching as they inhale their pancakes. I've been through hell to get here, and while there's still a dull ache that will forever reside in my chest, I've never been happier. I have the most beautiful children in the world and have a wife who blows me away every damn day.

My heart still hurts each and every time I think of Sara, but I know that it was her who has given me this life. She watches over us, and I don't know how, but I'm certain that she brought Gigi to me when I needed her most, and for that, I'll never be able to thank her enough.

My thoughts are cut short when Georgie bounces into my lap. "Can we get ready for my party now? Pleasssssssse Daddy."

Gigi laces her fingers through mine and gives them a squeeze. When I look over at my gorgeous wife, my heart races seeing the most radiant smile across her face. "Yeah, kid," I smile back down at Georgie, my heart never so full. "Let's get ready."

Thanks for reading

If you enjoyed reading this book as much as I enjoyed writing it, please consider leaving an Amazon review to let me know.

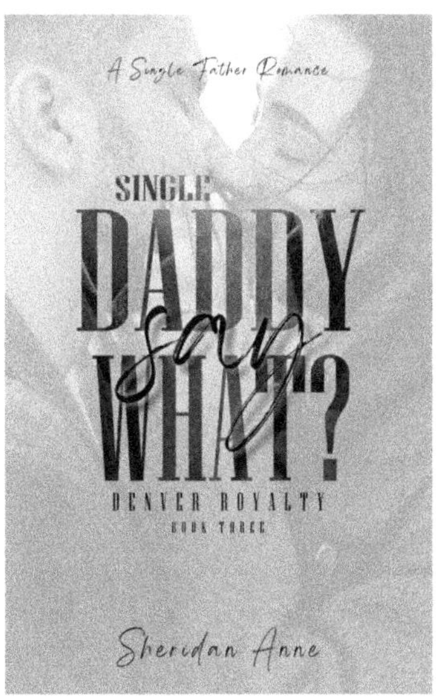

For more information on the Denver Royalty series, find me on Facebook –

www.facebook.com/sheridansbookishbabes

Stalk me

Join me online with the rest of the stalkers!!
I swear, I don't bite. Not unless you say please!

Facebook Reader Group

www.facebook.com/SheridansBookishBabes

Facebook Page

www.facebook.com/sheridan.anne.author1

Instagram

www.instagram.com/Sheridan.Anne.Author

TikTok

www.tiktok.com/@Sheridan.Anne.Author

Subscribe to my Newsletter

https://landing.mailerlite.com/webforms/landing/a8q0y0

More by Sheridan Anne

www.amazon.com/Sheridan-Anne/e/B079TLXN6K

DARK CONTEMPORARY ROMANCE - M/F

Broken Hill High | Haven Falls | Broken Hill Boys | Aston Creek High | Rejects Paradise | Bradford Bastard

DARK CONTEMPORARY ROMANCE - REVERSE HAREM

Boys of Winter | Depraved Sinners | Empire

NEW ADULT SPORTS ROMANCE

Kings of Denver | Denver Royalty | Rebels Advocate

CONTEMPORARY ROMANCE (standalones)

Play With Fire | Until Autumn (Happily Eva Alpha World)

PARANORMAL ROMANCE

Slayer Academy [Pen name - Cassidy Summers]

Ingram Content Group UK Ltd.
Milton Keynes UK
UKHW040807240723
425668UK00003B/203

9 781925 958805